Praise for the *New*

Magical Ca

"A charming small-town settir
ters, mystical cats, and muffins.

"Will delight fans of cat mysteries and Jenn McKinlay's Library Lover's series." —*Library Journal*

"Literary comfort food." —*Kirkus Reviews*

"Kathleen is a smart, resourceful heroine, and cat lovers will delight in the charming felines." —*Booklist*

"It's easy to get hooked on the two sleuthing felines featured in Sofie Kelly's Magical Cats Mysteries. Owen and Hercules may be two of the friskiest characters appearing in the cozy-mystery world." —Fresh Fiction

"Sofie's books add a new twist to the cat mystery. Her feline sleuths, Owen and Hercules, have a knack for solving crime that is literally magical." —The Big Thrill

"Owen and Hercules are a delight." —Kings River Life Magazine

"Small-town charm and a charming cat duo make this every cat fancier's dream." —The Mystery Reader

"The perfect balance of small-town relationships, interesting characters, and a historic library transports readers into the heart of the mystery. Owen and Hercules are my favorite fictional felines." —MyShelf.com

TITLES BY SOFIE KELLY

curiosity thrilled the cat

sleight of paw

copycat killing

cat trick

final catcall

a midwinter's tail

faux paw

paws and effect

a tale of two kitties

the cats came back

a night's tail

a case of cat and mouse

hooked on a feline

whiskers and lies

paws to remember

furever after

paws to remember

A MAGICAL CATS MYSTERY

SOFIE KELLY

BERKLEY PRIME CRIME
new york

BERKLEY PRIME CRIME
Published by Berkley
An imprint of Penguin Random House LLC
penguinrandomhouse.com

ISBN: 9780593548714

The Library of Congress has cataloged the Berkley Prime Crime hardcover edition of this book as follows:

Names: Kelly, Sofie, 1958- author.
Title: Paws to remember / Sofie Kelly.
Description: New York : Berkley Prime Crime, [2023] |
Series: A magical cats mystery
Identifiers: LCCN 2023005365 (print) | LCCN 2023005366 (ebook) |
ISBN 9780593548707 (hardcover) | ISBN 9780593548721 (ebook)
Subjects: LCSH: Cat owners--Fiction. | Librarians--Fiction. | Cats--Fiction. |
Murder--Investigation--Fiction. | LCGFT: Detective and mystery fiction. | Novels.
Classification: LCC PR9199.4.K453 P397 2023 (print) | LCC PR9199.4.K453 (ebook) |
DDC 813/.6--dc23/eng/20230210
LC record available at https://lccn.loc.gov/2023005365
LC ebook record available at https://lccn.loc.gov/2023005366

Berkley Prime Crime hardcover edition / October 2023
Berkley Prime Crime trade paperback edition / August 2024

Printed in the United States of America
1st Printing

paws to remember

chapter 1

It wasn't the first dead body I'd ever seen, so I didn't scream. It also helped that I had been expecting at least one—or possibly two. Owen looked up at me, an expression of self-satisfaction on his face that made him look rather smug—which I'm sure he was. He had one foot on the corpse, his way of claiming credit for the fact that it was lying there in the first place. Since the body was that of a fairly large rodent and Owen was a small cat, I had no problem with the way things had worked out.

Harry Taylor looked down at the little gray-and-white tabby. "Nice work," he said. Harry was in his late fifties, his face weathered from working outside in the sun and wind. Very little rattled him.

The cat dipped his head in gracious acknowledgment of his skills.

A couple of days of colder-than-usual weather—even for Minnesota in December—and a middle-of-the-night power failure downtown had caused a water pipe to burst in the old building where the artists' cooperative had their shop. My friend Maggie, who helped run the business, had been the one who'd gotten the call about the power failure, and she'd discovered both the broken pipe and the furry trespasser.

Maggie had called Harry, who was responsible for the maintenance on the building, and me because Maggie had a long-standing phobia of mice and other rodents. I knew it was connected to something that had happened when she was a child, but she had never shared any details and I had never pushed. I'd brought Owen because no rat, mouse, vole or mole was a match for him.

Harry glanced over at me. "Want me to take care of this?" he asked, indicating the dead animal. "Or is there someone you wanted to fling the dearly departed at?"

I'd been about to pick up Owen. I straightened and eyed Harry, my gaze narrowing in surprise. "How did you know about that incident?" I said. He had to be referring to the last time I'd been involved in disposing of a dead rodent, although I took issue with his use of the word "fling."

He laughed. "Well, you did lob a dead rat at Ruby's head," he said. "Not really the kind of thing people tend to keep to themselves."

"First of all, I didn't throw it at her head deliberately," I said. "She just sort of walked into the line of fire." I could feel my face getting red. "And second, it wasn't actually dead."

He was still laughing. "Doesn't help your case at all, Kathleen."

Harry's laughter was contagious. The incident Harry was talking about was the time the building's basement had been half-filled with water and what I thought was one very dead rodent floating near the stairs. Turned out it was only *mostly* dead. And as any fan of the book and the movie *The Princess Bride* will tell you, *mostly* dead is slightly alive.

I had scooped the animal out of the water with a snow shovel and then, because I hadn't thought ahead to what I was going to do next, ended up tossing it outside just as Ruby Blackthorne—one of the co-op artists—walked by. In my defense I didn't hit Ruby, who was startled but not at all angry, and the animal had scurried away the moment it landed on the pavement. Ruby had teased me about the whole thing for weeks.

"I'd be happy for you to take care of . . . this," I said in answer to Harry's original question. I bent down and scooped up Owen with one hand and raised an eyebrow at Harry as I headed for the door. "It's not like Ruby is in town."

Maggie was waiting in the entryway clutching a broom in one hand with her other arm wrapped tightly around her chest. "Is it . . . gone?" she asked. She glanced over my right shoulder and then her green eyes came back to my face.

Owen gave a loud and very definitive meow. I set him on the floor at my feet.

"Yes," I said. Maggie's shoulders immediately slumped in relief.

I gestured to the half-open door behind me. "Harry's just cleaning up."

Maggie leaned forward and smiled at Owen. "Thank you," she said. "You're my hero."

The cat smiled up at her. Owen adored Maggie.

"So now what?" she asked, looking up at me. I noticed she still had a tight grip on the broom handle.

"Harry's going to pull down the rest of the drywall on that back wall. He wants to see how much water damage there is and he wants to get things dried out before you end up with mold in there."

"There's never a good time for something like this to happen, but this close to Christmas . . ." Maggie shook her head. "I can think of three people off the top of my head who make as much of their income in December as they do during the summer tourist season."

"Is there somewhere you could set up a temporary shop until Harry gets this space usable again?" I asked.

"So far I've had no luck finding space. The Christmas Market is set up in the community center, so that's out."

Ruby was the president of the co-op, but she was in Minneapolis getting ready for an exhibit of her paintings. Since Maggie had had the job before Ruby, she'd stepped in to handle the water leak.

Maggie finally seemed to realize that she was still holding

the broom. She leaned it against the wall behind the front door and folded her arm up over her head, fingers playing with her blond curls. "I'm hoping Harry can put some kind of tarp or plastic over that wall and we can reopen early next week."

I could hear Harry moving around inside the shop. He must have disposed of the "dearly departed," as he'd put it, by now. "Owen and I are going to help Harry," I said to Maggie. "Why don't you go upstairs and have a cup of tea?"

"Maybe in a minute," she said. "I'd really like to get a good look at the damage. When I saw that flash of fur earlier I didn't spend any time looking around." She gave me a sheepish smile. "I'm sorry I woke you up so early."

"Merow!" Owen said.

I smiled. "Like he said, we don't mind. And I was awake anyway. Hercules has been waking up early and seems to think if he's up he should be having breakfast."

Owen meowed loudly again. Hercules was his brother. If one of them had something, the other wanted it, the only exception being catnip chickens, which Owen loved and Hercules was bored by.

"And if Hercules is having breakfast then Owen is having breakfast. And since neither one of them has figured out how to use a can opener, that means I have to get up, too." I'd woken up at ten to six to find Hercules breathing his kitty morning breath in my face. When Maggie had called at five past I was downstairs in the kitchen wrapped around a large cup of coffee while the boys ate their breakfast.

I put my arms around her shoulders now. "And even if you had woken me up I wouldn't have minded. That's what friends are for." Owen murped his agreement. "Let's go see if Harry is ready to get started."

Harry was set to tackle the rest of the old drywall, and since I didn't have to be at work at the library for a while, I'd offered to help. My parents had an old house back in Boston and I'd removed drywall before.

Harry had taken off his jacket but he was warmly dressed underneath it in heavy brown canvas pants and a red-and-brown-plaid flannel shirt over a long-sleeved T-shirt. He handed me a mask. "You got gloves?" he asked as he pulled on his own pair.

I nodded as I pulled mine out of the back pocket of my old, paint-spattered jeans. Like Harry I was wearing a flannel shirt over a double-layer long-sleeved T-shirt. There was heat on in the building, but since the electricity had come back on only half an hour ago, it was going to take a while to get the old structure warmed up again.

Maggie stood several steps behind us with Owen next to her as though he were her bodyguard, which in his little kitty mind he probably was. Neither Owen nor Hercules was exactly what you'd call an ordinary housecat.

I adjusted the mask Harry handed me and we got to work. The old drywall was wet and crumbly in some places and broke apart in small pieces in our hands. Harry had spread a couple of large tarps on the floor so we just dropped everything we pulled loose onto the floor. He grabbed the edge of a piece of Sheetrock and braced one foot against the wall for leverage. Harry had pulled off most of the trim in the room before I'd gotten down the hill. Once Owen and I had arrived to do rodent patrol, Harry had removed the last piece because the cat had scratched very insistently at it. Harry had also sucked up the water on the floor with his big, industrial Shop-Vac. Maggie and I had moved everything upstairs into the tai chi studio. The only water damage was to some holiday decorations and several paintings that had been hanging on the wall when the pipe burst.

Harry looked over his shoulder at Owen, whose golden eyes were fixed on the wall. I didn't hear or see anything that suggested there was anything else alive back there, but if there was, it didn't stand a chance against either one of them.

"Ready?" Harry asked.

Owen bobbed his head and meowed.

Harry grinned at me. "I swear your cat knows what I'm saying."

"Of course he does," Maggie said. "Owen is very smart."

The cat looked up at her and seemed to smile.

Harry would have been shocked if he'd known everything that Owen and Hercules as well could do. I wondered what he'd say—what anyone in town would say—if they knew that Owen could become invisible at will and Hercules could walk through walls. They'd probably wonder about my mental health. I glanced at Owen, hoping he wouldn't suddenly get the idea to demonstrate his talent. He liked to do things like that.

I grabbed a section of drywall next to the piece Harry had just ripped down. It wasn't quite as saturated with water as the previous piece I'd pulled loose had been, but it was wet enough that I managed to yank down a piece only about a foot wide.

There was something in the wall cavity between the studs, something behind the thin layer of old insulation. Whatever it was, was wrapped in heavy plastic.

"Harry," I said.

He turned to look at me. "Did you find something?" he asked.

Out of the corner of my eye I saw Owen move in front of Maggie. "Not what you're thinking," I said, realizing he probably thought I'd discovered another rat. "There's something wrapped up in plastic in between the studs."

"You sure it's not just insulation?"

I pulled a bit more of the Sheetrock loose so I could get a better look. "It's definitely plastic," I said.

Harry leaned in closer.

"Do you think it could be some sort of time capsule?" I asked, brushing dust from the front of my shirt.

Harry shrugged. "Last time these walls were back to the studs must be forty years ago now. I don't remember hearing about them putting anything like that in a wall, but it wouldn't have been the kind of thing I would have paid attention to back then. Might as well see what it is."

We worked together to pull the last of the drywall away from the studs and peel back the wet insulation. The wall cavity was deeper than I had thought. The plastic was thick and heavy and I could see it was wrapped around something but I couldn't tell what. The bundle was easily five feet long, wedged into the space between two wooden wall studs. Harry moved to lift the whole thing out.

He frowned. "Whatever this is, it's heavier than it looks," he said. I caught hold of the plastic about halfway down and helped Harry lower it to the floor, kicking some of the pieces of Sheetrock out of the way. I knelt down on the tarp as Owen made his way over to me. I pulled off my gloves and peeled back the first two layers of plastic, brushing a layer of dust and dirt from the outside one. Underneath the third one I could see what looked like a heavy gray wool blanket. My heart began to pound and all at once my mouth went dry. Owen meowed softly.

"I know," I said. I tried to swallow the lump at the back of my throat but I couldn't.

"What is it?" Harry asked.

"I . . . um . . . can you help me get more of this plastic undone?"

His eyes narrowed but all he said was, "Sure."

We managed to unwrap the third layer. I lifted up a corner of the blanket and let it fall again. I sat back on my heels and slowly let out a breath. Owen put a paw on my leg. Harry said an oath almost under his breath.

"What's wrong?" Maggie said. There was an edge of uncertainty to her voice.

Harry swiped a hand over the back of his neck. "I'll make the call," he said, pulling out his phone as he moved several steps away.

"Kathleen, what's wrong?" Maggie asked again.

I got to my feet. My stomach was doing somersaults. I turned to face her.

She looked past me at the . . . bundle on the floor. "Is that asbestos or something dangerous?"

I shook my head. "No. It's a body."

chapter 2

For a moment Maggie just stared at me, a frown creasing her forehead. Then her gaze flicked to the plastic-wrapped bundle on the floor behind me. "No," she said. "That doesn't make sense. How could a body have gotten into the wall? It's a mannequin or a doll." She gestured with one hand. "Every artist that's part of the co-op is in this building every week. It's someone's project or someone's very warped idea of a joke. It has to be."

I shook my head. "No. It's not." Unfortunately, I'd seen more than one dead body. I'd known what was wrapped in the heavy plastic as soon as I'd seen the gray blanket, even before

Harry had helped me peel back another layer of plastic, even as I'd fervently hoped I was wrong.

Maggie closed her eyes, took a slow, deep breath and then exhaled equally slowly before she looked at me again. "How could a body have ended up here, behind that wall?"

"I don't know," I said. What I didn't say was I couldn't think of any good explanation.

Harry rejoined us. "Police are on their way," he said, his expression somber.

By unspoken agreement we moved across the room to stand by the doorway. A police car arrived within minutes, although it seemed longer. I recognized the responding officer who climbed out. His name was Stephen Keller. He was ex-military, square-shouldered and serious. He dipped his head at me in recognition.

Marcus was right behind the squad car. "Kathleen, what's going on?" he asked. "You found a body?" Marcus Gordon was a detective with the Mayville Heights Police Department. He was also my fiancé.

"Harry and I did," I said. "There was a leak overnight. A pipe burst. It . . . the body . . . was behind a wall in the store."

Marcus glanced over at the plastic-wrapped bundle on the floor. Officer Keller had bent down and looked under the gray blanket. He looked up at Marcus and gave a slight nod.

Marcus turned his attention back to me. "Okay, start at the beginning," he said.

I explained about Maggie calling me and how Owen and I

had come down because she was certain she'd seen and heard something in the section of wall where the worst of the water damage was. Owen bobbed his gray tabby head in agreement.

"How did you find out about the leak in the first place?" Marcus asked Maggie.

"Eric called," she said.

Eric Cullen ran Eric's Place. The café was a block and a half away.

"He told me the power had been off for most of the night all along the street. I got dressed and came to check on things." She clasped her hands in front of her. "By the time I got here it was back on again. But it was freezing in here. All those hours with no heat and almost no insulation in the walls—I wasn't surprised a pipe had burst."

Maggie had been lobbying for the last year for the co-op to either renovate this old building or look for a new location.

"I shut off the water," she continued, "and I called Harry. Then I got the old Shop-Vac from the basement. It was less than five minutes after that when I realized I could hear something in the wall. Then I saw a flash of fur. I was pretty certain I knew what it was, so I called Kathleen. She and Owen—and Harry—got here about the same time."

Harry and I both nodded.

"Was there something in the wall?" Marcus said.

Before Maggie could answer, Owen gave a loud meow. She smiled at him and he seemed to smile back.

"Rat," Harry said, holding his hands about eight inches

apart. "Cat took care of it and I threw the remains in the garbage can in the alley." He went on to explain how the two of us had started pulling down the Sheetrock on the back wall so he could see just how much water damage there was behind it.

"We wouldn't have moved the body if we'd realized it *was* a body," I said.

"There's no way you could have known," Marcus said. "Show me exactly where it was."

I set Owen down on the floor. "Stay with Maggie," I told him.

"Mrrr," he said.

I led Marcus across the room and pointed out the wall cavity where the plastic-wrapped body had been hidden.

He pulled out a small flashlight and used it to get a better look at the space between the two wall studs. I saw him take note of the dust and bits of sawdust the same way I had.

"Aside from the Sheetrock and the plastic, Harry and I didn't touch anything," I said. "The two of us lifted the body out of the wall and laid it right there." I gestured at the plastic-wrapped bundle. Officer Keller had put on a pair of latex gloves and was going through the wet drywall Harry and I had pulled from the wall.

Marcus touched my arm. "It's all right. You couldn't have guessed what was going to be under that plastic." He looked back over his shoulder. "Harry, when was the last time there would have been any renovations in this space?"

Harry pulled off his cap and smoothed one hand over his mostly hairless scalp. "There's been a lot of painting and patching over the years. There was water damage in the basement when we had the flooding four years ago. And the display cases and shelving were put in must be ten years ago." He gave Maggie a questioning look.

"Eleven years in January," she said.

Harry settled his ball cap on his head again. "As far as I know, that wall has been intact since this whole downstairs area was renovated close to forty years ago. I can't tell you who the contractor was back then, but I wouldn't be surprised if Idris Blackthorne did the drywalling and painting."

"As long as I've been part of the co-op there hasn't been any major work done in here," Maggie added. "There was some painting and crack filling done last year. Before that I'd have to look back in our records."

"Talk to Oren," Harry added. "If anyone can tell you what's been done on this building, it's him."

Oren Kenyon was a very talented carpenter. He'd worked on most of the old buildings in Mayville Heights over the years and he could remember details of each project going back decades. If anyone could help the police figure out how long the body had been hidden in this building, it was Oren.

"I will," Marcus said. "Thanks." He glanced over at the plastic-wrapped bundle. "Give me a minute," he said, lowering his voice.

I gave his shoulder a squeeze and walked over to rejoin Maggie and Harry. Was it possible that the body had been hidden in the wall for decades? It seemed hard to believe, but based on what I'd seen under the blanket, it wasn't impossible. How had it ended up there in the first place? I couldn't think of any good explanation.

Marcus had leaned down to take a closer look at the corpse. The brief glimpse I'd gotten of the body left me thinking it was a woman wrapped up in all those layers of plastic. Had there been someone missing her for almost forty years?

Marcus had some questions for Mags about the store and the co-op. She stood with her arms wrapped tightly around her midsection as she answered them. Owen stayed right beside her like a sentinel, watching Marcus, his head cocked slightly to one side as though he was following every word of the conversation.

"Do you think it's possible that body has been in the wall all this time?" I asked Harry.

He shrugged. "As far-fetched as it seems, I do." He lowered his voice a little. "You saw that body, Kathleen. You probably got a better look at it than I did. It looked like it had been . . . mummified. You think that could be possible given how long it might have been there?"

The lump was back in my throat. I had to swallow before I could answer. "It is . . . possible," I said, "based on what I know of how the process works. It could be what's called spontaneous mummification."

"And that is?"

"In essence, the remains dry out faster than decomposition happens. You saw that heavy blanket around the body underneath the plastic."

I knew he must have. Harry didn't miss much.

He nodded.

"I saw the edge of what I'm pretty sure was another one as well. The blankets and the plastic would have helped keep the remains dry and protected them from bacteria, fungi, insects and . . . any animals." I swallowed. It felt as though that lump in my throat would choke me.

Harry swiped a hand over the stubble on his chin. "Don't take anything I come up with as gospel, but I seem to remember Idris's boys having trouble getting the drywall compound to dry properly on a project back about then and I think it might have been this one. Someone came and borrowed a couple of big fans from the old man. I didn't pay a lot of attention because all I was interested in back then was girls and guitars, but I do remember helping load the fans in somebody's truck. And it seems to me there was a portable heater as well."

"All those things probably contributed to preserving the body," I said.

"It makes some kind of sense," he said. He looked over at the tarps and the damp Sheetrock on the floor. "I hate to leave this mess behind, but I don't see Marcus letting me clean any of it up."

I pushed a stray strand of hair back off my face. "He needs

to figure out who that person was and how they ended up here. Everything is evidence." What I didn't say was we could be standing in a crime scene, albeit possibly nearly forty years after the crime was committed.

Marcus had finished talking to Maggie. "You can all leave now," he said. "I'll probably have more questions, but for now, we're good."

I nodded because I knew the routine. The crime scene techs would be here any minute, and at some point the body would be transported to the medical examiner's office. It wasn't the first time I'd ended up connected to one of Marcus's cases. I fervently wished that I had no idea how the whole process worked.

"Any idea how long it will be before I can get back in here to finish pulling down the drywall and get things dried up?" Harry asked.

Marcus pulled one hand through his dark, wavy hair, a sign he was already feeling a bit stressed over this new case. "I honestly don't know. A day or two for sure, maybe longer. It depends on a lot of things."

"I understand," Harry said. "I don't mean to push. It's just that I don't want to end up with mold growing on those damp walls."

Marcus nodded. "I get that. I promise as soon as the scene is released I'll call you."

"I appreciate that." Maggie, trailed by Owen, had joined us.

"As soon as I can get back inside I'll get everything cleaned up and get you an estimate on what else needs to be done," Harry said to her.

Maggie smiled. "Thank you. And thank you for coming down here so early."

He smiled back at her. "Anytime." He glanced at me. "I'll be in to the library later to take a look at the loading dock door."

"There's no rush," I said.

Harry left.

I bent down and picked up Owen. He wrinkled his whiskers at me. I was pretty sure that meant he expected a treat for dispatching the rat and for behaving himself.

"I'll be at the library if you have any more questions, and yes, I know you won't make it for lunch," I said to Marcus.

"I'm sorry," he began. His attention had drifted back to that plastic-wrapped bundle on the floor. He was in full detective mode now.

I held up one hand. "It's okay. Call me when you have a chance."

Maggie and I—and Owen, who I think would have been happy to join Marcus and do a little nosing around—moved out into the entryway.

"I thought it was bad when I got here and discovered the broken pipe," she said. "How could a body have ended up in that wall and whose is it?"

"I don't know," I said. "The police keep records of missing

persons. They'll figure all of this out." Owen squirmed in my arms and I tightened my grip on him. He was nosy, even for a cat, and I didn't want him traipsing all over Marcus's possible crime scene. "We should get out of here."

Maggie smiled. "You must be down at least half a gallon of coffee by now."

She was a tea drinker. She had a teapot in her art studio, in the yoga and tai chi studio upstairs, and half a dozen of them in her apartment. I, on the other hand, was a die-hard coffee fanatic.

"At least," I said, smiling back at her. I followed her up the steps to the second-floor space where she taught yoga and tai chi classes. Owen was still wriggling to get down. I set him on the floor. He gave me a pointed look, shook himself and headed in the direction of the low window on the other side of the room.

Maggie stretched both arms up over her head. "I know old buildings have secrets, but this is just so incredibly sad. Do you think there's someone out there who has been waiting all these years, wondering if that person—whoever they are—was alive or dead?"

"It's possible," I said slowly. "Maybe finding the body will at least give someone some peace of mind."

"I hope so." She dropped her arms and rolled her neck from one side to the other. "I need to get my jacket and my computer. "I'll have to cancel tai chi tomorrow, and yoga tonight and Friday. In fact, I'm thinking I might as well cancel everything the first of the week as well."

"I think that's a good idea." I stuffed my hands in my pockets. It was still a little cold in the old building. "It's freezing out there," I said. "I can drop you at River Arts. I'll take Owen to the library with me for the morning."

The furball in question walked over to us, sat down beside Maggie, looked up and meowed. Then he looked at me.

I shook my head. "Absolutely not."

He meowed again even louder and more insistently.

Maggie looked down at Owen. "What is it?" she asked as though she expected him to answer. Maggie talked to Owen all the time as if he were a person. I was pretty sure he thought he was.

"I think he wants to go to your studio with you."

She shrugged. "So why can't he?"

There was a look of triumph on the cat's face. I had no doubt he'd understood exactly what she'd said.

"Because he'll get into everything in your studio. He'll wander all over the building given half the chance. *You* won't get any work done."

Maggie looked down at Owen, whose expression had flipped to one of complete innocence. "He's good company," she said. "I have a dish I can use for water and a bag of cat crackers that I was going to give him in my backpack. We even have a bag of kitty litter by the back door."

Owen licked his lips when he heard about the cat crackers.

Maggie tilted her head to one side. "Say yes, Kathleen. How much trouble can one small cat get into?"

I eyed Owen, who had tipped his head in the same way. "You have no idea," I said, "but all right. I will pick him up on my lunch break, a bit after one." I pointed a finger at the cat and narrowed my eyes at him. "Behave yourself and stay out of trouble."

He gave me his most guileless look. I wasn't fooled.

Maggie grabbed her backpack and bag and jacket and we headed back down the stairs.

It was freezing outside, the air sharp with every breath I took. My hands were still cold, even inside my double-knit woolen mittens. Maggie pulled her hat down over her ears and turned up her collar. We hurried to my truck, which was parked one building away at the curb. Owen jumped in and settled himself on the seat. Maggie made a "move over" gesture with one hand and the cat obligingly slid over. I would have had to pick him up to move him.

Luckily the truck had an excellent heater and we were warm by the time we got to the River Arts building.

"Thank you for everything," Maggie said, leaning over Owen to hug me. "What would I do without you?"

Owen meowed loudly. Maggie smiled down at him. "Yes, and you, too."

"Anytime you need us, all you have to do is ask," I said.

"Marcus will let you know as soon as Harry can get back in the building, and Owen and I will come back to help."

Maggie climbed out of the truck. "Let's go," she said to Owen.

The cat jumped down onto the snowy pavement of the parking lot and followed her.

"I'll see you at lunchtime," I called after them. Owen didn't so much as twitch an ear or even break stride. Maggie waved a hand in acknowledgment. I waited until I saw they were inside and then I headed for the library. I hoped leaving Owen with Maggie wasn't going to be as bad an idea as I knew it could be.

Owen—and his brother, Hercules—had been feral. I'd found them out at the old Henderson estate shortly after I'd moved to Minnesota. Neither one of them let anyone but me touch them. As much as Owen loved Maggie, she knew better than to try to pick him up.

But the cat's touchiness about being touched wasn't the reason I was afraid I'd l made a mistake in letting Owen spend the morning in Maggie's studio. The cat's ability to . . . disappear was something only I and now Marcus knew about.

I hadn't believed it myself until I'd witnessed it happen more than once. Marcus had been afraid I was having some sort of psychological breakdown when I'd finally confessed the cats' special skills to him. (Marcus's own cat, Micah, had the same ability to vanish as Owen did. She, at least, was a little more circumspect about when she used her talent. She also seemed to understand every word that was said to her.) Marcus had read every physics book I'd been able to find for him in our library system trying to come up with a logical explanation. He hadn't found anything that had really satisfied him.

Owen had a tendency to disappear when he wasn't getting his own way. Or when he was bored. And even, I suspected, just to aggravate me. I hoped he wouldn't decide to play his version of hide-and-seek with Maggie.

I glanced at my watch. I was still old-school enough that I always wore it. I was actually going to be a few minutes early at the library. I'd have lots of time to make coffee and see if there were any of Mary's cinnamon rolls left.

I pulled into the parking lot, noting that Harry had sanded the entire area and the walkway to the front door. As always, I smiled as I looked at the brick building. We had started decorating for the holiday season on Monday. Harry had come and hung evergreen wreaths decorated with pinecones and berries in every window. The library looked very festive.

The Mayville Heights Free Public Library had been in dire need of repairs and updating the first time I'd seen it. I had applied for and accepted the short-term job of head librarian to supervise the restoration of the library in time for its centenary without seeing more than a few photos of the building. By the time the work was finished I'd fallen in love with the town and the people. Now I couldn't imagine living anywhere else.

I thought about the body we'd just discovered. Had that person been part of this town at one time? Had they gone to class in the River Arts building back when it was still a school? Had they climbed to the top of Wild Rose Bluff or borrowed books from the library?

And what about that person's family and friends? Had they been holding a tiny spark of hope all these years, believing that he or she was out there somewhere? Was that tiny spark about to go out?

chapter 3

I hurried across the parking lot, making a mental note to thank Harry for the sanding and for widening the path to the front door. I unlocked the main library doors, shut off the alarm system and turned on some lights. I had more than enough time to make coffee before opening the building for the day.

I started the coffee maker and changed into the gray trousers and red sweater I'd brought from home. When I came back downstairs, my hands wrapped around my mug to warm them up, Eric's wife, Susan, was waiting at the front door. She'd worked at the library for years and probably knew more about our book collection than I did. I hurried over to let her in. She was enveloped from neck to knee in a bright green hooded puffy coat. She was also wearing a gray hat and scarf that she'd proudly and painstakingly knit for herself and a pair of polar fleece mittens that matched her coat. If she'd had a set of pointy ears underneath that knit hat she could have passed for one of Santa's elves.

"Hi," she said. "I wasn't sure you would be here yet. I figured you'd probably stopped in to see how Maggie was doing at the shop."

She grabbed the faux fur pompom on her hat and pulled it off her head. Somehow the updo her hair was pulled into had stayed in place, secured by three tiny cocktail swords and a sparkly red-and-green barrette. Sometimes it seemed as though Susan's hair could defy gravity—and weather.

"I was over there," I said. "Maggie told me that Eric called about the power failure, and it's a good thing he did because it turns out a pipe burst in the shop."

"Aw, crap," she said, making a face. "I was afraid that might happen. There's almost no insulation in those walls and our winters aren't getting any warmer."

I took a sip of my coffee. I was finally starting to feel warm myself. "How are things at the café?"

Susan was unwinding her scarf from around her neck. It had to be more than six feet long. "Aside from a very small leak in the cellar, which had nothing to do with the power failure, and the loss of a batch of cinnamon rolls, things are fine. How bad are things at the co-op?"

I knew I couldn't tell her about the body. "It's hard to say yet," I hedged.

"Don't worry," Susan said, stuffing her scarf in the hood of her jacket. "Harry can fix anything."

I just nodded. There was no way Harry could fix what we'd found.

To my surprise the library was busy despite the bitter temperatures outside. People came in for stacks of books and a surprising number of movies on DVD. I attributed the latter to my part-time student employee, Levi, fixing a DVD player for Harry's father, Harrison Taylor Senior. Harry was so tickled that he had a way to watch his Hitchcock collection that he talked up Levi's skills to everyone he knew, which was pretty much everyone in town. That had led to Levi fixing several more DVD players for various library patrons, including one woman who, when Levi refused to accept payment, made him two dozen pumpkin spice donuts—which he had generously shared with the rest of the staff.

Levi liked to tinker with electronic devices. "It's fun," he'd told me when I'd asked why he wouldn't take any money for his efforts. "And in most of the cases the problem is just dust and dog hair." He'd grinned then. "And in one case three French fries."

I picked up Owen at lunchtime. I found him sitting on a

stool in front of Maggie's easel while she worked on a sketch. "Did he behave?" I asked as I picked Owen up off his seat.

"He was a perfect gentleman," Maggie said. She handed me the bag of crackers she'd mentioned earlier. "Don't forget these."

Owen meowed loudly. There wasn't much chance that I would forget anything that the cat considered to be his.

I noticed that Owen smelled like salmon and the little bag of fish crackers seemed to be about a third empty. It was easy to guess what had ensured his gentlemanly behavior all morning.

"Thanks for babysitting the furball," I said, giving Maggie a one-armed hug. Owen made a face as if to say he didn't need to be babysat.

"He really is good company," she said with a smile. "He has some strong opinions on assemblage art, but for the most part we agree. And he has an excellent eye for color."

"I'll keep that in mind when I start trying to decide what color to paint the bathroom," I said, smiling back at her.

I tucked Owen inside my jacket, his head poking out the front, above the zipper. I knew there was no way he'd walk across the parking lot for me the way he'd done for Maggie.

"Hey, since there's no tai chi tomorrow night, are you up for trying Eric's new sourdough pizza?" Maggie asked.

"Merow!" Owen said.

I leaned sideways to look at him. "She meant me, not you."

Pizza was one of Owen's favorite things. It was also something his veterinarian, my friend Roma, had warned me not to feed him. "Pizza is not cat food," she'd told Marcus the last time she'd caught him sneaking both cats a tiny bite of his slice. "It's not good for them." Marcus had looked contrite and Owen annoyed at her words.

"Sorry," Maggie said to Owen. "I did mean Kathleen."

The cat made a sound like a sigh and hung his head. He was such a drama queen.

"Maybe Roma knows of a recipe for cat pizza."

The cat kept his head down but I saw him lick his whiskers. Maggie was clearly forgiven.

"Call her and see if she can join us," I said.

"Already did and she already said yes." She gave me a satisfied grin.

We settled on a time and Owen and I headed out to my truck.

I realized when I pulled into the driveway that I had enough time to warm up some soup and eat it before returning to the library. I decided that was better than just making a sandwich to take back with me. Hercules was waiting in the sunporch. He eyed the little bag of crackers I was carrying. I could tell he knew what was inside.

"Yes, you can have a couple," I said as I went to unlock the kitchen door.

Owen gave an indignant meow of objection.

"Brothers share," I said firmly.

He glared at me.

I glared back.

Hercules simply walked through the door without waiting for me to open it.

I continued to eye his brother, who decided to end the stalemate by just disappearing.

"That's cheating," I said to the space where he'd been just a moment before. "And it doesn't change anything."

I hung up my coat and stepped out of my boots, padding around the kitchen in sock feet. I gave Hercules two crackers and both cats fresh water. Roma had suggested a water fountain since it seemed as though one cat or the other was always upending the wide, low dishes I had been using for water.

Hercules had refused to go anywhere near the device no matter what the enticement. Owen seemed to think it was a toy he could use to leave dirty, wet pawprints all over the kitchen floor. Neither one of them drank from the fountain as far as I could tell. After four days I'd given up and taken it out to Marcus's cat, Micah. She'd happily and daintily drunk from it, of course, and was still using it.

"Boys," I'd said to her.

She'd murped softly in agreement.

I warmed up a bowl of the tomato soup I'd made over the weekend. I'd gotten the recipe from my neighbor Rebecca, and it was delicious. I added some grated cheese and croutons and told Hercules about my morning as he kept me company at the table.

Harry Taylor came in to check the new loading dock door about half an hour after I'd gotten back to the library. It was working well and the seal was tight. "I'm so glad you were able to find us a used door," I said. "It was a fraction of the cost of a new one."

"So am I," Harry said. His expression became serious. "Are you going to see Marcus tonight?"

"I think so," I said. "He said he was going to try to make it for supper. Did you remember something?"

Harry looked uncomfortable. "Not exactly. It's more like I found something."

I frowned at him. "You found something? You mean this morning?"

He nodded, twisting the visor of his cap in his hands. "When I got the shovel to get rid of that rat, I noticed something on the floor." He reached into the pocket of his jacket and held out his hand.

He was holding what looked at first glance to be a tiny gold crescent moon on a thin gold chain. As I studied the piece of jewelry I realized the shape wasn't a crescent moon after all. It was half a heart.

"Do you think this might have belonged with the body?" I asked.

Harry shrugged. "I don't know. Remember I pulled off the baseboard before the cat went to work?"

I nodded. Harry had pulled a section of the trim away from the wall because Owen had been scratching furiously at it and we'd both thought the rat might be behind that part of the wall.

"I found this on the floor against the wall where the baseboard had been." He shrugged. "I didn't think anything of it. I picked it up meaning to give it to Maggie and it went right out of my head. Could you give it to Marcus? I don't want to spend the rest of the day with the two of us leaving each other messages."

"I'll give it to him," I said. The chances of there being any sort of fingerprint evidence on the necklace were slim. Even so, I went to the checkout desk and got one of the small envelopes we kept there for things that people left behind in the books they returned. Harry dropped the necklace inside and I sealed the flap and put it in my pocket.

Harry seemed relieved. "Tell Marcus to call me if he has any questions."

I promised I would and he left.

Marcus called just before I left for the day to say he could make supper. Before I could ask if he'd been able to talk to Oren, there was a loud crash from the children's section. Susan and I looked at each other. "Justasons," we both said at the same time. I told Marcus I'd see him later and said good-bye.

Mike Justason's boys had a lot of creative energy. They had a lot of energy period, and much of it seemed to end up leaving damaged library books in their wake. The boys loved books. Their father was always apologetic and quick to pay for the ones his boys destroyed.

I headed for the stacks. "Do you need any help?" Susan called after me.

I shook my head. "I've got this," I said.

I knew as soon as Ronan and Gavin saw me they'd both run. I'd watched them enough—and chased them enough—to know if Ronan went left he'd run a particular zigzag, like a wide receiver who had only one running pattern in his repertoire. Ronan went left about three-quarters of the time. Gavin, on the other hand, just put his head down and looked for the fastest route out of any situation.

As predicted, both boys bolted as soon as they caught sight of me. I snagged Gavin as he darted down the main aisle between two sets of bookshelves and I nabbed Ronan as he zigged around the magazine racks. I barely even broke a sweat. By the time Mike arrived the boys had reshelved the considerable number of books they'd used to play "library Jenga."

"The two of you act like you were raised by wolves," Mike said. His expression was anything but happy.

Gavin shook his head. "We weren't raised by wolves. We were raised by you."

"Maybe you dropped us on our heads when we were babies," Ronan added.

Susan's lips twitched as she tried not to laugh. She had two boys of her own with genius-level IQs. Library Jenga would have been way too tame for them.

Mike looked back over his shoulder at me. "Let me know what I owe you, Kathleen," he said.

It wasn't until all three of the Justasons were out the door that I realized I hadn't told Marcus about the necklace.

I headed home shortly after. Once again I was grateful for the warmth of the old truck, which had been a gift from Harry's father, Harrison. My first winter in Mayville Heights I'd walked to work every day because I'd sold my car when I left Boston to come to Minnesota.

Almost every house along Mountain Road was decked out for Christmas. Snow decorated the tree branches, frost sparkled in the corners of windowpanes, and there seemed to be a snowman in every second yard. I thought it would be nice to walk the length of the street some night to get a good look at the decorations, as long as it was a little warmer and as long as the trek ended at Eric's Place with a dish of his chocolate pudding cake.

There were cat paw prints in the dusting of snow on the back steps and a few larger prints in the driveway. The latter likely belonged to the Justasons' dog, Fifi. The Justasons were also my next-door neighbors. Contrary to the type of dog the name Fifi conjured up, the dog was in reality a large German shepherd mixed breed with an intimidating bark—a he, not a she—who was absolutely terrified of my cats. Mike and I had been trying to get the dog to at least get a little more comfortable with Owen and Hercules, but it was slow going.

I had bribed Hercules with sardine crackers to get him to sit on the back landing while Mike stood in the driveway with the dog. Fifi had looked like he was going to bolt at any time and then had, all but dragging Mike with him. Since I saw dog paw prints but no sign of people footprints, maybe Fifi was getting bolder. And maybe Hercules had been inside the porch looking out the window, which had made the dog feel safer.

I looked in the refrigerator and saw that I had all the ingredients I needed to make chicken corn chowder. I set the table, and while the chowder simmered I sat and made a list of everything I could remember from that morning. Hercules jumped onto my lap to help, which mostly meant he got in the way.

At one point the light caught my engagement ring and I stopped to stare at it, something I still did all the time even though I had been wearing the ring for over a month. Marcus had chosen the design, an entwined Celtic love knot around a single diamond solitaire. It was beautiful.

I had actually been the one to first propose to him, a tradition in the Gordon family, I'd learned. A week later Marcus had given me the ring I now wore. We were heading to Boston to spend Christmas with my family on the twenty-third. My mother wanted to start planning the wedding. All I wanted was to be married to Marcus. I didn't care about the details around how it happened, just that it happened. I'd already explained that what I pictured was a wedding that was small and simple, not something over-the-top.

My parents didn't really do small or simple. They had married each other twice. The second time when my mother was hugely pregnant with twins—my brother Ethan and sister Sarah—much to the embarrassment of a teenage me.

Mom and Dad were actors, primarily onstage, although Mom had a recurring role on the soap opera *The Wild and the Wonderful* and Dad had a cult following from a commercial he'd done years ago in which he'd been a dancing raisin. Marcus had spent time with my family before, but he'd never experienced a Paulson Christmas. I'd warned him my father would be deep into creating his role as Harold Hill for a production of *The Music Man* starting in mid-January—and possibly bursting into song at any moment—and my mom would be tweaking his interpretation since she was directing. It basically meant they'd be feuding or suddenly dancing to a song on the radio and sneaking kisses in the pantry while they made Christmas dinner.

We were spending New Year's back here in Mayville Heights with Marcus's parents, Elliot and Celeste, and his sister, Hannah. I was overjoyed that I'd get so much family time over the holidays. Once again my thoughts turned to the remains we'd discovered at the co-op store. Had that person left a family behind that loved and missed them? I couldn't think of any innocent reason for that body being where it was, and I knew that for whatever loved ones he or she had left behind, finding out what happened to them would bring just as much pain as long-awaited answers.

I was still sitting at the table lost in thought when Marcus arrived. He looked tired. He kissed me and turned to the stove. "Whatever that is, it smells delicious."

"Chicken corn chowder," I said. I noticed Hercules had already stationed himself next to the other chair at the table. He knew Marcus was his best chance of being slipped a bit of chicken.

The envelope containing the necklace Harry had found was sitting on the counter. I handed it to Marcus and explained about Harry finding it and then forgetting he had it in all the shock of finding the body. Marcus tore the end off the envelope, looked inside and then folded down the open end.

"Thanks," he said.

"Do you think it's important?"

He blew out a breath. "At this point it's too early to tell what's important and what isn't, so for now I just assume everything is important. It'll be days before we have a cause of death and a positive ID on the body."

I studied his face. "But you think you know who those remains belong to."

Marcus picked up a baking powder biscuit from the plate by the sink. "I'm not having this conversation," he said before taking a big bite.

I smiled. "I'm just making an observation." I felt sure he'd talked to Oren by now, and I noticed when I'd said he already knew whom we'd found, he might not have said yes, but he hadn't said no, either.

"People are already speculating about what was going on this morning," I said.

Marcus nodded. "I know. And I'm sure by morning Bridget will be adding fuel to the fire."

Bridget Lowe was the publisher of the *Mayville Heights Chronicle*. She seemed to know what was happening in any major investigation long before the police released any details. Marcus was convinced someone in the department was feeding her information. I suspected he was right.

The next morning, in a front-page story, the *Chronicle* speculated that the remains we'd found were those of Lily Abbott, who had disappeared almost thirty-six years ago on the night of the winter solstice. No sign of Lily, who had been seven months pregnant, was ever found, and police at the time suspected the eighteen-year-old had run away after an argument with her parents. There was no evidence of foul play, Lily had talked about running away to some of her friends, and a few of her things were missing from her bedroom. Lily's brother had always insisted that his sister's former boyfriend had done something to her. He had gone to his own grave certain that Lily was dead. I realized it was possible he'd been right.

chapter 4

By seven thirty Thursday morning the police department had posted a statement on the department's website and all their social media that they were still investigating the discovery of a body at the co-op store and had not yet made a positive ID of the remains. Susan and I arrived at the library at the same time and she told me that there was a lot of wild speculation about what exactly had been discovered at the shop.

"What do you mean?" I asked as I stomped snow off of my boots before disarming the security system.

"I was at the café before I walked over here and I accidentally overheard two men talking." She started the process of unwinding her scarf. "Okay, well, I accidentally overheard them and then I deliberately listened after that. You're not going to believe what they said."

"They thought the body belonged to Jimmy Hoffa?" I said dryly.

Susan made a face at me. "Of course not. They were too young to know who Jimmy Hoffa was. They were talking about a rumor that's going around that Harry actually found money under the floorboards in the shop. A lot of money."

I stuffed my mittens in one of my coat pockets. "So why did the van from the medical examiner's office show up?"

"That's how they snuck all the money out of the building."

"Very creative," I said. We headed upstairs.

I unlocked my office door, dumped my things on a chair and followed Susan to the staff room.

I started the coffee maker and leaned against the counter while it did its thing. "I wish Harry had found a million dollars in the shop instead of what was there."

Susan was putting her things in her locker. She turned to look at me, her smile fading. "Kathleen, please tell me there's an innocuous reason that a body ended up in that building."

I shook my head. "I wish I could," I said.

It was another busy day. Marcus called just before lunch. I could feel his frustration even through the phone. "This time Bridget has gone too far," he said. "Between you and me, that body could be Lily Abbott's but at this point we don't know. We haven't even spoken to her next of kin because we don't have anything to share."

"I don't disagree with you," I said, sitting on the edge of my desk. "But Bridget is going to say this falls under the public's right to know."

"And I might agree with her if there were actually any *facts* to know."

"What are you going to do?" I asked.

He blew out a breath. "I don't know, but I need to do something."

At the end of the day I drove over to meet Maggie and Roma for dinner. Surprisingly I found a parking space in front of the bookstore. I climbed out of the truck to see Maggie coming up the sidewalk from the opposite direction wearing her fuzzy teddy bear coat.

"How are you?" I asked as we hugged.

"I'm fine," she said. "Ruby is back, and as the current president of the co-op she's handling everything now." She looked past me for a moment but there was no sign of Roma yet. "Do you want to wait for Roma inside?"

"Yes," I said, jamming my hands in my pockets. "It's so cold." Now that the sun had gone down, so had the temperature.

We started for the door.

"So cold is better than freezing cold," Maggie said.

I shot her a look. "I don't think there's a difference."

She gave me a look of mock indignation. "Of course there's a difference. Don't you know anything about winter after living in Minnesota for several of them?"

We stepped inside and I pushed my hood back. "It seems I don't," I said.

Eric was at the counter pouring a cup of coffee. "Kathleen doesn't think there's a difference between so cold and freezing cold," Maggie said to him.

"Of course there is," he said.

Maggie gave me a smirk.

"So where does bitterly cold fall in this so-called ranking system?" I asked.

Maggie gave a theatrical sigh and Eric shook his head. "I think we may have to revoke her status as an honorary Minnesotan," he said.

Claire, who was my favorite waitress at the restaurant, had come out of the kitchen. She smiled and gestured at a table by the window. "I'll show you to a table." She leaned her head close to mine. "You don't want them to get started on the four categories of snow."

"Five categories," Eric called after us. "You keep forgetting they added a new one last year!"

I took off my jacket and hung it on the back of my chair.

Claire handed me a menu. "Is Roma coming?"

"Yes," Maggie and I said in unison.

Claire gave Maggie a menu and set one on the table for Roma. Maggie ordered a pot of tea, as usual, and I ordered decaf, also as usual for this time of day.

"There actually *are* five types of snow," I said as I sat down.

Maggie smiled. "I love that you know that. What are they?"

"Graupel, plates, needles, columns and dendrites."

"Graupel. I like that word."

I realized I still had my scarf around my neck. I pulled it loose and turned to stuff it in the sleeve of my jacket. "It's from the German word *Graupe*, which means pearl barley."

Maggie frowned. "So graupel is hail."

"More like a mix of snow and hail," I said. "It's also called soft hail or tapioca snow. Because it's so soft it's not destructive like regular hail."

"You have the most interesting brain I've ever met," she said, lifting the lid of the teapot Claire had set in front of her and peering inside.

I loved watching the ritual of Maggie pouring a cup of tea. It was almost as enjoyable as Commander Will Riker calling "Red alert!" on an episode of *Star Trek: The Next Generation.*

I smiled across the table at her. "My brain says thank you for the compliment."

Maggie's attention shifted to something behind me. I turned to see that Roma had just come in the door. She spotted us and came over to the table, pulling off her gloves and pushing down her hood. She was wearing her sleek brown hair a little longer these days.

"Tea?" Claire asked.

"Please," Roma said.

Claire nodded. "I'll be right back."

"I'm sorry I'm late," Roma said as she took off her coat and sat down. "I had a patient—dog—that made the mistake of poking its nose in a porcupine's den."

"Ouch!" I said.

Maggie made a sympathetic face.

"What have I missed?" Roma asked.

"Maggie and Eric were trying to convince me that there's a difference between so cold, freezing cold and bitterly cold."

Roma gave me a blank look. "Well, of course there is. Everyone knows that."

I stuck out my tongue at her.

Claire returned with Roma's tea and we ordered pizza with spinach and turkey sausage.

"I'm guessing Marcus wasn't happy about Bridget's editorial this morning," Roma said.

I took a sip of my coffee. "I don't think anyone in the police department is happy about what Bridget wrote."

Roma leaned back in her chair and wrapped both hands around her cup. "I remember when Lily Abbott went missing. Everyone was talking about her running away."

"So no one thought anything had happened to her?" Maggie asked.

Roma shrugged. "I know it's hard to believe, but no. No one did. I think today people would look more seriously at that being a possibility, but not then."

"Lily had a brother," I said.

"Tim. He was in college, home for Christmas vacation. I remember my mother on the phone with someone saying that Tim was going around telling everyone he thought something bad had happened to Lily and how crazy that seemed to her. I don't think it seriously crossed anyone's mind that she might have been abducted, or heaven forbid, killed. That kind of thing just didn't happen. Not here in Mayville Heights. Back then most people didn't even lock their doors at night, as much of a cliché as that sounds."

"Maybe no one wanted to believe anything bad could have happened to her because if it could happen to someone else's child, it could happen to theirs," I said.

The three of us were silent for a moment. Finally Roma cleared her throat. "I'm just going to have faith that Marcus will figure out what happened."

Maggie nodded. "Me too."

"I'm changing the subject," I said. I gestured at Maggie. "Tell me how the igloo is coming along."

She smiled. "Better than I'd hoped for. We're more than halfway to the top."

Roma frowned. "You're building an igloo?"

Maggie reached for her tea. "Uh-huh. Out of packages of toilet paper. A couple of art classes at the high school are doing the work. I'm helping with the design. It's a charity challenge some of the area schools are taking part in. Everything they collect goes to the food bank."

"That's a great idea," Roma said. "Could I drop off a donation at your studio?"

Maggie smiled. "Yes. Thank you."

I looked over my shoulder then to see Claire coming with our pizza. She set it in the middle of the table and Roma served us all.

Maggie took the first bite and gave a little grunt of happiness. "It's better than mine," she said.

Claire grinned. "That's high praise. I'll tell Eric you like it."

Mags was right. The pizza was good, especially the sourdough crust. "This is good," I said, pulling a long string of mozzarella cheese from my slice. "But so is yours."

Maggie raised her slice in acknowledgment. "You're good for my ego."

Roma was frowning. "I really think I'd have to have your pizza again sometime soon, while the memory of this one is fresh on my taste buds, before I could make any kind of a fair comparison."

My mouth was full so I settled for nodding vigorously and pointing at Roma with my free hand.

Somehow as we ate, the topic turned to the fashions Roma wore when she was a teen. "Leg warmers with everything and those big oversize sweaters with the neck stretched out so they slid down on one shoulder." Roma gestured with her free hand. "Oh, and spandex leggings in hot pink and lime green."

"I need to see photos," Maggie said.

Roma shook her head. "No. No. And no."

"Not a problem," I said. "I have her mother's phone number."

Maggie gave me a thumbs-up.

"Did you have a Swatch watch?" I asked, tapping my own wrist.

"You know, I did," Roma said. "And I bought it myself with money I made cleaning out horse stalls. My mother said I already had a perfectly good watch and I didn't need another one. What I really wanted was a broken-heart necklace, but you could only get those from a guy, although I did know one girl who bought herself one of those necklaces and pretended her boyfriend—that no one had ever seen because he didn't actually exist—gave it to her." She traced a finger around the edge of her cup. "I can't believe those things meant so much to us. I remember being so angry at my mother because she didn't understand why I needed the 'right' pair of neon leggings. Can you picture me coming to tai chi in a pair of lime green leggings and hot pink leg warmers?"

"I think you'd look good," Maggie said.

Roma laughed. "I think I'd glow in the dark."

"What is a broken-heart necklace?" I asked. From the moment Roma had first said "broken-heart necklace," an unsettling sensation had curled up the back of my neck.

Roma shifted in my direction. "It's actually intended to be

more romantic than the name sounds. A broken-heart necklace was something a guy gave a girl when they were dating. It was just a small heart on a chain. The heart separated into two pieces. The girl was supposed to wear one half on the chain around her neck and the guy wore his on his key chain." She put a hand on her chest. "It was a 'you always have a piece of my heart' thing."

Claire had come back with the coffeepot. "A boy once gave me a pink flamingo Beanie Baby," she said.

"That's romantic," I said.

She made a face. "Not really. What he really wanted was the answers on our math sheet. And he swiped the flamingo from a girl in our class. On the other hand, we were six."

Everyone laughed and then we turned our attention back to what we were going to have for dessert. I couldn't get Roma's description of the broken-heart necklace out of my head. It sounded an awful lot like the necklace Harry had found.

Friday was my late day at the library. I was in the kitchen taking cinnamon rolls out of the oven with two very attentive and furry helpers when there was a knock at the back door.

"Merow," Hercules said. Both cats looked expectantly at me.

I put the pan of rolls on the rack I'd set on the counter. "No, you two stay right there," I said as I took off my big oven mitts. "I'll get that. Don't put yourselves out."

Ella King was standing on the steps in a heavy blue parka

and red earmuffs. She'd cut her hair since the last time I'd seen her and she'd added a blue streak in the front.

"I'm sorry to stop by without calling first," she said. "I need to talk to you, and I figured since it was Friday I'd just take a chance you'd be here."

"It's all right," I said. "C'mon in."

Ella kicked off her boots and stepped into the kitchen. "It smells wonderful in here," she said.

I gestured at the counter. "Rebecca's cinnamon roll recipe."

"So you still haven't managed to wheedle Mary's recipe out of her yet?"

Mary Lowe worked at the library with me. She made the best cinnamon rolls I'd ever tasted but refused to share the secret to them. I'd been trying to duplicate them for ages but never quite got there.

I smiled. "Not yet, but I'm going to keep working on her. In the meantime I'm trying everyone else's recipe."

Hercules murped "hello" to Ella. She leaned down to talk to him for a moment. Owen had disappeared. Quite possibly, literally.

"Taylor will be here this weekend," Ella said as she straightened up. "She said to tell you she'll be by the library tomorrow. Just between Thanksgiving and now she seems to have grown up so much."

Taylor was Ella and her husband Keith's only child. She had worked in the job Levi had now before she left for college, and we all missed her.

I smiled. "Everyone is going to be happy to see her."

I noticed how Ella kept twisting her wedding ring around her finger. Something was bothering her.

"How about a cup of coffee and a cinnamon roll?" I said. "I can't vouch for the cinnamon rolls, but I can promise the coffee is excellent."

"That sounds good," Ella said. "Since the recipe is Rebecca's I know they'll be delicious."

Once we'd sat down, plates and cups in front of us, Ella put both hands flat on the table and stared down at them for a moment. Hercules sat next to her chair, his green eyes fixed on her face.

"What did you want to talk to me about?" I asked.

Ella looked up at me then. "I need your help. You read the editorial in yesterday's paper."

Even though she hadn't phrased the words as a question, I nodded.

"I believe Bridget is right. I think the body found at the co-op shop is Lily Abbott." She paused and swallowed a couple of times. "I believe Lily was my mother."

chapter 5

For a long moment I just stared at Ella.

She pulled one leg up underneath her, smiling down at Hercules as she did. He was still watching her, head tipped to one side.

"I, uh, I don't understand," I finally said.

"I should tell you my backstory."

I nodded. "Please."

"You know I'm adopted."

"Taylor told me a couple of years ago when we were working on a display for World Adoption Day." I reached for my coffee.

Ella smiled. "I had wonderful parents and a happy childhood. I was loved and wanted and I can't imagine anyone else as my mother and father. I miss them both every day. And I want to make it clear that they were always supportive of me finding my birth parents." She paused and pressed her lips together for a moment. "My mom used to say that you can never have too many people who love you."

I smiled back at her. "I think your mother was right."

Ella picked up her mug.

"What makes you think Lily Abbott is your birth mother?" I asked.

"I was left in the manger of St. Luke's Church in Red Wing on December twenty-first, almost thirty-six years ago."

"The same night Lily disappeared."

"Yes." Ella set her mug back on the table without taking a drink.

"And no one made the connection between a missing pregnant woman in Mayville Heights and a newborn baby that turned up in Red Wing?"

"The minister who found me didn't get the authorities involved right away. He's dead now but I talked to his wife. They looked after me for two days, hoping whoever left me would come back. She told me that they didn't want my mother to pay for a decision that they believed she might have made at what felt like a very hopeless moment."

"They wanted to give her the chance to change her mind if she had second thoughts," I said.

Ella nodded again. "For those first two days no one knew about me, so no one made the connection. On top of that, the minister's wife said that I was clearly a full-term baby and Lily was supposedly seven months pregnant."

I raised an eyebrow. "Supposedly?"

"I think Lily was lying about how far along she was. She'd refused to tell anyone who her baby's father was. The night she disappeared she'd argued with her parents about that again." She played with the scarf at her neck with one hand. "And most importantly our blood types didn't match."

Again she had taken me by surprise. "I don't understand," I said. If their blood types were different, why did Ella think she was Lily Abbott's child?

"A baby turning up in Red Wing, even two days after a pregnant teenager disappeared, was too much of a coincidence," she said, "so they compared my blood type with Lily's blood type. Her family knew Lily's because she'd had surgery. She was type O and I'm type AB."

I flipped through the various possibilities in my mind. "So you think there was a mistake in the bloodwork."

Ella shook her head. "No. They ran mine twice and they checked Lily's mother and father in case there had been a problem with hers. Her parents both had type O blood. As far as the police and child protective services were concerned, there was no way the baby the minister had found in the manger could be Lily Abbott's child."

I twisted my engagement ring around my finger, trying

to remember some of the things I'd learned about genetics over the summer. There are four main blood groups: A, B, AB and O. A person's blood type is inherited from their parents and most of the time follows a predictable pattern. But there are rare exceptions. "Taylor has type AB blood, the same as you do."

"She does," Ella said, taking a sip of her coffee. Her eyes never left my face.

"Both of you have the cis-AB allele," I said slowly. One of those rare exceptions.

"We do."

"And since we know Lily had type O blood, you had to have inherited that from your biological father."

She nodded in agreement. "It's the only thing that makes sense. I inherited it from him and Taylor got it from me."

"I don't know much about cis-AB," I said, getting up for more coffee, "other than it's an extremely rare blood type." I gestured at Ella's cup and she shook her head.

"The cis-AB allele results in AB blood for a child that inherits it, no matter what blood type the other parent has," Ella said. "That's the most important thing to know. It shows up most often in Korean and Japanese populations. If I inherited that blood type from my father, then Lily could have been my mother and I'm convinced that she was."

Hercules was still watching Ella. He seemed engrossed in the conversation.

I came back to the table with my cup. "How did you figure it out?" I asked.

Ella shook her head. "For a long time I didn't. A couple of months ago Taylor went to a blood drive on campus. When I talked to her afterward she told me she was the same blood type as I am. She didn't think much of it, but I knew something was off because I knew Keith had type O blood.

"I went to see my doctor and she sent me to a genetic counselor. At first I thought they'd gotten my blood type wrong when they did the test when I was a baby. The counselor explained I must have inherited my blood type from my father."

"What did you do next?" I asked, adding cream and sugar to my cup.

"I went to see Lily's former high school boyfriend, Bryan James. I asked him to do a DNA test." She shifted in her seat again. She had a sort of restless energy, as though staying still took work. "I was prepared for him to say no, but he didn't. From the beginning I just had this feeling that he wasn't my father, and I was right."

Ella sighed. "Kathleen, you have a brother and a sister, don't you?"

I nodded and automatically smiled. "Ethan and Sarah. They're twins."

"I could have siblings out there somewhere. My father could easily still be alive. I just want to know where I came from—*who*

I came from. It doesn't mean I didn't love my mom and dad. I just want answers."

She dropped her head for a moment, and when she lifted it to look at me I could see the resolve and the sadness in her face. "I always thought my mother—my birth mother—left me at the church because she didn't want me. Otherwise, she would have at least tried to find me. But if I'm right and Lily was my mother, she couldn't come back for me or try to find me because she was dead. And maybe the reason she left me in the manger that night was because she was trying to keep me safe."

I felt a knot in the pit of my stomach. I didn't see any way that I could help Ella find the answers she was looking for. I tried to choose my words carefully. "I think you should talk to Marcus," I said. "It's possible they can do a DNA test to show whether or not Lily was your mother. It could help them with their identification."

Ella was already nodding. "I was going to talk to him but I wanted to talk to you first. Everyone knows you're good at finding out things—things the police can't discover so easily. People trust you. They'll talk to you. I want to know who killed my mother, Kathleen. You're my best hope for finding answers."

I rubbed the bridge of my nose with two fingers. "First of all you need to find out for certain that Lily is your biological mother."

Ella leaned forward. "Given what I know now about my blood type and given that I was left at the church on the night Lily disappeared, it seems pretty clear I'm her child."

I held up one hand. "I'm not disagreeing with you," I said, "but you need proof."

"I'll get it," she said. "Then you'll help me?"

I took a slow breath and let it out. "Ella, I don't have the skills or the resources for something like that. I don't even know how to start."

"You figured out who killed Simon Janes's father and you helped Harrison find his daughter."

"I found some papers that helped Harrison," I said. I was treading carefully. "That's all. And as for figuring out who killed Simon's father, some of that was just luck."

"I don't think it was luck." Ella raised her chin. She wasn't going to be dissuaded. "And even if it was, who's to say you couldn't get lucky again?"

I put both of my hands flat on the table as I struggled to find the right words to let her down easy. "This is a case that's close to forty years old. Some of the people involved are dead. And the ones who aren't probably won't remember the details of something that happened so many years ago. It's not the same as asking someone where they were a week from last Tuesday, and even in those circumstances people can't always remember. Trying to find out what happen so long ago is going to be a challenge, even for the police with all their resources."

Ella waved away my words. "I don't need resources. What I need is someone who understands people, someone other people instinctively trust. I'm going to go talk to Marcus when I leave here. I'll get proof that Lily Abbott was my mother. Please, don't close the door completely yet."

"Keep in mind the police haven't identified those remains yet. And even if they do turn out to be Lily's, you still need real proof that she was your biological mother. You can't do anything else until you have those two answers."

Ella was nodding, but I felt as though she really wasn't listening. It was more like she was waiting for me to stop talking so she could speak. "Fine, then," she said. "I'll get them."

We both got to our feet and Hercules finally moved, coming to stand beside me. He continued to watch Ella with curiosity. I wondered how much of the conversation he had actually understood. Certainly more than the average feline.

Ella pulled on her coat and then, to my surprise, wrapped me in a quick hug. "Thank you," she said. "I *will* get those answers."

She gave Hercules a little wave and he responded with a soft meow. I was left with the feeling that somehow my no had turned into a yes, or at least a maybe.

When the back door closed Hercules finally looked at me. "I don't see how I can help Ella," I said.

He continued to look at me, seemingly without blinking. I turned to get a bit more coffee and I could feel the cat's green eyes still on me. I turned and looked back at him. He hadn't so much as twitched a whisker.

"I can't do anything until Marcus can say whether or not the body is Lily's," I said, "and that could take a week or more."

"Mrrr," he said.

The next day the body was identified as Lily Abbott's.

chapter 6

It was cold again on Saturday morning and I wondered if Maggie would classify this as so cold, freezing cold or bitterly cold. Hercules decided it was too cold, period. He poked his furry nose out the back door, at least waiting for me to open it first, gave his head a shake and retreated to his favorite seat by the window. I decided if there was anything to reincarnation, I was coming back in my next life as a cat.

There was a dusting of snow on the back steps. I grabbed the broom and swept them clean. Then I used the shovel to make quick work of clearing the path to the driveway. I brushed the snow off my truck and then went back inside for my messenger bag and my travel mug of coffee.

Hercules had given up looking out the porch window and had gone back into the kitchen. I gave him a scratch behind his left ear and one of the kitty crackers that Maggie had bought. "Don't tell your brother," I whispered.

"Mrrr," he said softly, butting my hand with his head.

As usual Harry had been and gone at the library. The walkway and steps were cleared of snow and there was a thin layer of sand in the parking lot. I let myself into the building and went upstairs to my office. Once I'd replaced my boots with shoes and hung up my things, I sat down at my desk with my coffee and opened my laptop. I'd headed down early deliberately so I could reread the police statement and see what response Bridget had made.

Bridget's comments were brief and to the point. She chastised the police department for what she called a lackadaisical investigation thirty-six years ago. She went on to say that she was confident that the current investigation would be far more extensive and urged people to assist the police in any way they could.

Ella had gone to talk to Marcus after she'd left me Friday morning, and arrangements had been made for the DNA test to determine whether or not Lily was Ella's biological mother.

"She made a convincing argument," Marcus had said, "and if Ella is Lily's child, there could be a connection between her being left in the church manger and Lily's death, so determining their connection is part of the investigation."

Marcus had been sitting at my feet while I worked on a knot

in his left shoulder that had probably come from being checked into the boards at hockey practice. He helped coach the girls' high school hockey team and they played hard and fast. When I didn't say anything, he had tilted his head to look up at me. "You think Ella will be proved right, don't you?" he said.

I sighed and nodded. "I do. I think you'd have to put too many coincidences together to have things work out any other way." I leaned down to kiss him before getting back to his shoulder. "Lily was murdered, wasn't she?" I asked.

"Yes. Bridget will have a statement from the department in the paper tomorrow."

I felt his body stiffen a little under my fingers. "Have you talked to her?"

"I didn't, but someone from the department did."

"Do you know who has been feeding Bridget information?"

Marcus had raked a hand back through his hair, a sure sign this was a stressful subject. "No. I don't even know why this person—whoever they are—is helping her." The muscles along his jawline had tightened. "But I am going to find out."

I shut my computer off and went downstairs. Mary was just coming up the steps carrying a Christmas cookie tin along with her tote bag. I hurried to get the front door and hold it open for her. "Thank you," she said with a smile.

"Could I carry that for you?" I asked, indicating the large round container in her left hand.

"Well, now, that would be a bit like getting the fox to herd all the chickens into the henhouse, wouldn't it?" she said. She was bundled up in a black wool duffle coat.

I laughed. "Yes, it probably would." I had a sweet tooth and Mary was an excellent baker. I took her tote bag instead, which she had no problem surrendering.

Once we were upstairs in the staff room, Mary set the cookie tin on the counter and unfastened her coat. Underneath she was wearing one of her many holiday sweaters. Mary had sweaters for every holiday including a few I'd never heard of before. This one had Rudolph's head on the right front side with a nose that lit up. It was actually one of her more sedate cardigans.

"Are you going to give me grief about Bridget?" she asked as she hung her coat in her locker. "Everyone else seems to be." Bridget was Mary's daughter.

I shook my head. "No. As far as I'm concerned our friendship is separate from anything Bridget does at the newspaper."

Mary smiled. "I appreciate that." She closed her locker door and gestured at the tin on the counter beside me. "One," she said, holding up a single finger.

I opened the lid to find the container was filled with gingerbread stars decorated with thin stripes of icing. I took one. As usual they were delicious.

"You make the best cookies," I said.

Mary was getting herself a cup of coffee. "Yes, I do," she said. "That doesn't change the fact that you don't need more than one of them."

I grinned at her and put the lid back on the tin. "Taylor is coming to see us sometime this morning."

Mary smiled again. "I heard she was home this weekend. I was hoping to see her." She narrowed her gaze at me. "Do not get into those cookies again before that child gets here." She shook a finger at me.

I ducked my head. "Yes, ma'am," I said.

"Have the police released the crime scene?" Mary asked a few minutes later as I turned on the lights downstairs before opening the building for the day.

"Not yet," I said. "Maggie is hoping she'll be able to get back in by Monday."

"I can't imagine Harry being happy about not being able to get the damage from that leak repaired."

"He's not, but at this point there's nothing he or anyone else can do except figure out how to clean things up when the building is free again."

"I remember when Lily disappeared," Mary said as she went to empty the book deposit. "Bridget was just a toddler."

I plugged in the snowflake lights that wrapped around the checkout desk. "Did you know Lily's family?" I asked.

"My younger brother, Ben, was friends with her brother, Tim. Ben said Tim told him that Lily was fighting with her mother and father because of the baby. They wanted Lily to place the baby for adoption and go on to college. They at least wanted the father to take some responsibility, but Lily refused to name him."

"Didn't Lily have a boyfriend?" I moved toward the computer area to turn the machines on.

Mary pushed the bin full of books over to the circulation desk. "Ex-boyfriend. But he had an alibi for the time Lily was believed to have disappeared. Her brother, Tim, always said something bad had happened to Lily. They were close. It looks like he was the only one with half a clue."

Once the computers were all up and running I walked back to join Mary.

"Which playlist are we using?" she asked.

"Mine," I said with a smile.

We had decided to play holiday music (softly) every Saturday morning for the month of December. It had been Susan's suggestion. Larry Taylor had set up a temporary sound system for us and there were three speakers spread throughout the first floor. The only problem we'd run into was that Susan and I had very different opinions on holiday music. The rest of the staff didn't seem to care.

To my surprise, Susan was a traditionalist when it came to Christmas. Her idea of holiday music was songs like "White Christmas" and "O Holy Night." My taste ran to funny songs like "I Want a Hippopotamus for Christmas" and "Santa Never Brings Me a Banjo." After a lot of back-and-forth and some blatant bribery with Eric's chocolate chip cookies on Susan's part, we had decided to alternate playlists on alternate Saturdays.

We'd resorted to Rock, Paper, Scissors to decide who got the first Saturday.

Mary turned on the music, checked in the books from the book drop and then spent some time helping two high schoolers figure out how to format the history essays they had due after Christmas break. Levi put out the new magazines and then got to work cleaning gum from the tables in the children's department. I helped a harried mom find picture books for her two toddlers while Abigail was at the front desk checking out books and answering questions. I had just finished adding a few more books to our holiday reading shelf when Taylor King walked in. Abigail darted around the desk to wrap her in a hug, and I was next.

"It's so good to see you," I said. She wore jeans, a black puffer coat and one of her mother's knitted scarves at her neck. I thought that Ella was right. In just the short time since Thanksgiving, Taylor somehow seemed older.

Mary came over and gave Taylor a hug. "Kathleen's right," she said. "It is good to see you." Rudolph's nose was blinking merrily on her sweater.

"Thank you all for the care package you sent," Taylor said. "The cookies made me very popular and so did the socks."

Abigail grinned at Mary. "See?" she said. "I told you socks would be useful."

Mary made a dismissive motion like she was shooing away a bug. "There are cookies upstairs," she said.

"I was hoping there would be," Taylor said with a smile.

"First I want to know about Reading Buddies." Taylor had volunteered a lot of her time with the kids in the program designed to help foster a love of books. The little ones were crazy about her.

"We have more kids than we did last year," I said. "More little ones and more older ones for mentors."

"I have the card they made me up on my bulletin board," she said. "Anytime I'm having a bad day I just look at it and it makes me smile."

The mom I'd helped approached the desk with an armload of books. Abigail went to check her out.

"Is it all right if I walk around and look at all this year's decorations?" Taylor asked.

I smiled. "Of course. I think Susan outdid herself this year. She roped Levi and Riley Hollister into helping her."

"Make sure she sees the Cookie Monster tree," Mary said.

Taylor frowned. "You have a tree devoted to Cookie Monster?"

"Well, sort of," I said. "You really need to see it."

I walked her over to the children's department, where Susan and her co-conspirators had set up the tree. Levi waved hello from under a table—they knew each other from school. The Cookie Monster tree had been his idea.

Taylor laughed when she spotted the tree. "It's Cookie Monster!" she said as she walked all around it.

The tree was bright blue and lit with clear LED lights. At the top there was a Santa hat. The tree had eyes and a wide-open mouth. Levi had made the mouth from black poster board and the eyes from two white plastic balls and black felt. The tree had been a big hit with everyone, not just the kids.

"I miss this place," Taylor said, shoving her hands in her jacket pockets.

"We miss you," I said.

She smiled. "So when's the wedding going to be?"

"I'm still not certain. Marcus and I are going to Boston for Christmas and we'll set a date then. At least I think we will."

Taylor's expression grew serious. "I'm glad you're getting your happy ending." She cleared her throat. "My mom needs a happy ending, or at least some answers."

"And I hope she'll get them when the results of the DNA test come back," I said.

"That's not enough." She looked down at the floor for a moment. "C'mon, Kathleen. You know that DNA test is going to show that Lily Abbott was my mother's mother. You put everything together and it's the only thing that makes sense. But it's not enough. Someone took away my mom's chance to get to know her birth mother. She needs to know who. She needs to know why. She can't get those answers from a DNA test. But you can get them for her."

I was already shaking my head. "You're giving me way too much credit. I'm not a detective."

I barely got the words out. "I know," Taylor said. "That's why people tell you things. How would you feel if you found out you had family that you never got to know, and not because it was your choice or theirs?"

Inwardly I sighed. "You're not being fair," I said.

"I'm not trying to be fair." Her eyes met mine. "Please." She continued to look at me without saying anything more.

I felt a tangle of emotions knotted in my chest. "It was thirty-six years ago."

Taylor still didn't speak; she just continued to look at me. It was somehow harder than if she'd tried to argue her case.

I wanted to say no. But . . .

"I'm not making any promises, but I'll ask a few questions."

Taylor threw her arms around me. "I know you can figure this out," she said.

I wasn't sure at all that I could, but if I found any answers to Ella's questions, would they be the ones Ella and her family wanted?

chapter 7

It was snowing hard with several inches already on the ground when I got up on Sunday morning—earlier than I'd wanted to because Owen subscribed to the theory that if he was up everyone should be up. I'd been planning on going out to Marcus's house to beat him at his new rod hockey game and eat beef stew.

He called while Owen and I were looking in the refrigerator trying to decide what to put in a breakfast omelet. "It's really crappy out there and the forecast is for snow all day," he said.

"Move your giant head. I'm closing the door," I said sharply.

"My head is nowhere near the door and it's perfectly normal size," he said.

"Sorry. I was talking to Owen, not you."

The cat wrinkled his whiskers at me and I made a face back at him.

I set two tiny tomatoes, a handful of spinach and a chunk of cheddar on the counter next to the eggs. My backyard neighbor, Rebecca, had grown the tomatoes and spinach in the new greenhouse window in her dining room.

"The truck has new snow tires and a little snow doesn't bother me," I said.

"The thing is, it's not a little snow. It's a lot of snow and it's slippery; I've already helped get two cars out of the ditch. I don't think you should chance it."

I reluctantly agreed not to risk the weather. Marcus promised a rematch on the rod hockey and some leftover stew and we said good-bye.

I made my omelet and ate it with a slice of oatmeal bread and more coffee. Owen went to the kitchen door and meowed.

"It's snowing," I said.

He meowed, loudly, again. "Fine, you can go out if you want to." I opened the door into the porch, crossed the space and opened the back door. The steps and landing were covered with snow and a gust of wind blew it into our faces.

Owen shook his head, made a U-turn and headed for the kitchen. I wiped my face on the sleeve of my sweatshirt. Hercules, who had trailed us but wisely stayed behind me, gave a murp of sympathy and also retreated back to the warmth of the kitchen.

Since I had some time, I decided to make chicken soup in

the slow cooker. Once it was set up on the counter, I got out my laptop to see what else I could learn about Lily and baby Ella. Owen had wandered off but Hercules immediately settled on my lap, as he often did. As usual he seemed to be reading the screen and occasionally he clicked on something that invariably helped.

Someone matching Lily's description had been seen at the bus station early on December 22, I discovered. The young woman was wearing a green Mayville Heights High School hoodie and a gray knit beanie, both items that Lily Abbott owned and was regularly seen in. She also carried a dark blue backpack just like Lily's. The woman who saw her had noticed the tiny turquoise Care Bear clipped to the zipper pull of the backpack. She noticed it because her own little girl had the same one. Lily's mother confirmed Lily had one as well.

Hercules looked at me, his green eyes narrowed in curiosity.

"Wish Bear," I said. That seemed to satisfy him.

I leaned back in my chair, stretching first one arm and then the other over my head. According to the newspaper article, the sighting of Lily at the bus station was considered credible. There were just too many details like the hooded sweatshirt and the toy bear to be a coincidence. I could see why everyone thought Lily ran away. So how had she ended up dead? Had she left the bus station with someone she met there? Had she been abducted?

"We need to make a timeline with what we know so far," I told Hercules.

He gave a murp of agreement.

I got a piece of cardboard from the recycling bin and a heavy black marker from my messenger bag. I flattened the cardboard on the kitchen table. To my amusement the cat put his paw on one corner.

I wrote "bus station" and the approximate time Lily had been seen there at the far right end. From what I'd seen online, the last person *definitely* known to have seen Lily—other than whoever killed her—was her friend Mila. They had both been on the volleyball team. According to Mila it was snowing when Lily got in her car to head home. I put Mila's name at the corresponding time she'd been with Lily in the center of the cardboard.

Hercules moved his paw and his attention back to my laptop and clicked on something. We were back to an article about baby Ella, with the headline AWAY IN A MANGER.

I nodded. "You're right. When did Lily have the baby?" From what I'd read the minister had discovered baby Ella sometime just after midnight. Lily had been seen at the bus station later than that. I wrote "Ella born" in the space between Mila's name and the words "bus station." I added the other few facts I'd been able to glean from the newspaper accounts. Lily watching volleyball practice. Lily stopping for fast-food fries.

I studied the timeline. Hercules leaned sideways and seemed to do the same. Then he looked at me.

"I know," I said, rubbing the back of my neck with one hand. "It doesn't make things any clearer, does it?" What was I missing? "Where was Lily after she left her friend and before she showed up at the bus station?"

Hercules didn't seem to know.

"Wait a minute." I jabbed the air with the marker and the cat jumped. "Sorry," I said, reaching over to stroke his fur. "The bus station. Why was Lily at the bus station? Where was her car?"

I picked up Hercules and sat down at the computer again. A little more time in the *Chronicle*'s archives and we had the answer to my question. Lily's car had slid into the ditch not far from the high school. It had a damaged tire and wouldn't have been drivable even if she had somehow gotten pulled out. Since the car was covered in snow, no one knew how long it had been there, but at least overnight based on how much snow the storm had dumped.

I picked up the marker again, looked at the timeline for a moment and wrote "car in ditch" before "Ella born." So far the timeline wasn't much help, but maybe as I learned more it would be. "I need to talk to the minister's wife," I said to Hercules. "Maybe she'll be able to narrow down the time that her husband found Ella."

"Mrrr," he said. I decided to take that as support for my plan.

I felt the best way forward was to ask Ella to make the introduction to Ruth Hansen, hoping that would help her feel more comfortable talking to me. Before I shut down the laptop I made a note of the names of Lily's former boyfriend, Bryan James, and her best friend, Mila Serrano.

I wondered, was Bryan James the same Bryan James who had a child in Reading Buddies? I'd talked to the man a couple of times. He was an older dad, married for the second time. He had a seven-year-old son with big blue eyes and a love of dinosaurs. There was an excellent chance they were the same man.

Mila Serrano's name sounded familiar but I couldn't place it. Once again Hercules came to the rescue. Somehow his paw on the keyboard found a photo of the woman. Mila was one of the newest artists in the co-op. She created mixed-media, stylized portraits of people. I'd seen her work in the store, I realized.

"Thank you for your help," I said to Hercules. "You have very good research skills." He bowed his head, modestly accepting the praise.

I shut down the computer, put Hercules on the floor and went into the living room to check on the storm. It seemed to me that the snow was letting up a little. Owen wandered in and I bent over to pick him up. He looked outside and made a face.

"I think the worst is over," I said. "The sky seems to be a little brighter."

Owen wasn't impressed with my assessment of the weather. He squirmed to get down and stalked toward the kitchen, probably headed to his basement lair, where among other things he hid some of his stash of catnip chickens.

Hercules and I decided we needed cheese biscuits with the chicken soup. I was just taking them out of the oven when my phone rang. It was Ella.

"I'm sorry Taylor pressured you yesterday," she said without preamble. "I didn't send her to do that."

"I know," I said, sliding the biscuits onto the rack I'd put on the counter. "I'm glad you called. Would you call Ruth Hansen and vouch for me? I'd like to talk to her. And do you have Bryan James's contact information? Even though he isn't your biological father, I'd still like to talk to him."

For a moment there was silence on the other end of the phone. "I . . . uh . . . yes. Yes to everything. Absolutely." I wasn't sure if she was going to cry or laugh.

"I make no promises," I said. "And anything I learn I share with Marcus."

"I have no problem with that," Ella said. "I don't know how to say thank you."

I smiled even though she couldn't see me. "You just did."

Ella promised that she'd get in touch with Ruth Hansen right away and that she'd find Bryan James's phone number and e-mail. She thanked me again and we said good-bye. Ella called back in fifteen minutes to say Mrs. Hansen was going to be in Mayville Heights on Tuesday and would come to the library about two o'clock. She also read off Bryan's e-mail address and phone number.

"But if you want to talk to him in person you're going to have to wait. He coaches the middle school boys' basketball team and they're in St. Cloud at a tournament."

I thanked her and we said good-bye again.

By the time I'd eaten lunch and done the dishes it had

stopped snowing and I could see patches of blue sky. I pulled on my snow pants and parka so I could clear off the steps and the truck.

I was just starting to shovel the walkway when Fifi came over. I stopped what I was doing to pet the dog and talk to him. Hercules watched from the window and then to my surprise came through the door—literally. He stayed up on the stoop since he hated having wet feet. I wasn't sure if he was a bit jealous, a bit curious or actually interested in making friends with the big dog. Back before Halloween the dog had made several overtures.

There was no question that Fifi was afraid of the cat. He moved behind me and I bent down in the snow next to him and put one arm around his neck. He gave a small whine.

"Hercules won't hurt you," I said.

The dog kept his eyes locked on the cat. The tension I could feel in his body told me he was ready to bolt at any time.

After a moment Hercules began to nonchalantly wash his face. I noticed his gaze flick to Fifi from time to time. I kept patting the dog's side and talking to him and he seemed to settle a little. I got to my feet and picked up my shovel again. Fifi stayed close to me, watching Hercules all the time.

I was almost at the end of the walkway when I heard Mike calling the dog. "He's over here," I called.

Mike waded up my snowy driveway, saw the situation and smiled. "Well, it's more progress than you and I made the two times we tried to get Fifi used to Hercules."

I leaned down and took the dog's face in my hands. "You did a great job of facing your fears," I told him. He went over to Mike, tail wagging, and leaned against his leg. Mike patted Fifi's side. "Kathleen's right. You're a good dog," he said.

I thought how happy I was that I lived in a place where no one cared that you talked to your animals like they were people.

Mike and Fifi went home. The plow went by just as I finished the walkway. I went to clear off the truck because I knew Harry would be coming soon to do the driveway. Hercules meowed loudly from the stairs. He had ventured as far as the top one.

"C'mon," I said. No surprise he held up one paw and shook it.

I sighed. Also no surprise, I went and got him.

I brushed the snow off the driver's door, unlocked it and set Hercules on the front seat. Once the hood was free of snow Hercules came through the windshield to sit in a patch of sunshine. I looked around to see if anyone might have seen him, but the coast was clear.

I leaned my face close to his. "One of these days you're going to get caught," I said. He licked my chin.

Harry arrived about five minutes later as I was trying to decide whether to shovel the snow out of the bed of the truck or leave it and hope the sun would melt it. He climbed out of the truck and walked over to me. "I talked to Maggie, and Marcus is going to release the co-op space in the morning," he said. "I'm going down to get started first thing. You think I could borrow your cat? I don't think there's any more wildlife, but it wouldn't hurt to have him on standby."

"Sure," I said.

"Seven thirty too early?" Harry asked.

"Not for Owen," I said.

I moved the truck so Harry could blow out the driveway and clear the front steps. Then I scooped up Hercules and headed for the house. Once inside I called Marcus.

"Is your road plowed?" I asked.

"It is," he said, "and I just came in from clearing the driveway."

"Harry is just finishing mine. Would you like some company after all?"

"If the company is you, absolutely."

"You're such a romantic," I teased.

He laughed. "If you think I sound romantic you should see me. I'm very manly after shoveling the driveway."

It was my turn to laugh. "Let me guess. You're standing in the kitchen, unshaven, in a sweaty T-shirt and long underwear."

"But it's my Batman long underwear," he said. "Doesn't that increase my manly quotient?"

"I'll see you soon," I said. I was still laughing as I ended the call.

As I headed out to Marcus's the sun was high in the sky, melting the bits of snow the plow had left behind on the roads, helped along by salt and sand. I arrived to find that Marcus had showered and was wearing jeans and a long-sleeved red thermal T-shirt. He'd already started cooking.

I kissed him and settled at the table with a cup of coffee. Micah climbed onto my lap. "Tell me about the Batman underwear," I stage-whispered to the cat.

She shook her furry head and covered her face with a paw.

I laughed.

Marcus looked over his shoulder at us and pointed a spoon at the cat. "You might want to remember who dispenses the treats in this house," he said.

She stretched up and nuzzled my chin.

Micah spent a couple more minutes on my lap before jumping down and moving to sit closer to Marcus. I knew she was hoping he'd drop something like a bit of meat. Both of the boys did the same thing.

"We have a small problem with our trip to Boston," Marcus said, stirring something in the bottom of the Dutch oven.

"What do you mean 'small problem'?" I asked. Our tickets had been booked for months.

"The flight has been canceled."

"Why?"

"Scheduling, as far as I know. Contract negotiations with the airline aren't going well and the pilots are refusing extra flights." He glanced over at me.

I sighed.

"We'll find another flight," he said. "Could you leave a day earlier if we needed to?"

I nodded. "I'm pretty sure Susan would cover for me."

"Would you mind a couple of plane changes?"

I'd been looking forward to going to Boston for Christmas for months. I missed my crazy family. "I will change planes half a dozen times if I have to," I said. I really hoped I didn't have to.

Once the stew was simmering, we set Marcus's rod hockey game on the table and I beat him three games in a row.

"Why do I play with you?" he asked.

"I've asked myself that question more than once," I said, flipping the tiny puck in the air and catching it again.

"And why is it that someone who can't skate can beat me at floor hockey and tabletop hockey?"

"I have fast reflexes and I've been playing both since I was six." I grinned at him.

"Did you ever go outside when you were a kid?"

My parents were actors. They had done summer theater all up and down the East Coast for pretty much all the years of my childhood. I had spent a lot of time hanging around backstage. I'd played a lot of floor hockey, pinball and rod hockey when I was a kid, among other things. "Of course I went outside," I said with mock indignation. "How do you think I got to the library?"

Marcus put the game away and then peered at his stew. "I forgot to tell you," he said. "We're releasing the co-op in the morning."

I wrapped my arms around his waist and kissed the side of

his jaw. "I already know," I said. "Harry told me when he came to do the driveway." I gave him a second kiss and pulled out my phone. "I need to call Susan and ask if she can open tomorrow and I think I'll see if Levi can come in early. He's off. Teacher's meetings."

"No problem," Susan said when I reached her.

I could hear her sons' voices in the background.

"Can I ask what you're doing?"

"Eric and the boys are building a giant snowman in the backyard and there's some disagreement on the math. There may be calculus involved."

Knowing the boys, there *could* easily be calculus involved. I thanked her again and called Levi, who happily said yes to extra hours.

I set my phone on the table and it rang. It was Maggie.

"You've probably heard Harry can start work in the morning," she said.

"I have and Owen will be happy to see you."

I told her I'd meet her at seven thirty and we said good-bye.

Marcus was at the counter, head in one of the cupboards. "Do you want dumplings?" he asked.

"Please," I said. "Could I help?"

Micah appeared at my feet, literally, and meowed.

Marcus turned to look at us. "Thank you to both of you but I've got this."

I decided I could set the table. "Where did the dancing-reindeer place mats come from?" I asked.

He smiled. "Hannah."

Marcus's sister was always trying to loosen up her big brother. Since we were going to be in Boston he didn't have a tree. I had convinced him to put lights on the big evergreen in the front yard and candles in the front windows.

"I'm looking forward to seeing her at New Year's."

He took a large mixing bowl from the cupboard. "Me too. It's been a long time since I've seen her at any holiday."

"I think Burtis is planning some kind of a get-together for New Year's Eve."

Marcus shot me a look. "Please tell me it won't involve any singing."

Marcus's dad, Elliot Gordon, and Burtis Chapman had been friends since they were boys. The fact that Elliot was a well-respected lawyer and Burtis once worked for the town boot-legger had never affected the strong bond of loyalty between the two of them. On one of Elliot's visits the two of them had ended up entertaining the crowd in the bar at the St. James Hotel. A fair amount of alcohol had been involved.

"I can't promise no singing, but at least your mom will be here. There may be some pinball. Your father and I still haven't played."

Burtis's son, Brady, kept his pinball machine out at his father's house. I'd bested Burtis at the game multiple times. Marcus refused to play me but the last time Elliot had been in town he'd challenged me to a match.

"Dad's really good at pinball," Marcus warned.

I smiled. "I'm better."

Micah trailed me while I found knives and forks, salt and pepper, and some of the green tomato pickles I'd made a few months ago.

"Do you want some of this stew to take for lunch on Monday?" Marcus asked. He had flour on his T-shirt and on his chin.

"Yes, please," I said. "I'll probably work up an appetite at the shop."

"You won't find anything."

I turned to look at him, still holding the dish of pickles in one hand. "Why do you think I'm looking for anything?"

"I know you and I know Ella is looking for answers."

I set the pickles on the table. "I just want to look around. Why did Lily's body end up there, of all places?"

Marcus made a face at the contents of the bowl in front of him. "Maybe her killer knew the building. Maybe they had easy access to it. It was December. There aren't a lot of places to dump a body and not have it be found in December."

"That suggests whoever killed her knew this town," I said slowly.

Marcus turned to look at me. "Yes, it does."

The killer knew Mayville Heights. The killer was likely *from* Mayville Heights. The thought made my chest hurt.

chapter 8

Monday morning was clear and cold. I pulled on my paint-spattered jeans and a faded T-shirt and topped that with an old sweatshirt that had a hole in one elbow. Owen ate his breakfast, washed his face and then went to sit by the kitchen door, shooting me impatient looks every few minutes. We pulled in behind Harry's truck at twenty-five minutes after seven. Maggie was waiting for me just inside the door.

"Good morning," she said. She leaned closer and smiled at Owen. "Good morning to you, too."

He dipped his head toward her and smiled back. I set him down on the floor and he immediately headed through the open door into the shop.

"You must be happy to finally get started in here," I said.

She nodded. "I am. We all are. People don't want to buy art from a website. They want to see it in person."

"Where's Ruby? Is she still in Minneapolis?"

"She was back but she's gone again. They wanted another piece for the show."

We walked inside to join Harry. He and Owen were just finishing up a circuit of the space with the cat leading the way, peering into every corner and sniffing everything.

"Hi, Harry. How are you?" I said.

He smiled. "Morning, Kathleen." He glanced at Maggie. "As far as either of us can tell, there's no more wildlife in here."

"Thank you," she said. "Both of you." I saw her shoulders relax.

Harry had brought in several large garbage bins and I pulled on the work gloves I'd brought with me and helped him clean up the mess we'd left behind the last time. "I'm surprised all of this isn't covered with mold," I said to Harry.

"You and me both," he said. "I think the fact that the heat was on helped a lot." He gestured at what I had assumed was some kind of fan. "I borrowed that air cleaner from Burtis and I think I'll run it for a few hours just to be on the safe side."

Harry and I made short work of removing the remaining drywall. He stuffed the last piece into a bin. Maggie had been walking around the room making notes about what needed to be done, with Owen adding commentary. I stood in front of the space where we'd found Lily Abbott's body. Marcus was right. I didn't see a single thing that would help me figure out who had done this.

"I know what you're doing," Harry said.

"I'm looking for answers," I said. "But I can't seem to find any. Why did the person who killed Lily put her body here of all places?"

Harry looked at the wall cavity. Then he looked at me. "Are you going to stop for coffee at Eric's on your way to the library?" he asked.

It was a bit of an abrupt change in the conversation, but I nodded as I pushed my hair back off my face. "I probably will."

"A small one or a large one?"

"You know me," I said. "I'll get the largest size. I always do. A small coffee would be gone before I made it to the library parking lot. The large one is just more convenient."

Harry gave an indifferent shrug and reached for the shovel we'd been using to get up the small chunks of broken Sheetrock.

It took a moment for me to see what he was getting at. For some reason the co-op location had been a convenient place for the killer to leave Lily. Maybe if I could figure out the why of that I could figure out the who.

"Okay, I get it," I said.

Harry dumped a shovelful of debris into a bin. "Pretty much figured you would," he said.

We got most of the small pieces of drywall off the floor and I started sweeping with the push broom Harry had brought in.

"I just want to take a quick look in the basement," he said.

"Go ahead," I said. "I've got this."

Maggie fished her keys out of her pocket and handed them to him. "Could I borrow your assistant?" he asked.

She looked down at Owen. "Would you please go help Harry?"

The cat cocked his head to one side and meowed.

"I'll be fine," she said. "And Kathleen is here."

Owen's golden eyes flicked to me, but he dutifully followed Harry.

I made short work of the sweeping, using the shovel as a dustpan. Then I joined Maggie, who was sitting on the windowsill of one of the front windows. "What's on your list?" I asked.

"Fix that wall, of course," she said. "Replace the light fixture that we know was damaged by the water." She indicated the overhead light at the far end of the room. "Repair the two receptacles on that wall. See if those shelves that are down in the basement will work there, and since two of the walls will have to be painted, paint the whole dang space."

"That shouldn't take long," I said.

"Do you think it's too ambitious to hope we could be open in a week or so?"

I shook my head. "I don't think so, but see what Harry says."

Harry and Owen returned, the cat leading the way, just as Maggie and I were measuring the wall to see if the shelving units that had been in the basement for the last six months would fit in the space.

"They should fit," I said to her.

"What should fit?" Harry asked.

"Did you see those two metal shelving units in the basement?" Maggie asked.

He nodded. "I saw them. Are they coming up here?"

"We'd like to bring them up. We need the extra storage space."

"I took a look at them while I was down there," Harry said, pulling a small notebook and a pencil out of his pocket. "They'll definitely fit in that space. I do think they should be anchored to the wall so they don't accidentally get pulled down." Harry had an uncanny ability to look at something and figure out whether or not it would fit in the back of a truck, under a set of stairs or along a wall.

"That's a good idea," Maggie said. "Did you find what you were looking for in the basement?"

Owen meowed loudly before Harry could answer.

I bent down and picked him up. "Maggie wasn't talking to you," I said.

He wrinkled his whiskers at me.

"We found a small space between one of the windows and the foundation where I think wildlife has been getting in."

"Can you fix it?" Maggie asked.

He nodded. "I need to go get a couple of things but it's an easy repair."

"So you can do it now?" Maggie asked.

"As soon as I get what I need," he said. "I'll put together an estimate for everything else."

Maggie held her list out to Harry. He read it over, nodding as he did so. "None of this is complicated. I recommend you get Oren to do the painting. I know he's around and he does a much better job than I do and he's fast."

"That will work," Maggie said. "Ruby had to do a last-minute trip to Minneapolis to take another piece for the show. She'll be back tonight."

"I'll get the estimate to you by the end of the day," Harry said.

Maggie put the list back in her pocket. "The co-op board has a meeting planned for tonight. Ruby will be in touch tomorrow morning."

Harry indicated the air cleaner. "Run that for the rest of the day. Just to be on the safe side."

"I will," she said.

Harry looked at me. "Thank you for your help. Both of you."

I smiled. "Anytime."

"I'll be back," he said to Maggie, and he was gone.

Maggie and I went upstairs to the studio. "I think I'll wait and start yoga on Wednesday and tai chi on Thursday. I need to clean up a little. There's dust everywhere."

"I have some time," I said. "What can I do?"

I vacuumed the studio floor while Maggie dusted every flat surface with help—of sorts—from Owen. Then I worked my way down the stairs with the vacuum while she mopped the studio floor with Owen supervising from the bench just outside the studio door where we changed our shoes.

"I'll do the steps and the entryway after Harry gets finished," she said.

"Mags, you know Mila Serrano, don't you?" I asked.

"Not really well, but yes, I know her. Her studio is just down the hall from mine. She does these incredible stylized portraits." Her eyes narrowed. "Why are you asking?"

"She was friends with Lily Abbott." I hesitated for a moment. "I'd like to talk to her."

Maggie didn't ask why, though she must have been curious. All she said was, "I'll introduce you. Just tell me when."

"Thank you," I said. I looked at Owen. "We need to get going."

He immediately became engrossed with his left foot.

I reached over and picked him up before he could disappear into the studio—or disappear altogether.

"Thank you for coming," Maggie said. "I'm keeping my fingers crossed that Harry has figured out where those unwanted visitors came from."

"Merow," Owen said.

I gave Maggie a one-armed hug. "Like the furball said, we'll be here anytime you need us."

I had time so I drove Owen home and gave him a sardine cracker as a reward. He ate while I changed and he breathed fish breath on me when I bent down to say good-bye. There was no sign of Hercules, which probably meant he'd braved the snow in the backyard to mooch a second breakfast from Everett and Rebecca.

I drove down to the library, stopping at Eric's for coffee. I thanked Susan and Levi for filling in for me.

"How do things look at the store?" Susan asked, pushing her cat's-eye-framed glasses up her nose.

"Better than I expected," I said. "Harry should be able to get going as early as tomorrow."

"So they could be open again before Christmas?"

I nodded. "If everything works out. Yes."

Susan held up one hand with her fingers crossed.

"How did the math for the snowman work out?" I asked.

"Fine," she said. "Which may not be a good thing. When I put the boys to bed they were talking about scaffolding."

It was a quiet day, even for a Monday. I had plenty of time at lunch to eat the container of stew Marcus had sent home with me—it was even better the second day—and see what I could learn about Reverend Richard Hansen. Very little, it turned out. He was the minister at St. Luke's for thirty-four years. I read condolences online from his obituary page, and over and over again people mentioned his kind heart and his generosity. It sounded like the person Ella had described.

I also tried Bryan James and got his voice mail. I left a brief message explaining I was helping Ella search for her biological family and was hoping to ask him a few questions about Lily Abbott. That was true as far as it went.

Tuesday morning when I got to the library I discovered that the book drop was frozen shut again. I couldn't get it open, not even trying to force it from the inside using my booted foot. After pulling and pushing and almost getting my entire left leg stuck inside, I gave up and called Harry.

"Leave if for now," he said. "If it gets a little warmer, that may be enough to help you open it."

"I don't mean to be the voice of doom," I said, "but this is as warm as it's supposed to get today." I wondered where Harry came down on the so cold, freezing cold, bitterly cold debate.

He promised he'd stop by just before lunch. "I'm starting work at the co-op store this afternoon."

"Best news I've had all day," I said. I told him I'd see him later and we said good-bye.

Ruth Hansen arrived at five minutes to two. She walked over to the desk where I was talking to Levi and introduced herself to me.

"Thank you for coming," I said. I still hadn't heard back

from Bryan and I was happy that at least I wouldn't have to chase down Ruth. I knew none of these people were obligated to talk to me, but in my experience most people wanted to help when a crime had been committed.

"It's my pleasure," she said. "I'm happy to help Ella in any way I can. She's a lovely person." I noticed she was wearing one of Ella's scarves at the neck of her charcoal gray coat. I heard a hint of a British accent in her voice.

Ruth Hansen was a little taller than my own five six. We were eye to eye standing at the desk and I was wearing heels, albeit not high ones. She had snow white hair pulled back in a French twist, high cheekbones and gorgeous, creamy skin that made me think of a sheet of fine Japanese paper.

"I'm taking my break," I said to Levi. I turned to Ruth. "Let's go up to my office."

Once we were upstairs, I asked, "Would you like coffee or tea?"

"Coffee, please," she said. "If it's not too much trouble. Don't let the accent fool you. I've been here so long I'm a die-hard coffee drinker."

I smiled. "You're a kindred soul."

I got a cup of coffee for both of us and we settled in the two chairs in front of my desk.

"You're helping Ella look for her birth family," Ruth said.

Strictly speaking, that was true. "A lot of time has passed," I said. "What do you remember from the night she was left at your church?"

Ruth took a sip of coffee. "What I remember most is the snow. It had snowed all afternoon and Richard had thought about canceling the service, but the plows seemed to be keeping the road passable and the longest-night service is important to a lot of people. The snow had stopped before the service began, and Richard and Joe Cairns, our sexton, had managed to clear the steps and the church parking lot before people arrived.

"There were more people than we'd expected, and after we got home Richard was restless. He decided to stay up a little longer. He came in and woke me sometime after midnight and he was holding the baby. For a moment I didn't realize it was a real baby in his arms."

"What did he say happened?" I asked.

"He told me that he had been looking across the street at the church—it and the rectory were across from each other—and had seen some small movement in the manger. He put on his coat and boots and walked over to have a look, thinking it was some animal, and he found Ella. I remember him saying he didn't really think to look for anyone. It was cold and he brought her home."

"So he didn't see Ella being left in the manger?"

Ruth shook her head. "No. Like I said, he just wanted to get the baby in out of the cold. She was wrapped in a towel and a gray wool blanket. I was a nurse. I looked her over and she seemed fine and certainly not premature."

"But you didn't call the police," I said.

Ruth's gaze slid away from mine for a moment. "I know it was wrong," she said. "Richard was insistent that it was almost Christmas and we needed to keep the baby for at least a day or two because the mother might change her mind." She looked at me again. "Leaving the baby in the manger that way made me think the mother wasn't very old. I was twenty when our first child was born. I knew how overwhelming it could be to have a child when you were barely an adult yourself, so I didn't put up much of an argument."

I took a sip of my own coffee to buy some time. The story Ruth had just told me sounded just like the one she'd told the reporter who had interviewed her. It sounded *exactly* like that story, as though she'd memorized it thirty-six years ago and stuck with it ever since.

"Ella speaks very highly of your husband," I said. "He was a good man."

She nodded. "Yes, he was. He was a man of faith even if sometimes that faith was misplaced."

"When did you figure out that he hadn't told you the whole story?" I asked gently.

Ruth reached for her cup. "In thirty-six years you're the first person to figure that out. What gave me away?"

I'd spent my whole life watching my mother and father create characters, from the smallest details to the broadest strokes. Over time I'd just instinctively learned what rang true and what seemed false.

"Partly gut feeling," I said with a smile. "And partly that your story sounded just a bit too rehearsed."

"I've told it a surprising number of times over the years," she said. "Richard did wake me up the way I said, but I knew very quickly that he wasn't being straight with me. The man couldn't tell a lie to save his life."

"That's a good quality to have as a minister," I said.

Ruth smiled. "And he was a good one, kind and compassionate. He told me a young woman had come to the door carrying the baby. She had been going to leave Ella at the church but she saw the light on at our house and she knew it was the rectory. She told Richard that she couldn't keep the baby but wanted her to have a good home. He tried to convince her to come inside, but he said she seemed jumpy. She stayed down on the steps, in the shadows, after she handed him the baby, and she had a scarf wrapped around her face so he couldn't make out her features. Richard told her that we could keep the baby with us for two days before we called the police so she could come back if she changed her mind, no questions asked."

She exhaled slowly. "He was certain she would. He kept putting off making the call, so finally I did it."

I leaned forward, my coffee forgotten. "Did he tell you anything about the young woman?" I asked.

Ruth twisted her gold wedding band around her finger. "I remember he said that she wore a green Mayville Heights High

School sweatshirt with a hood, which he noticed because he didn't think it was warm enough. She had some kind of knit hat on her head with a no-ghosts pin on the brim and Black Dog boots."

The description matched the description of the young woman at the bus station whom the police had believed was Lily. "Do you think it was Lily Abbott?" I asked.

"I assumed it was," Ruth said. "Richard couldn't be sure. As I said, she'd had a scarf covering most of her face and she stayed out of the light. And he wasn't wearing his glasses. I assumed it was her because who else could it have been? Richard said the mother had blond hair like the baby. I was shocked when the blood tests showed they couldn't be related."

Lily Abbott had had blond hair. I'd seen a photo of the girls' high school volleyball team online.

"We should have called the police and child protective services right away, but Richard had made a promise. He couldn't tell a lie but he also couldn't break a promise, either. He had integrity. I don't want people to think badly of my husband."

"I don't think calling the police right away would have made a difference," I said. "No one knew that Lily Abbott was missing at that point." What I didn't say was that very soon after that, she was likely dead.

chapter 9

For the next week there was really nothing to do but wait for Ella to get the DNA test results. I wasn't sure whether to hope Ella would learn that Lily was her mother or to wish for a different outcome. To me there were too many reasons to believe they were parent and child, but that didn't mean it was definitely the case.

Ella's husband, Keith, stopped in at the library on Thursday afternoon, ostensibly to see how our new computers were working. Keith was one of the newer members on the library board and he'd been a big help when I'd finally decided we couldn't get by wiggling connector cords, thumping monitors and crossing our fingers any longer. I showed him our unofficial stats, which indicated computer usage was up about twenty percent. I also shared my idea for offering a couple of workshops on basic computer skills and pitched the idea of Keith doing a talk on researching his family tree to tie in with the presentations we'd been doing on the history of Mayville Heights and this whole area of Minnesota.

"I'm completely behind the idea of doing a class or two on basic computer skills," he said. We were standing at the far end of the computer room, in front of the windows looking out over the water. "Can I say maybe on the other thing?"

"You can say no. Not everyone likes public speaking."

"It's not that," he said. "It's just . . . do you really think there would be anyone interested in listening to me talk about how to research your family tree? I mean, all of that is online."

"Harrison Taylor said the same thing to me when I asked him to give a talk about the history of the town. He didn't believe anyone would show up. We even made a small wager over it."

Keith narrowed his eyes. "And?"

I smiled. "And I didn't lose."

Keith laughed. "I'm sticking with my maybe for now, but I will think about it. And no, I'm not getting involved in any wager with you over how many people might show up."

I shook my head in mock dismay. "I knew I shouldn't have told you about Harrison."

Keith looked around the space again. I had the sense he wanted to talk.

"How's Ella doing?" I asked.

He blew out a breath. "The wait for the DNA tests isn't easy," he said. "The uncertainty about Lily has been eating at Ella since the possibility opened that Lily actually could be her biological mother."

"It raised just as many questions as it answered."

Keith nodded. "Don't get me wrong, no one could have loved Ella more than her parents did, and Ella loved . . . loves them. It's not that she's trying to replace them. It's the not knowing that gets to her. Her mom always told her she was loved because she was left at a safe place, the church. I sometimes think she needs to hear that from the person who put her there."

I wondered if Ruth had shared the full story of how baby Ella ended up with the Hansens that winter night. It wasn't my place to tell Ella what Ruth had told me. And did it really change things that much?

Keith patted the pocket where I'd seen him stow his phone. "I don't mean to put any pressure on you, but if you can find any answers, please, Ella deserves to have them."

"She does," I said. "And if I come up with anything—anything—I promise I'll share it."

He nodded. "I don't know if this will help, but Tim Abbott's widow, Emily, still lives here. I'd hazard a guess she's been in the library a few times. You've probably seen her. Pretty much everyone knew that Tim was obsessed with the idea that Lily was murdered, and he got even more that way as time went by and no one heard from her. I've heard more than one person say he kept boxes of information about the case. Maybe his wife threw all of that out after Tim died last year, but maybe she didn't."

"That's good to know," I said. I didn't want to make any promises beyond that.

The rest of the week passed uneventfully. Marcus and I went out to dinner Saturday night and talked in very general terms about our wedding. Neither one of us wanted anything fancy or formal.

"What if we asked Roma and Eddie if we could be married out at Wisteria Hill?" I suggested. Roma was one of my closest friends and I wasn't sure any other veterinarian would have put up with all of Hercules's and Owen's idiosyncrasies. Roma had bought Wisteria Hill, which had been the Henderson family estate, from Everett Henderson before she married. She'd done a lot of work on the property. Roma had proposed to Eddie in the middle of my kitchen and married him in the living room in the old farmhouse. In fact, Everett and Rebecca had also gotten married in Roma's living room just a couple of years before that. And given that Roma and Maggie had worked hard to push Marcus and me together, I didn't see Roma saying no.

"I like that idea," Marcus said. "You know I'd marry you anywhere, anytime."

I reached across the table and gave his hand a squeeze. "Any luck on finding us another flight?" I asked.

"Not yet, but I'm still looking. The dispute with the pilots seems to be spreading to other airlines. But don't panic, I'll find something."

"This isn't my panicked face," I said. "This is my slightly worried face. You won't see my panicked face for at least another week."

Marcus smiled. "Good to know."

I decided that I couldn't go talk to Emily Abbott until Ella got the results of the DNA test and I'd gotten her okay. When I came out of the library after work on Monday, Ella was standing in front of the building looking at the holiday lights. She had the DNA results, I realized. I walked down the stairs to join her.

Ella pointed toward the right side of the brick building, where a large sun made of twinkling lights hung above the windows. "Why do you have a sun hanging there?" she asked. "Shouldn't it be a star?"

"There's a star on the other side," I said, gesturing toward the left side of the building. "The sun was Susan's suggestion. It's a reminder that even though it's getting a little darker each day, very soon that will end and the days will begin to lengthen and get brighter."

Ella nodded. "A metaphor for life. Dark times won't last forever. The light will eventually come back."

I nodded. "Yes. That's why some people burn a Yule log—to welcome back the sun."

Ella finally looked at me. "She was my mother," she said.

I wasn't sure what to say. "I'm glad you found out," I finally said.

She gave a helpless shrug. "I'm not so sure I am. Lily is dead and so are her parents—my grandparents. Even her brother"—she shook her head—"my uncle is gone. He died of a heart attack. And I can't help wondering if the constant stress from looking for Lily had something to do with that. I can't get any answers because the people who have them are all dead."

I put a hand on her shoulder and swallowed against my own sudden urge to cry.

"I can't stop thinking about all the times that I was in the co-op store and my . . . Lily . . ." She choked on the next words and couldn't get any more out.

I wrapped both my arms around her and we stood there, silent in the darkness.

Finally Ella pulled away from me. She wrapped her arms around her midsection after swiping at her cheeks with one hand. "I want my mom," she said in a small, quiet voice. "Finding out one mother is dead makes me miss the other one so much. My mom would know what to say to make this not feel so . . . awful."

"So tell me what you think that would be," I said. I kept one hand on her shoulder.

"First, she'd tell me she loves me. She always did that. And she always said that my other mother—I guess now I should say Lily—loved me, too, because she wouldn't have taken me to the church, a safe place, if she hadn't cared about me. And I think my mom truly believed that."

She reached over and put her hand on top of mine. "Then Mom would tell me not to quit. To keep looking for the answers I need."

"It sounds like good advice to me."

"She used to say that we weren't quitters and then my dad would say yes, we were, and he'd start listing off things that we'd all quit. He and Mom quit line dancing because they were both awful at remembering when to go right and when to go left. He said they once knocked down a whole row of people like they were dominos, dancing to 'Achy Breaky Heart.' And he'd remind us that I quit nursery school because I categorically refused to lie on the mats for quiet time."

"Because?"

"Why would I sleep on the floor when I had a perfectly good bed?"

"I can't argue with that," I said.

Ella gave me a small smile. "My dad would list off four or five things we'd quit between us and Mom would finally stuff a cookie in his mouth and tell him she was trying to make a point and he was ruining it. I think he just did it for the cookie."

I smiled.

"Mom would stand in the middle of the kitchen—because these conversations always seemed to happen in the kitchen—

waving a spatula or a wooden spoon and say yes, we had quit some things that relied on an overemphasis on directionality or excessive adherence to the status quo—me and the naptime, in case you couldn't guess—but we didn't quit on the things and people that mattered to us." Ella straightened her shoulders and her chin came up. "I'm not quitting on Lily . . . on my mother."

The words seem a little unfamiliar to her mouth.

"You're still going to help me. You're not going to quit, are you?" Ella asked.

I realized then how much I wanted to do this. I wanted to find the person who had killed Lily Abbott. I wanted to find the person who had robbed Ella of her chance to know her birth family.

I took a deep breath and put my hands on Ella's shoulders. "I quit skating lessons because even with a sofa cushion stuffed down the back of my pants it still hurt when I fell. And I fell a lot." I gave her a wry smile. "And as an aside, putting a pillow down the back of your pants will only make the cutest guy in sixth grade think you are a dork."

Ella ducked her head to hide her grin.

"I quit choir because I lack even a basic ability to sing anywhere close to on key. I only sing around Hercules, who is either tone-deaf, too polite to yowl and hurt my feelings or, since he's a cat, just doesn't care. But I'm not quitting on you."

"Thank you," Ella whispered, putting her hand over her

heart for a moment. She cleared her throat. "I'm not going to keep my connection to Lily a secret. Share that with anyone you need to. Just find out who killed my mother."

I nodded. "I will," I said. I hoped I hadn't made a promise I wouldn't be able to keep.

chapter 10

I woke up Tuesday morning and decided the best place to start was with Tim Abbott's widow. I'd been trying for a week to connect with Bryan James. I'd left two messages and I suspected he was avoiding me. I didn't want to ambush him, but if all else failed I would look for him at the Reading Buddies Christmas party.

"Do you by any chance know Emily Abbott?" I asked Abigail as we emptied the book drop.

She narrowed her eyes and looked a little puzzled. "Yes, and so do you," she said. "Emily gave Harry tomato seedlings from her greenhouse to replace the ones the kids planted that all died."

"Wait a minute. Greenhouse Emily is Emily Abbott?"

Abigail nodded. "Yes. You really didn't know her last name?"

I pulled apart two books that seemed to be stuck together with strawberry-scented Play-Doh and handed them to her. "I honestly don't remember ever hearing it."

She took the books and set them to one side to be cleaned later.

The fact that I sort of knew Emily Abbott made me feel a little better.

All told, there were two books stuck together with strawberry Play-Doh, two more with grape-scented, and one book in which someone had used a candy cane as a bookmark—a candy cane that had likely been in someone's mouth before it ended up between the pages of the book.

Once we were open I walked around the building checking on our holiday decorations. One of Cookie Monster's eyes had slipped down about a foot, and I made quick work of putting it back in place again. The center black candle in the Kwanzaa candleholder had broken in the middle, and the top half hung to one side. One of the red candles was missing altogether. We kept extra candles at the checkout desk, so that problem was easily fixed as well. The string of reindeer lights around the magazine carousel was a bigger issue. They wouldn't light at all. Neither would the first bulb on the menorah. I got a new bulb for the menorah and took down the reindeer lights, replacing them with a string of clear twinkle lights until I could find a replacement reindeer set. As I worked I thought about how I wanted to approach Emily Abbott. It felt wrong to just show up at her front door and I decided I'd call first.

At lunchtime I drove over to the co-op store to meet Maggie. Oren was painting the storage closet and Maggie and several others were getting the shop ready to reopen on Wednesday. The space had been painted a soft blue-gray with all the trim white, and the back wall had been repaired.

"Harry did a good job," I said to Maggie. "Oren, too."

She smiled and I noticed that she looked more relaxed than she had in days. "We couldn't have been opening again so fast without both of them," she said.

Ruby walked over to join us. Her hair was highlighted with streaks of green and she was wearing her favorite red sweater with the words "Dear Santa, Define Good" across the front. "Hey, Kathleen, what do you think?" she asked.

"Everything looks wonderful," I said. I noticed that someone had cleaned the windows—probably Harry.

Ruby smiled. "It does, doesn't it? The color was Oren's suggestion."

"I like it." The space seemed bigger and warmer somehow.

"It feels peaceful," Maggie said.

"If you're looking for any holiday decorations, come over to the library," I said. "We haven't used everything we have. I think it all multiplies after we put things away in January."

"I might do that," Ruby said. "I know that some of our lights and those big paper snowflakes Nic made were ruined by the water."

Nic was an assemblage artist who worked with recycled metal and paper. His three-dimensional snowflakes were intricate artworks and Maggie had told me that they could have sold every one of the six that had been hanging from the ceiling in the shop. I hated that they had all been ruined by the leak.

"Anytime," I said. "If I'm not around, just ask Susan or Abigail to let you into the workroom."

"Thanks," Ruby said. "I'll see you at class tonight for sure."

"The shelves fit perfectly," I said to Maggie.

She nodded. "Harry brought them upstairs and made sure all the connections were tight, and I washed off all the dust. I know we measured the space and Harry has a good eye for that sort of thing, but I was holding my breath as we set them in place."

Behind the two sets of shelves I noticed a tiny hand-painted plaque. I stepped closer to read what was written on it: "Lily Abbott, 'And flights of angels sing thee to thy rest.'"

"*Hamlet*," I said softly.

"We all agreed that while we're not going to talk about Lily to any customers who come in just to be salacious, we couldn't just ignore what happened here, either," Maggie said. "If anyone asks—some of the tourists might—we're going to say that Lily was the mother of one of our artists, which she was."

"It's a beautiful gesture," I said. Maggie had said "we" more than once, but I felt sure this had been her idea. It was the kind of thing she did.

"Do you mind if I go say hello to Oren?" I asked.

She shook her head. "Go ahead. He's just around the corner finishing that storage closet."

I found Oren crouched in the closet, painting the trim that no one would ever see with the same meticulous care he'd used in the shop. He looked up at the sound of my footsteps and got to his feet when he caught sight of me. "Kathleen. This is a lovely surprise," he said with a smile. He was wearing white painter's pants and a long-sleeved white T-shirt with the sleeves pushed back to his elbows.

I smiled back, remembering how long it had taken to get Oren to stop calling me Miss Paulson and how much more time before he'd use my given name. "The shop looks wonderful," I said.

He ducked his head. "Most of the credit for that goes to Harry. You'd never know that whole wall had been replaced. He has a fine touch with the crack filling."

Oren Kenyon was in his fifties, tall and lean, with sandy hair that lightened in the summer sun and was darker this time of year. He didn't say a lot but I didn't think he was capable of lying and I knew his word was his bond. He'd been a musical prodigy as a child but the pressure and other people's expectations had been too much for him. He was happier working with his hands and playing music for small groups of people when it suited him.

Oren had carved the beautiful wooden sun that hung over the front door of the library. It seemed to me that no matter what he did, his creative spirit always shone through.

"He does," I said. "But you did a fine job painting. I like the new color very much."

He smiled again. "To tell the truth, I've been itching to change the paint color in here for years." His smile faded. "I'm sorry you and Harry had to be the ones who found Lily Abbott, but I'm glad she was found. I never believed she ran away."

"Oren, did you know Lily?" I asked.

He nodded. "Yes, I did." He rubbed a smudge of paint off the handle of his brush.

"What was she like?" I knew more than anyone else Oren could be counted on to tell me who Lily Abbott had really been.

"Lily was a good person. She was kind to everyone. She was kind to me. A lot of people weren't. I never believed she would have hurt her family by running away like everyone said she did. And as for the baby, Lily wanted her. The only way she would have left her at St. Luke's is because she thought it was the safest place for her."

I nodded. "Thank you," I said. Oren's words fit with what I'd been feeling for a while. Why and how baby Ella ended up with the Hansens on that snowy longest night was important. If I could figure that part out, maybe I could figure out all the rest.

I said good-bye to Oren and stopped to tell Maggie I'd see her at tai chi.

I got back to the library with just enough time to eat my sandwich. I decided I would call Emily after supper. There was a rush of people looking for books at the end of the day and I was a bit late leaving the library. I got home to find Fifi's footprints in the driveway again and more cat footprints on the back landing. I wondered, were Fifi and Hercules getting any more friendly?

In the kitchen I found Owen sitting on one chair at the table and Hercules on the other, as though they were waiting for someone to serve them a meal.

"What are you doing?" I asked.

Owen meowed and looked over at the cupboard where I kept the cat crackers.

"Number one, you don't need a treat. And number two, if you were getting one, it would not be served like you were at a restaurant." I folded my arms over my chest and glared at them.

Owen meowed again.

"People eat at this table. Cats do not."

They both look blankly at me.

"That means get down," I said. I made a "move along" gesture with my hand. They both jumped to the floor, making little grumbling noises almost under their breath.

I heated up a bowl of chicken soup for supper and ate it with the last cheese biscuit. Hercules came wandering back in from the living room and sat at my feet, watching me eat. I finally gave him a bite of chicken.

"This doesn't set a precedent," I warned. He ignored my words, although his green eyes flicked to my face for a moment. He knew the precedent had been set a long time ago.

As I started to clear the table, Hercules went over to the back door, sat down and meowed loudly. "You can go out into the porch if you want to. It's cold."

He looked at the door and looked at me again.

I set my bowl and spoon on the counter and went to open the door. "Now all of a sudden you can't just walk through like you usually do?" I asked.

He ignored me. He was a cat with a purpose, walking across the porch to the back door without stopping. He meowed again and looked back at me.

I shook my head and unlocked the door. "I know which one of us is the smarter one in this interaction, and it's not me," I said.

Hercules poked his head out and looked across the backyard but made no move to actually go outside.

"Go if you're going," I said. "You're letting all the cold in."

He seemed to be looking at Everett and Rebecca's house. "I'm not carrying you over there if that's what you're asking."

He wrinkled his whiskers and flicked his tail, which suggested that was not what he was trying to say.

"I'll be seeing Rebecca in a little while at class," I said. Rebecca was one of the boys' favorite people. She bought catnip chickens for Owen and poached chicken for Hercules.

A gust of wind swirled around the side of the house, blowing snow into Hercules's face. That was enough to get him to pull his head back inside. I closed the door and locked it again. If he really did want to go outside he could just walk through the door.

I leaned down and wiped the dusting of snow off his face. Then he looked at the back door again. I was missing something.

I knew that Hercules often had a second breakfast with Everett, but it wasn't breakfast time. In the good weather he often trailed Rebecca while she worked in her garden.

Rebecca. She had lived in Mayville Heights all her life. She might be able to give me some idea of who to talk to about Lily besides Emily Abbott.

I looked down at the cat. "Are you trying to tell me I should talk to Rebecca?" I said.

His response was a loud meow and a flick of his tail as he turned and went back to the kitchen. Had he really been trying to tell me to talk to Rebecca or was he just being a cat?

I grabbed my boots, deciding to bring them inside the kitchen to warm up by the heat vent before I put them on to head back downtown to tai chi.

In the minute he'd been in the kitchen without me, Hercules had managed to pull down my multicolored scarf and get his claws tangled in the fabric. He gave me a sheepish look and held up his paw.

I set my boots down and went to rescue him, thinking maybe he hadn't been trying to tell me to talk to Rebecca after all. Maybe he *had* just been being a cat.

I stacked the dishes in the sink and went upstairs to change my clothes. When I came back downstairs there was no sign of either cat. I grabbed my bag, pulled on my big parka and stepped into my now warm boots.

"I'm leaving," I called. After a moment I heard an answering meow from upstairs and another one from the basement.

I had to park a bit farther down the street than usual, so I pulled up my hood and hurried down the sidewalk, happy that I'd worn the big coat. Roma was sitting on the bench at the top of the stairs, changing her shoes and singing softly to herself.

"Hi," I said. "You're in an extra-good mood."

She smiled up at me. "That's because Olivia is coming for Christmas."

I smiled back at her as I took off my coat. Olivia was Roma's daughter from her first marriage. "That's wonderful news."

"She's staying for the week. Will you and Marcus come to dinner when you get back from Boston?"

I hung up my jacket. "We will, although there's a chance we might not get to Boston after all."

Roma frowned. "Why? You've had this trip planned for months."

I explained about the pilots' dispute with the airline.

"I wondered why Olivia was taking the train," she said.

"Marcus and I might end up having to do the same thing."

"If you don't get to go see your family, come have Christmas dinner with us. Sydney will be here, too. Eddie is brining a huge turkey."

Sydney was Eddie's daughter. After a bit of a bumpy start, she and Olivia had gotten very close. She and Roma had bonded from the moment they met, and when Roma and Eddie had almost broken up, Sydney had lobbied hard for the two of them to get back together.

Sydney was also an avid reader, and whenever I saw her I came away with more insight into what middle schoolers were reading and several suggestions for books to order for the library.

I nodded as I pulled my slip-on shoes out of my bag and stepped into them. "I'd like that," I said. "If we end up staying here, yes, we'll come for Christmas dinner. And thank you for asking."

We both got to our feet and went into the studio. Even though we hadn't missed a lot of classes, I had missed being here.

"I need to talk to Ruby," Roma said. She headed across the floor to where Ruby was standing by the window pulling her green-streaked hair back into a stubby ponytail. I walked over to Maggie. She wore a pale gray sweatshirt with the words "Peace on Earth" stitched across the chest and charcoal gray leggings.

"Hi," I said. "Will you be ready to open the shop in the morning?"

She smiled. "We will. We have more stock and I'm really happy with the way everything looks." She stretched one arm up over her head. "Oh, and Ruby is going to come by the library sometime in the morning to take a look at your decorations. We need something for the front windows."

"I'll be there."

Maggie looked at her watch, then clapped her hands and called, "Circle, everyone."

I walked across the floor to stand next to Roma, and Rebecca joined me on my other side, smiling hello.

Maggie worked us hard, correcting posture, demonstrating a movement, giving encouragement and a nudge wherever it was needed. Even though I had practiced—a little—I still felt the loss of the canceled classes. By the time we'd finished the whole form at the end, I wasn't cold anymore. I tugged at the front of my shirt, trying to cool down a little. Rebecca stretched one arm in front of her and then the other. She had been practicing tai chi a lot longer than I had.

"I made your cinnamon roll recipe," I said. "It's the best recipe I've tried yet."

"That's because it was my mother's recipe," Rebecca said. "All of my best recipes come from her."

No one was standing near us and it occurred to me that this would be a good time to talk to her about Lily. "Rebecca, could I ask you a few questions about Lily Abbott?" I said.

"You're helping Ella," she said. She said the words as if they were fact and not question.

I pulled at the neck of my shirt. "I'm trying."

We walked over to the window, away from the others. "What do you need to know?" she asked.

I shrugged. "I'm not sure."

"I cut Maura Abbott's hair for years."

"So you knew her, then?"

Rebecca shook her head. "Maura was quiet and soft-spoken, so I never really felt I knew her at all. After Lily disappeared, Maura seemed to cling to the idea that her daughter had just run away. I think maybe it was easier than facing the idea that she might be dead."

"I can understand that," I said.

"You've probably heard that Tim Abbott, Lily's brother, didn't agree with his parents or the police."

I nodded. "I know that he thought something bad had happened to Lily."

"I hate that he turned out to be right," Rebecca said, "but he and Lily were close, and he probably knew her better than anyone else."

"Tell me about her," I said.

She smiled again. "Lily was an A student and a very talented volleyball player who was being recruited by some top colleges. More than that, she was a sweet girl. She volunteered at the seniors' center—not to look good for a college application, but because when her grandmother had spent time there, Lily had noticed how lonely some of the people were."

"So why would anyone have wanted to hurt her?"

Rebecca shook her head. "I don't know. It never made sense. I think that was one of the reasons so many people were so quick to embrace the idea that she'd just run away." She narrowed her eyes. "You should talk to Ann McKinnon."

"Was she a friend of Lily's?" I asked.

"She's the current girls' volleyball coach; back then she was an assistant. Ann became a mentor to the girls because she was in her first year of teaching/coaching and she was close to their age."

"I'll talk to her," I said. "Thank you."

"I need to talk to Maggie before I leave," Rebecca said. "If you think of anything else you want to ask me, just put on your snowshoes and come knock on my back door. And tell Hercules I have some of that thick-cut bacon that he and Everett like."

Anyone who heard our conversation would think Hercules

was a person, not a cat. "Thank you," I said, "for the information, the cinnamon roll recipe and for . . . everything."

She gave me a hug and whispered, "You can do this. I'm certain of it."

I watched her walk over to Maggie and wondered if, for once, Rebecca was going to be wrong.

chapter 11

When I got home I made myself a piece of peanut butter toast and a mug of hot chocolate—my favorite comfort foods. Owen came and sat at my feet and I gave him a sardine cracker for no other reason than I was happy to have his company.

I decided to stop putting off calling Emily Abbott. I felt a bit uncomfortable, nosing into the woman's life and family, but if I didn't, I might not be able to help Ella, and doing that was important to me.

All I got was Emily's voice mail, and I didn't think this was a request that should be made that way. Owen, who had been sitting on my lap, wrinkled his nose at me.

"Don't look at me like that," I said, giving the top of his head a scratch. "I'm not avoiding talking to her. I just want to do it in person."

He didn't look convinced.

I had a restless night and woke up early. There was no sign of the boys in the kitchen when I got downstairs. I'd made the coffee and was trying to decide what I wanted for breakfast when Owen walked in, a dust bunny stuck to his tail, and yawned. He was followed by Hercules, who was also yawning. It seemed like no one had gotten enough sleep.

I got to the library just as Susan was arriving. She held up a large red insulated bag as she got out of her car. "Eric sent over a new recipe for everyone to test."

"I can't wait," I said as we walked across the parking lot.

Susan laughed and the dangling earrings she wore, which flashed red and green, swung back and forth. "You don't even know what he sent."

"And I don't care," I said, unlocking the door. "If Eric made it, it will be good."

She pushed the door open with her hip. "That's true, but for the record there are spinach-and-cheese hand pies in this cooler bag."

I smiled. "Cheese, pastry and spinach, so I can say I'm eating a vegetable. There's no chance I'm not going to like this recipe."

I shut off the alarm system and let us into the building proper.

Susan took off her red earmuffs and wrapped them around her left wrist. "Eric is trying two different variations of the recipe. Tomorrow I'm bringing the other one."

"Eric is one of my favorite people," I said.

Susan smiled. "Funny," she said, "he's one of mine, too."

We went upstairs and put two of the hand pies in the toaster oven to heat because Eric had told Susan not to use the microwave.

"It's butter pastry," she said. "According to Eric it will lose its flakiness if we put the pies in the microwave. And I never argue with him about cooking unless it's about the merits of Cheez Whiz." She was wearing black trousers and a black sweater covered in dancing penguins with reindeer antlers. Her topknot sported two candy canes and a plastic icicle.

"For or against?" I asked as the scent of pastry and cheese began to fill the staff room.

"For," she said with a frown, as though it was obvious.

The pies were delicious, which I'd known they would be. The pastry was light and flaky and the spinach-and-cheese filling had a bit of a bite to it.

"Pepper Jack cheese," Susan said when I asked about the extra flavor boost.

"This recipe gets a ten out of ten from me," I said.

Susan licked a dab of cheese from her thumb. "Nine from me because I'm not a big fan of spinach, although if it came with cheese and butter pastry all the time I might become one."

Ruby showed up half an hour after we opened and I took her up to our workroom to look in the bins of decorations we had stored there. She left with two strings of clear twinkle lights, a small menorah and several blue glass ornaments.

Marcus arrived midmorning to let me know he was going to Minneapolis to check out a lead and wasn't sure how late he'd be back. I kissed him at the door, for once not caring if it seemed unprofessional. When I turned back around, Susan was grinning. "You two are so cute," she said.

Right before lunch I tried Emily Abbott again and again got her voice mail. I realized I might have to just show up at her door after all.

Susan had found another string of reindeer lights and I decided to replace the twinkle lights I'd put around the magazine carousel with them and frame the bulletin board with the twinkle lights. I'd just gotten the new reindeer lights plugged in when I glanced idly over at the circulation desk and realized Emily Abbott was standing there talking to Susan.

I walked over to join them. "Kathleen, hello," Emily said. "I was just asking Susan to thank you for tracking down a copy of *I Start Counting* for me. I read it when I was a teenager and the book has stayed with me all this time."

"You're welcome," I said. "I knew some library somewhere had to have a copy and I liked the challenge of finding it."

Emily Abbott was in her late fifties by my calculations. She had dark, chin-length hair with a streak of white at the front that she wore in loose curls. She was maybe five foot five or so and she wore a leopard-print jacket that I knew Maggie would have loved.

"Could I talk to you for a moment?" I asked.

Emily looked puzzled, but all she said was, "Of course."

I led her over to one of the meeting rooms and we stepped inside.

"Is this is about next summer's garden for the kids?" she asked. "Because I already told Harry I'd be happy to help."

"I appreciate the offer and I may take you up on it," I said, "but this is about Ella King. She's my friend."

Emily's face became guarded. "You know about her . . . connection to my husband's family."

"I know that Tim was Ella's uncle, yes. She needs to know what happened to her mother." I hoped I had chosen my words carefully enough. "If you don't feel comfortable talking to me, I get it. But would you talk to Ella?"

Emily closed her eyes for a brief moment. "I know that you helped Georgia Tepper a few months ago when she was accused of killing her former mother-in-law. What do you want to know?"

I hadn't expected it to be this easy. "I've heard that your husband was the only person who didn't believe his sister ran away."

She nodded. "That's right. Tim and Lily were close. Even though she was fighting with their parents over the baby, she wouldn't have run off without telling him and I don't think she would have been so cruel to her parents."

"He tried to find out what happened to her."

Emily twisted the wedding ring she still wore around her finger. "Tim was a newspaper reporter for years. In his spare time he kept investigating Lily's case. He never stopped trying to figure out what happened to her. And he never found anything that made him believe Lily ran away."

"Do you know if he had any leads?" Over my shoulder through the windows I could see it was snowing.

"He always felt that Lily's former boyfriend was involved."

"Bryan James."

Emily nodded. "Tim thought he wasn't good enough for Lily and told her not to settle, that she deserved better than Bryan. Tim was suspicious of Bryan's alibi, but he could never break his friends or family, as much as he tried. Those boys, they were a tight group, according to Tim, and they all took Bryan's side when he and Lily broke up and again when it came out that she was pregnant. One of them, Jake Andersen, had apparently gotten into it with Lily shortly before she died. I know Tim looked at Jake, but in the end he always came back to Bryan. He couldn't come up with anyone else who would have wanted to hurt her."

"What about the baby's father? It wasn't Bryan James," I said.

She hesitated and I wondered if I'd pushed too far. "Tim thought there was a possibility Lily had been . . . assaulted."

"It would explain why she wouldn't tell anyone who the baby's father was."

"Yes. I hate to think she went through something so awful all alone, but it is possible."

My heart sank.

Emily was still playing with her wedding ring. "I don't know if you know that Lily was supposedly seen at the bus station."

Supposedly.

"Tim was skeptical about that actually being her. He thought the woman who IDed her got too caught up in the story and probably saw someone who looked a bit similar to Lily."

I nodded because I knew from Marcus that kind of witness ID often wasn't reliable.

"And Tim refused to believe Lily had been abducted by a stranger because he didn't think anyone would grab a pregnant young woman and then take the baby and leave it in a church manger."

I agreed, mainly because I knew baby Ella hadn't been left in the manger, but I didn't say anything.

Emily looked past me for a moment, then her gaze met mine again. She cleared her throat. "Even though I couldn't believe Lily would stay away so long without at least letting Tim know she was okay, a tiny part of me always hoped that she was out there somewhere. It broke my heart a little, even after so many years, to find out I was wrong."

I couldn't think of anything else to ask. Then I remembered the necklace Harry had picked up from the floor. "Do you remember Lily having a gold broken-heart necklace?"

Emily shook her head. "I don't. I never really saw her wear much jewelry. Is it important?"

"Probably not," I said. "I appreciate you answering my questions."

Emily nodded. "I hope you'll succeed where Tim didn't."

We started walking toward the front doors when Emily suddenly stopped. "Kathleen, I have a couple of boxes of Tim's papers that the police didn't want. He kept notes on everything he did. Would you like them?"

"Are you sure?' I asked.

"I'm sure," she said. "They've been sitting in the closet ever since Tim died."

"Then, yes. Thank you. I'll take care of everything and return it all to you."

Emily took her gloves out of her pocket and pulled them on. "You don't have to return anything. Give it all to Ella if she wants it. Burn it all. All those boxes hold is years and years of pain. I'm convinced they helped shorten Tim's life." She started for the door again and then turned to look at me. "Tell Ella to call me if she'd like to hear about Lily. I got to know her in the months before she disappeared." She stopped. "I mean before she died. I have a few photos Ella might like to see."

"Thank you," I said. "I know it will mean a lot to Ella."

I offered to pick up the boxes, but Emily said she'd drop them off before we closed.

About an hour later I came downstairs to find two large banker's boxes waiting for me at the circulation desk.

"The woman who was here earlier dropped them off for you," Levi said. "I'll help you carry them up to your office."

He grabbed one box and I picked up the other. "This is heavy," he said. "What's inside?"

"A lot of unanswered questions," I said.

chapter 12

I took the boxes home, planning to start going through them after supper. I set them on the floor in front of the sofa. Both Owen and Hercules came in for a look. Hercules walked slowly around both boxes, sniffing cautiously. Owen tried to get a paw under the edge of the lid on one carton.

"Stay out of those boxes," I said. Hercules stopped what he was doing long enough to look at me and meow an objection. Owen didn't pay the slightest bit of attention.

I could see how this was going to end. I went down into the basement and got two bricks. I brought them upstairs and set one on top of each box. That resulted in a lot of annoyed grumbling from Owen. Hercules finished sniffing the boxes and proceeded to sniff the bricks instead.

Owen continued to give me the cold shoulder while I had supper and did the dishes. He thawed a little when I set a sardine cracker in his dish. Hercules happily sat by my chair and ate his own cracker before wandering off. I was about to look inside the boxes when Marcus walked in.

"Hi," I exclaimed. "I didn't think I'd get to see you tonight." I stretched up on tiptoes to kiss him. His face was cold.

"Things went faster than expected so I got back early." He gave me a sly grin. "And I managed to get train tickets to Boston for the two of us. We leave on the twenty-second and it will take a day and a half but we'll make it in time for Christmas."

I stared at him wide-eyed. "Really?"

"Really," he said.

I did my happy dance, which looked a lot like I was having a foot cramp. Then I kissed him. I kissed him a second time and a third. I stopped to catch my breath.

"You can keep going," he said.

I laughed and threw my arms around him. We were going to Boston for Christmas. "I love you," I said.

He kissed the top of my head. "I love you, too," he said.

"What can I get you?" I asked. "There's some chicken soup left."

Marcus started taking off his jacket. "That sounds good," he said.

I got the soup out of the refrigerator, which brought Owen in to see what was going on.

"How was your day?" Marcus asked. Owen's golden eyes immediately focused on me and he meowed. Loudly.

"I'm sorry to hear that," Marcus said. He looked at me. "How was your day?"

"I talked to Emily Abbott," I said as I got a bowl out of the cupboard. "She gave me a couple of boxes of her husband's papers, his notes on everything he did to try to find out what happened to his sister. Do you want them?"

He shook his head. "No. They were already looked at. They're all yours." He pulled out a chair and sat down. "Are you getting anywhere?"

I blew out a breath. "Not really. What about you?"

He hesitated, then did his hand/hair thing. "No. Ruth Hansen called me."

"I take it she told you that their story about Ella being left in the manger wasn't what really happened." I put his soup in the microwave.

"She did. For all the good it does."

I looked over my shoulder at him. "What do you mean?"

He made a face. "It doesn't really help. Now we know that Lily likely handed the baby to Reverend Hansen instead of leaving her in the manger. She didn't say anything that's going to help us figure out who killed Lily."

"I think it might be important."

"Why?"

I shrugged. "I don't know. And I know what you're going to say." I took the soup out of the microwave and set it on the table in front of him. "Feelings aren't facts."

Marcus reached out and caught my arm. "Hey," he said. "I would never negate your instincts, but I have to deal with facts."

"Okay," I said. "Was Lily suffocated?"

He let go of my arm and I pulled out a chair and sat down. "Why do you think that?"

"Simple. If she had been stabbed or shot, I don't think the body would have been preserved the way it was."

"She could have been hit over the head." He picked up his spoon. "She could have been poisoned."

"Was she?"

Marcus didn't say anything. I waited. I'd learned a lot about waiting from Owen and Hercules. "No," he finally said.

"So she was suffocated," I said.

I didn't think he was going to answer, but finally he nodded.

I watched as he tried the soup and smiled. "This is good," he said. "Thank you."

"You're welcome," I said. I studied his face. He looked tired. There were lines around his eyes and stubble on his chin. "I don't suppose you can tell me why you went to Minneapolis."

"I can tell you that Bryan James may have an alibi."

"Lily's ex-boyfriend?" I still needed to talk to him.

He nodded.

"That's what you went to check."

"It could have been."

I got up to get Marcus a glass of milk and pretended not to see him slip Owen a bit of chicken and a small piece of carrot.

"You said he *may* have an alibi," I said. "So you're not certain?"

Marcus shook his head. "Not yet."

I sighed. Were we ever going to figure out who killed Lily?

I spent a chunk of Thursday working on my report about the library's new computers, as well as going over plans for the summer reading program with Rebecca and Abigail. Rebecca brought turtle cookies—rich with pecans, caramel and chocolate.

"I love this time of year because everyone brings us treats," Abigail said as she reached for a second cookie. "I hope someone brings us an exercise bike for January."

Once again I was late leaving the library. I looked in the refrigerator when I got home and decided to use up some leftovers to make fried rice. Hercules wandered in, meowed hello, rubbed against my legs and wandered out again. There was no sign of Owen. When I headed upstairs to change for class I discovered him sitting on one of the bricks on top of the boxes.

"You're persistent, I'll give you that," I said.

It was snowing lightly as I drove down the hill, which

meant it was a little warmer. There were no storms in the forecast and I decided I would happily brush a bit of snow off the truck and the steps if it wasn't so cold.

Class went better than it had the last time. Maggie and Rebecca helped me work on my Cloud Hands. The movement had always given me grief. After class I thought about going over to Eddie's training center, where he was teaching Marcus and Brady some skills drills for the hockey team, but the pull of a cup of hot chocolate with Ella's homemade marshmallows was stronger than the idea of standing in a chilly hockey rink.

I got home, made the hot chocolate—putting three marshmallows on top—and took it into the living room, sitting on the floor beside Tim Abbott's boxes with my back against the couch. I took the brick and the lid off the closer carton. Owen suddenly appeared. I wondered if he'd been lurking since I got home, waiting to see what was inside.

"Your invisible lurking skills are improving," I said.

He was too busy looking in the box to even twitch his whiskers at me. On top were several hardcover steno pads. I flipped through one and realized these were Tim's notes from over the years. He had tight angular writing and wrote everything in black ink. Each entry was dated on the left side, day, month and year with dashes between the numbers. He also seemed to be using some kind of shorthand and/or abbreviations as he wrote that I'd need to study to figure out.

Owen was keen to look in the other box. I pulled it closer and lifted off the brick and the lid. This box seemed, for the most part, to hold copies of every news story written about Lily's disappearance. There were also articles about the baby left at the church. I saw several of the pieces I'd read online. Something caught Owen's eye and he suddenly jumped inside the box.

"Get out of there right now," I said sharply. I moved to lift him out and he pawed insistently in one corner. I nudged him back with one hand and reached into the corner of the box with the other. "Whatever is in there better be dead."

It turned out what Owen had been after was a small, padded manila envelope. The end wasn't sealed. I pulled out an old disposable camera. Owen sneezed, startled himself and almost fell out of the box. I lifted him out and set him on the floor. He eyed my hot chocolate.

"Don't even think about it," I warned. He washed his face instead.

I wondered about the significance of the camera. Why had Tim Abbott kept it? Had Emily noticed it? Had the police? Should I give the camera back to Emily? She'd been very clear that she wanted none of the contents of the two boxes. Marcus had said the same thing. I decided to see if there were any photos on the camera that could be developed. If I found anything I thought Emily or Marcus would want, I'd give it to them.

I put the camera in my messenger bag and decided I'd take it to Bell's before work. I wondered why Tim had kept it and why he had never had the film developed.

I got up early the next morning to sunshine and (slightly)

warmer temperatures. I did a load of laundry and washed the kitchen floor. When I got the bucket out Hercules headed purposefully across the floor out to the porch.

"You're out there for the next fifteen minutes," I called after him.

I was halfway done with the floor when Owen came to the living room doorway, annoyed because he couldn't get into the kitchen.

"There's nothing you can't wait for," I said. I suspected he wanted to get to his catnip chicken stash in the basement. He made a sound like a sigh and continued to sit just inside the living room and glare at me.

I looked out the front window. The sun was melting the frost on the windshield of the truck—less scraping for me later. I glanced at the boxes again. Emily Abbott had mentioned two names—Lily's boyfriend and his friend Jake Andersen. I thought about what she had said about Jake. He "had apparently gotten into it with Lily shortly before she died." Tim Abbott had dismissed Jake as a suspect. Had he been too focused on Bryan James?

I reached for my computer. I had a few minutes while I waited for the floor to dry.

Searching online for information without help from Hercules felt a little odd. He'd often send me off on a tangent that always seemed to turn out to be useful.

Thanks to social media it wasn't difficult to track down Jake

Andersen. He was a structural engineer, living in Minneapolis. I felt certain I had found the right man. He'd gone to Mayville Heights High School and counted Bryan James as one of his friends. I pulled a hand across the back of my neck. Now that I'd found Jake, how was I going to get him to talk to me about Lily? Why should he? I hadn't had any success with Bryan. Based on what I'd learned from Emily, it didn't seem like he'd been Lily's friend. His loyalty had been with her former boyfriend and I was looking at him as a possible suspect. I needed some other way to initiate a conversation with the man.

What did I know about Jake Andersen? He'd grown up in Mayville Heights. He'd gone to school here. He was a structural engineer.

Jake Andersen was a structural engineer.

The library was over a hundred years old. Jake was exactly the type of person the library board would hire if they ever decided to add on to the building. That idea had been tossed around in the last couple of years but it had never gotten past the what-if stage. Since I was the head librarian it made sense that I'd want some questions answered before the discussion went any further.

Jake Andersen wasn't in his office in Minneapolis, it turned out. He was in Mayville Heights consulting on a project. All I needed to find out was what the project was and I could talk to him in person. I had a pretty good idea how to do that.

Everett Henderson was more than my backyard neighbor.

He had hired me to come to Mayville Heights to supervise the library renovations—his gift to the town. He was a successful businessman, born and raised here. His assistant, Lita, knew everything that was going on in the area, in no small part because she was related to pretty much everyone in Mayville Heights in one way or another. I reached for the phone again.

"I hear you have a Cookie Monster Christmas tree at the library," Lita said.

"We do," I said. "You should come over and see it. You might even get an actual cookie. Eric and Mary have been baking pretty much nonstop since Thanksgiving."

"So have I," she said. Lita was an excellent baker in her own right. "But I'm lucky to get to eat one cookie out of a batch. Burtis and the boys seem to inhale them as fast as they come out of the oven."

"Hey, I've had your inside-out chocolate chip cookies," I said. "I'd pretty much inhale them, too, given the chance."

She laughed. "Ah, flattery. You're after something."

"It's hardly flattery when it's the truth," I countered, "but yes, I am after something. I need a little information."

"What do you need to know?" she asked.

"I'm looking for a man named Jake Andersen. He's an engineer consulting on a project here in town."

"I know," Lita said. "I take it you want to talk to him about something."

I nodded even though she couldn't see me. "I do."

"Does it have anything to do with Lily Abbott?"

I hesitated. "Yes . . . maybe. I'm not sure yet."

It wasn't much of an answer but it was good enough for Lita.

"Jake's parents still live here but he's staying at the St. James. He's here in town to look at one of the old warehouses down along the waterfront for a client. In fact, he should be down there today. You might be able to catch him this morning."

"Thanks," I said.

"Kathleen, a word of warning," Lita said. "Jake Andersen is a rather . . . abrasive person."

"He won't be the first person I've come across who isn't exactly warm and cuddly," I said. "But thanks for the warning."

I hadn't asked Lita which of the old warehouses Jake Andersen was looking at, so I decided to start with the ones near the Sweeney Center, the hockey training center run by former NHL player Eddie Sweeney, who was also Roma's husband. It turned out to be a good choice. There was a black Ford truck, extended cab, in the parking lot of the building on the upriver side of the Sweeney Center. It said "Andersen Consulting" in white letters on the driver's-side door. There were no other vehicles.

I left two spaces between my truck and Jake Andersen's when I parked. His vehicle was a lot cleaner; in fact, I guessed it had been washed since he'd arrived in town. That suggested he was someone who cared about appearances.

There was no sign of Jake outside the warehouse. I sat for maybe five minutes watching the main doors at the front before he came out. He was alone and I knew from the photos I'd seen on social media that I had the right man. I got out of the truck and headed across the pavement.

"Mr. Andersen," I called out once I was close enough for him to hear me.

He turned to look at me.

Jake Andersen was taller than I'd guessed from his social media photos. He wore an olive green quilted jacket with a caramel-colored scarf at the neck and dark jeans. A pair of brown leather gloves poked out of one of the jacket pockets. He looked to be in good shape. He wasn't skinny but he didn't carry any extra weight, either. His dark blond hair was flecked with gray and had been expertly cut and he had a chiseled jaw and bright blue eyes. He had the kind of appearance that would make a lot of women and men take a second look.

"Mr. Andersen, my name is Kathleen Paulson," I said.

He frowned. "I don't know you."

I nodded. "No, you don't." I didn't get a chance to say anything else.

Jake held up one hand. "I don't contribute to any cause when I'm accosted on the street, no matter how noble you may think yours is." He said the word "noble" with a decidedly sarcastic edge.

Lita had been right. The man was abrasive.

"I don't have a cause," I said. "I do have a few questions . . . about Lily Abbott."

His blue eyes narrowed and the lines around them tightened. "I don't have anything to say about her. We weren't friends."

"You were friends with her boyfriend, Bryan James."

The muscles along his jawline clenched. "I'm not answering any questions about Bryan or Lily or anyone else," he said as he moved around me. "This conversation is over."

He cut across the parking lot in long strides, but to my surprise he didn't turn toward his truck; instead he headed for the Sweeney Center.

This was the only chance I was going to get to talk to Jake Andersen. There was no way going forward that he would talk to me on the phone or see me if I made an appointment. I had to make this opportunity count. I followed him.

He tried the main doors. They were locked since Eddie was out of town.

"Eddie will be back tomorrow," I said, stuffing my gloved hands in the pockets of my jacket. It was cold close to the water. "He's playing in a charity hockey game in Chicago."

Jake swore and smacked the tempered glass with the heel of his hand. "I need to get inside today," he said. He shifted his weight from one leg to the other, hands jammed in his pockets.

Burtis had an expression that struck me as perfect for this moment: "Some days you eat the bear. Some days the bear eats you." This time I was the one holding the fork. "I can get you inside," I said.

He gave a snort of humorless laughter. "Because you're what? Some kind of cat burglar who can pick locks?"

I almost laughed myself because with their unique skills Owen and Hercules had acted as feline thieves more than once. "No," I said. "But I do know Eddie."

"You know Eddie Sweeney?" The disdain in his voice made it clear that he didn't believe me.

I nodded.

Jake pulled his phone out, studied the screen for a moment and then stuffed it back in his pocket. "Let me guess. You have his keys because you're watering the plants while he's gone."

I shrugged. "Suit yourself, then," I said. I started walking back to my car, fingers crossed—literally as well as figuratively—that he wouldn't let me leave.

He didn't, but he did wait until I'd reached the edge of the parking lot before he called after me. "What do you want?"

I took my time turning around to look at him. "Just answer some questions about Lily Abbott."

"I already told you. We weren't friends."

"I know," I said.

"Why does she matter to you?" he asked.

I took a breath and let it out before I answered. "I found her body."

Jake looked out over the water. His body language and the way he'd already spoken to me told me he didn't like to lose.

"Fine," he said at last, his gaze coming back to my face. "Get me into the building and I'll answer your questions."

I shook my head. "Answer my questions and then I'll get you inside."

"Why should I believe you'll keep your side of the deal once I talk to you? How do I even know you can deliver on your promise?"

"No guts, no glory," I said. I sounded like Burtis. I'd picked up a little of his competitive attitude from our most recent pinball battle. I turned back around and started for my truck.

"Hang on," Jake said.

I didn't stop. I didn't turn around. This was getting tiresome.

"Hey, I'm serious," he called. "Hang on."

I could hear him hurrying after me. He reached me just as I reached the truck. "Ask your questions," he said, a flash of annoyance in his eyes.

"You argued with Lily not long before she died," I said.

"Yeah, we argued. So what?"

"What about?"

He looked away for a moment. "She was part of a group that was pushing school administration for more funding for the girls' sports teams. All I did was tell her what everyone else knew but no one would say: It was never going to happen. She was being a bitch about the whole thing, about it not being fair. It wasn't my fault that fans cared more about the guys' game. It was just the way of the world. Hell, it still is."

"You picked a fight with her on purpose," I said. It was a guess but I felt certain I was right.

"No. *She* wouldn't shut up. I got sick of listening to her so I set her straight. That's it." He swiped a hand over his mouth. "If it turns out that they've found her body after all this time, I'm sorry things ended up that way."

I folded my arms over my chest and studied him for a moment. He actually did look sorry, mouth downturned and tight lines pulling at the corners of his eyes.

"Where were you the night Lily disappeared?" I asked.

Jake gave a snort of laughter, but there was no real humor in it. "You honestly think I could have killed her?"

I raised an eyebrow. "Did you?"

"No. Yeah, I admit I liked getting a rise out of her, but that's all."

"So where were you?"

"Hanging with my buddies."

"Do those buddies have names?"

He smirked. "They do."

He wasn't going to give me any names, I realized. Why had I made this Faustian bargain in the first place? Jake Andersen wasn't just abrasive. He was also a jerk.

"Good luck," I said, jerking my head in the direction of the Sweeney Center.

Jake shook his head. "Oh for f—" He stopped himself. "Bryan James. Carter Reznik. Nick Gonzalez. Bryan and Rez are still in town. Nick's in Minneapolis."

"They were all teenage boys at the time?" I asked.

He frowned. "Yeah. What does that have to do with anything?"

"I know about loyalty, especially at that age."

"My friends didn't need to lie about where I was back then or now," Jake said, "because I didn't have anything to do with Lily's death. Talk to them. Talk to Lily's friends. I didn't kill her."

I looked at him for a long moment. Then I pulled out my phone and called Roma. I was lucky that she was between patients. I briefly explained where I was and the deal I'd made with Jake Andersen. Some people would have asked a lot of questions. Roma wasn't one of those people. "I'll be there in ten minutes," she said. "You'll have to lock up."

"Thank you," I said. I turned away from Jake and lowered my voice. "I owe you."

"I'm sensing there's a story here," she said. "I can't wait to hear it. Probably with a plate of brownies."

I laughed. "That I can do."

I ended the call with Roma, put my phone away and turned to Jake. "Ten minutes," I said.

He nodded. He didn't say thank you.

Jake spent the time on his phone. I spent it watching him, trying to decide if he could have killed Lily. The best I could come up with was maybe.

Roma pulled into the parking lot at the Sweeney Center nine minutes after our phone call had ended, which meant she'd probably broken a speed limit or two on the way over. She gave Jake a quick, appraising look, held out her hand and introduced herself. Then she let us in the main doors, disarmed the alarm system and showed me how to turn it back on once we were done. It was very similar to the system we had at the library so I didn't think I'd have any problem.

"I'll talk to you later," she said.

I nodded. "Thank you."

Jake Andersen's main interests seemed to be the roof trusses in the ice area and the heating system in the training rooms. He took some photos of the trusses and I gave him the name of the contractor who had overseen the project.

We spent less than twenty minutes in the building. I reset the alarm and locked up. "Did you get what you needed?" I asked.

"Yes," he said. He didn't thank me. "I didn't kill Lily."

I fished my keys out of my pocket. "You already said that." I started for the truck and he fell into step beside me.

"You don't believe me." There was a challenge in his blue eyes and the set of his shoulders.

"I haven't decided yet."

He swiped a hand over his face again. "Why would I kill Lily? I barely knew her."

I shook my head. "People kill other people they barely know all the time—by accident or for what they think are good reasons in the moment. Or because they're not thinking it through at all."

We reached our vehicles and I unlocked the driver's door of the truck. "Talk to my friends," Jake said. "Talk to anyone who knew me back then. They'll tell you that I didn't kill Lily Abbott."

"I will," I said. I slid behind the wheel and started the truck. I wasn't sure I'd learned anything useful other than the fact that it seemed very important to Jake that I believe he had nothing to do with Lily's disappearance. I wondered why that mattered so much.

There was no sign of Owen or Hercules when I got home. I got a cup of coffee and an oatmeal raisin cookie and then I vacuumed the bedrooms and bathroom. Once the vacuum was put away I called Maggie. "Are you at River Arts?" I asked. I still had time to get some things done before I needed to be at the library.

"I'm here," she said. I pictured her walking around the studio as she talked to me. "I'm staring at a tourist map I'm doing for the Red Wing civic pride committee. I have three mock-ups and I need to get that down to two, but I can't decide which one to eliminate."

"Would you like a second set of eyes?"

"I would. And I'd like them in the back of my head."

I laughed. "How about another set in the front of *my* head?"

"That would be a close second," she said.

Owen appeared out of nowhere then and jumped onto my lap. He seemed to have some instinct for when I was talking to Maggie. He nuzzled the edge of the receiver.

"Owen says hello," I said. I knew what was coming next.

"Put him on," she said. I held the phone up to Owen's furry face. He listened, meowed once and then jumped down to the floor.

"What do you two talk about?" I asked.

"I'm can't say," Maggie said. "That's personal."

"Sorry," I said.

"Are you coming down?" she asked.

I stretched my legs out onto the footstool. "Probably in about an hour, if that works. I have a couple of things I want to do before I go to work, so I thought I'd stop by after if that's okay."

"It's more than okay," Maggie said. "I really could use a second opinion. I'm guessing you'd like to talk to Mila while you're here."

"If she's there."

"She is. I saw her car in the parking lot when I came in."

"I'll see you in about an hour," I said.

I went upstairs to make my bed and put clean towels in the bathroom. When I came down again Owen had resumed not patiently waiting by the kitchen doorway.

"The floor has been dry for ages," I said. "Go do whatever it is you were going to do."

Owen started for the basement. I followed him down to get the laundry. He hopped up on top of the dryer, one of his favorite places to sit in the wintertime because it was warm. I still suspected what he really wanted was one of his catnip chickens. Owen guarded his stash zealously, hiding the soggy, half-chewed little birds in places he thought I would never find them because he knew I would consign the oldest and mangiest to the garbage can.

"I know you're hiding two chickens behind a can of paint on the workbench," I said as I picked up the laundry basket.

He pointedly turned his back on me and began to wash his face. I wondered if Fifi did this kind of thing.

Hercules was still in the porch when I was ready to leave. The sun was streaming through the windows and I was surprised by how warm it felt. I leaned down to scratch the top of his head and he meowed at me.

"You have a good day as well," I said.

I went to Bell's Camera Shop first. Jon Bell turned the old disposable camera over in his hands. "I haven't seen one like this in years," he said. "Assuming there actually are any photos on it, we may be able to develop them. It appears the camera's been kept dry."

I left it with him, mentally crossing my fingers. I walked down to the bookstore and bought a couple of markers. Then

I drove over to River Arts. Maggie came to let me in and went up to her studio.

Sunlight filled the room, and the space smelled like cinnamon. She had three of Nic's snowflakes hanging from the ceiling over her worktable.

"These are the three mock-ups," she said, indicating three large rectangles of what looked to me like watercolor paper spread out on her work space.

"This one for sure." I pointed at the middle drawing. "I like the sketch itself and I like your color choices."

Mags nodded. "That's my first choice, too." She moved the sketch off to one side.

I studied the other two. There were things I liked about each drawing, but neither one caught my attention the way the first sketch had. I twisted my watch around my arm as I thought. "I like the map in this one," I said, pointing to the sketch on the left. "But I like the lettering and the colors from this one." I tapped the edge of the drawing to my right with one finger. "Could you put all that together in one sketch?"

Maggie propped her elbows on the table and studied both sketches. She began to nod. "I could." She looked at me and smiled. "I could. Thank you."

I smiled back at her. "I'm glad I could help, especially since my artistic talents are limited to drawing stick men."

"Oh, but they're very good stick men," Maggie said. She straightened up. "Would you like to go see if Mila has time to talk to you?"

I nodded. "I would."

We walked down the hall to Mila Serrano's studio. Her door was partly open. Maggie knocked. Mila looked up and smiled. "Come in, please," she said.

The studio was slightly smaller than Maggie's space. Mila had an easel near the windows and a long, high workspace that was similar to Maggie's. There were a number of portraits laid out on her worktable.

"These are wonderful," Maggie said, walking around the table to get a better look at the artwork.

Mila smiled and a flush of color came to her cheeks at the compliment. "I'm trying to decide on an arrangement to display them."

I studied the portraits and realized I recognized some of the faces. I spotted Keith King; Sandra, my mail carrier; and Jon Bell, whom I'd just seen at the camera shop. Mila's portraits weren't realistic images. She used color and various drawing techniques to create a face that was recognizable and creative at the same time. I loved the vibrant colors she used for shading and shadows.

"Maggie's right," I said. "These are wonderful."

"Mila, this is my friend Kathleen Paulson," Maggie said.

Mila smiled. "I've seen you in the library."

She was probably a couple of inches over five feet, with dark eyes and dark hair streaked with just a few strands of silver. Her hair was pulled back in a braid and she was wearing jeans and a men's gray flannel shirt over a pink sweater. She had the kind of face that looked happy even when she wasn't smiling.

"Do you mind me asking how you got started doing this?" I asked, gesturing at the table. "I've never seen portraits like this before."

"I was a fiber artist for a long time," Mila said. She pointed at the opposite wall, where a large wall hanging was displayed, a knotted chevron design that was probably four feet wide and five feet or more long. "That's one of my early designs."

"You're very talented," I said. I was a bit in awe of people like Maggie and Mila. I hadn't been kidding when I'd said that my skills were limited to stick people.

Mila smiled again. "Thank you. I always drew, just for fun, little sketches of my friends and my family. But I never liked traditional, realistic portraits. Mine always seemed so . . . well . . . boring. I started adding more color and working with different media like colored pencils and watercolor paint. It just went from there."

"The colors you chose for Keith's portrait captured his energy."

She nodded. "That's the idea. This series of portraits is called the People in My Neighborhood."

"Keith's wife, Ella, is a friend of mine," I said.

"You want to talk to me about Lily."

"Yes. I just have a few questions."

Mila was sliding a silver ring with a moon and stars design

up and down her right finger. "Now that I know Lily was Ella's mother, I wonder why I didn't see the connection sooner. Ella has Lily's smile and her way of seeing the best in people."

Maggie had walked over to get a closer look at the wall hanging and likely to give us at least the illusion of privacy.

"Did you believe Lily ran away?" I said.

Mila shook her head and continued to play with her ring. "At first I didn't. She talked about leaving town occasionally, but I never took her that seriously. We all complained about our lives when we were teenagers. Later, I think I started to believe she'd just taken off, because the alternative was that something horrible had happened to her, and what seventeen-year-old wants to believe that?"

"Did you and Lily have plans that day?"

She shook her head. "Lily had a fight with her parents. They wanted her to place the baby up for adoption. She came to hang out for a while just to get out of the house. She left because we were getting ready to go to a family party. My mom invited her to come with us, but Lily said she was going home." Mila smiled. "Mom didn't treat Lily any differently because she was pregnant. She said that whoever the baby's father was wasn't being shamed, so why should it happen to Lily? Anyway, I thought she *was* home until her brother, Tim, called early the next morning."

"Was there anyone who might have wanted to hurt Lily?"

Mila was shaking her head before I got the words out. "The

police asked the same questions. There wasn't. We were kids. We were going to school, playing volleyball and waiting to get away to college. I know it sounds silly now, but I just somehow thought Lily would come with us. She talked about keeping the baby but I didn't really think she would. I thought in the end she'd listen to her parents. The only thing I remember that happened was Lily had a stupid fight with Jake Andersen a couple of days before she disappeared, but it didn't mean anything and they were friends again."

The argument Emily had mentioned. I tucked a strand of hair behind one ear. "Do you have any idea who Ella's father might be?"

Mila look away for a moment. "At first I thought it was someone she'd met at this volleyball tournament we went to that spring, but she said no and the timing seemed to be wrong. I thought it could be Bryan, even though they'd been broken up for a long time, but Lily said it wasn't. And she wouldn't tell me who it was." Her mouth moved as though she was trying the feel of something before she said the actual words.

I waited without trying to fill the silence. Mila's gaze shifted from the door to the floor before she looked at me again. "She was supposed to be about seven months pregnant when she disappeared. She wore a lot of baggy clothes so you couldn't really tell how big her baby bump was. I think she was lying about how far along she was."

"Why would she do that?"

"I don't know. Maybe she thought if anyone knew, they would figure out who the baby's father was, and for some reason Lily didn't want that."

"One more thing," I said. "Do you remember Lily wearing a broken heart necklace?"

Mila shook her head. "I remember those necklaces. They were really popular for a while but I don't remember ever seeing Lily wearing one."

I didn't have any other questions. "Thank you," I said.

"I wish I knew something that could help," she said. "I know it's been a long time, but I want to see the person who killed Lily punished. I hope you find something that helps that happen."

"Did you get what you needed?" Maggie asked as we walked back to her studio.

"Maybe," I said. I really needed to track down Bryan James.

I put my coat on and thanked Maggie for her help.

She tipped her head in the direction of her worktable. "Thanks for yours."

She walked me downstairs and I hurried across the parking lot to the truck. I climbed inside but didn't immediately start it up. I went over the conversation with Mila. That tournament was somewhere to keep digging and trying to figure out who Ella's father was and maybe who had killed Lily. I felt certain the baby and Lily's death were connected. Marcus would say that was a feeling, not a fact, but I was going to follow it anyway. I was convinced Mila was hiding something. I'd noticed how she had looked away briefly when I asked if she knew who the father of Lily's baby was. And she hadn't actually answered the question. All she'd said was Lily didn't tell her anything. Did Mila know who it was? Had she guessed? And could that person be Lily's killer?

chapter 13

I drove over to the library and had just enough time to eat the sandwich I'd brought with me and call Roma to thank her once more for her help with Jake Andersen.

"Do you actually think he could have hurt Lily?" she asked.

"I don't know," I said. "But I don't exactly have a lot of suspects, so I'm not taking him off my list until I have a good reason to."

I had decided first chance I got I would look for information about the volleyball tournament Mila had mentioned. I wasn't sure what to do with my suspicions that she hadn't been completely honest with me.

Marcus arrived at five to six with meatloaf from Fern's Diner for my supper.

"Fern's meatloaf is my favorite food," I said.

"I thought chocolate pudding cake was your favorite food," Marcus said.

"I have more than one favorite."

"You have about a hundred and forty-seven favorite foods," he teased as we walked upstairs.

"But I only have one favorite fiancé," I said. I leaned sideways and kissed him.

In the staff room I took the brown paper take-out bag from him and began unpacking the contents. There was meatloaf, mashed potatoes, roasted carrots, and French-style green beans. And gravy. Gravy was one of my hundred and forty-seven favorite foods.

"Remember those two boxes I got from Emily Abbott?" I said. "I found a disposable camera in one of them."

"Were there any pictures on it?" Marcus asked.

I got a plate out of the cupboard and began transferring food to it. "I don't know yet. I took the camera over to Jon Bell. If there are any photos you can have them."

He leaned against the counter, crossing one leg over the other. "Thank you, but I don't see how they can help unless you happen to have a photo of Lily Abbott's killer."

"I'm hoping that maybe there will be a photo of Lily with her baby's father." I snagged one of the roasted carrots and took a bite. Even cold it was delicious.

"Unless he's holding up a sign that says that, it's not going to help."

I sighed. "I know, but since Lily was killed so long ago, maybe it's going to take a little luck to find out what happened." I turned to look at him. "And don't tell me police officers don't believe in luck because I've heard you say more than once that you got lucky during an investigation."

"Oh, we believe in luck," he said, reaching over to snare one of my carrots for himself. "What we don't believe in is coincidence."

I stuck my plate in the microwave.

"I need to get going," Marcus said, straightening up. "I'll see you later?"

I nodded. "I need to check on Owen and Hercules and then I'll be out."

He leaned over to kiss me and he was gone.

By the time the library closed I was tired. I hadn't learned much about Jake Andersen from the small amount of time I'd spent with him other than he was a challenging person to deal with. I had ambushed him and now I was regretting that, but I also wondered why he had been so reluctant to talk to me if he had nothing to hide.

The library had a collection of yearbooks from the high school that went back decades. Before I left for the night I unearthed the volumes from Jake's last three years of school and took them with me.

I got home, changed into jeans and a sweater and spent a few minutes with the cats. Owen made it clear he wanted to look in the boxes again. "Tomorrow," I told him.

I saw the timeline I'd made and picked it up to look at what I'd written. All it did was confuse me. I put the piece of cardboard in the recycling bin. I looked at the clock. I didn't have to drive out to Marcus's house right away. I got the yearbooks from my messenger bag and set them on the table. Owen watched me, his head cocked to one side in curiosity.

"Want to help me take a look through these?" I asked, raising an eyebrow at him.

He gave an enthusiastic meow.

I leaned down to scoop him up, pulled out a chair and sat down at the table. We started with the last yearbook, flipping slowly through the pages. I smiled at the hair and the clothes. "No one, including you, is ever seeing my yearbook," I said to Owen.

He glanced up at the ceiling and then stared at me without blinking, and it crossed my mind that he might somehow have found the box at the back of my closet. I made a mental note to make sure it was still securely sealed with duct tape. No one needed to see teenage me with crimped hair. Not even my cat.

Midway through the yearbook I found several photos of the boys' volleyball team and I also learned that Jake had been a wrestler. He had been the heaviest player on both teams, with wide shoulders and muscular arms. "He was more than capable of putting Lily's body in that wall cavity," I said to Owen. "But what was his motive? I find it hard to believe one teenager killed another over a disagreement about funding their sports teams."

Owen wrinkled his whiskers. I took that to mean he agreed.

We found several more photographs of both volleyball teams, casual shots at practices and school events. There was one image from what looked to be some sort of Christmas party, based on the decorations and the Santa hats a number of the players were wearing. I found Jake easily since he was at least a couple of inches taller than everyone else. Based on the formal team photo, which had all the players' names listed underneath, I was able to pick out the boys whose names Jake had given me, including Bryan James.

Lily was also in the photo. Everyone seemed to be laughing at something that was happening off-camera.

I tilted the book up a little and studied the image for a long moment. Then Owen and I exchanged a look. "Do you see what I see?" I asked.

"Merow," he said, putting a paw on the page, I knew that could mean yes and it could also mean "let's have a snack."

I decided it was the former. I set the yearbook back on the table and leaned back in my chair, hands linked behind my head. Owen watched me, head cocked quizzically to one side.

Everyone in that picture was laughing. Everyone except Jake, who was looking sideways.

At Lily.

Even in the old black-and-white photo I could see the longing on his face.

"Jake had a thing for Lily," I said aloud.

Could he be Ella's father? I wondered.

Could he be Lily's killer?

As I drove out to Marcus's house I went over what I knew. It didn't take very long. After Lily left Mila's house, no one knew what she did or where she was until she showed up at the church with baby Ella. At some point after she left the Serranos', her car had gone in the ditch. Was that before or after she had the baby and before or after she went to Red Wing? Her car had been described as being covered in snow, which suggested it had been there for a while. So how did she get to Red Wing? And sometime in those hours Lily had given birth. After she left the Hansens' she might have gone to the bus station, assuming the person who had identified her was right—which wasn't a given. None of it made sense.

How on earth was I going to find answers for Ella?

Micah was waiting for me on the back deck. I leaned down to say hello to her. Marcus was in the kitchen pouring milk into a mug.

"I'm tired and grumpy and not good company," I said.

He came and took my coat as I stepped out of my boots. "I. Don't. Care," he said, kissing me after each word. He pointed at the table. "Sit." He made me a mug of hot chocolate with two marshmallows and rubbed my shoulders while I drank it.

"What did I do to deserve you?" I asked, tipping my head back to look up at him.

Marcus grinned. "I don't know but it must have been something really terrific."

"Do you ever think about all the things that had to happen for us to meet, from me deciding to leave Boston to the library needing a new librarian on very short notice to Maggie setting us up to sit next to each other at the music festival?"

"No." He shook his head. "All of those things had to happen so we would happen. Some things are just meant to be. We're just meant to be, and what's meant to be will always find a way."

The girls' hockey team had a practice in the morning. Marcus was up early, and after breakfast I headed home. It felt odd not to be going to work. We'd been having plumbing issues for several weeks and finally the library board had decided to close the building for a day and get them dealt with all at once. We were getting a new sink in the staff room and new toilets in all three washrooms. "No more going into the washrooms a dozen times a day to jiggle the toilet handles," Susan had crowed. "No more trying to plunge the staff-room sink with my hand so it will drain," Levi had added.

As soon as she'd heard I was off on Saturday, Maggie had asked me to go Christmas shopping with her. She was looking for something special for Rebecca, who had been spending a lot of time recently teaching Maggie how to make bread. Since a lot of Maggie's baking efforts ended up at my back door, I was more than happy to help.

Owen and I spent some time looking through the box of newspaper clippings. I discovered that the woman who had seen Lily at the bus station was a former police officer. That had to have given her more credibility in everyone's eyes. I looked through a few more clippings but didn't learn anything new. I picked up one of Tim Abbott's notebooks and studied his notes. It was easier than I'd expected to figure out his shorthand. Basically he wrote words the way they sounded, with a few other refinements. His writings were a record of everything that the police had done when Lily disappeared. They evolved into what he'd done to find his sister. I didn't learn a lot from Tim's notes other than he was convinced Lily had not run away.

After a while I put the notebook back in the box and got up to get the yearbooks, which I'd set on the footstool. I wanted to see if there were any more informal photos with both Jake Andersen and Lily. Owen jumped up next to me and leaned over my arm so he could see as well. Neither one of us found even one more photograph that the two of them were in together.

Still, I was convinced that Jake had had feelings for Lily. I took another look at the image that had first stirred my suspicions. "I'm not wrong, am I?" I said to Owen.

He leaned over the page, seemingly studying the photo. Then he looked at me and meowed.

I took that as a vote of confidence.

"So how am I going to find out if I'm right?" I said. Unless Jake wanted to get into some other building here in town I had no incentive to offer to get him to talk to me again.

Owen wrinkled his whiskers at me. He didn't have any ideas, either.

My phone rang while I was getting another cup of coffee. The photos were ready. I decided I'd stop and get them before I met Maggie. Owen had gotten bored and gone upstairs, probably to move the shoes around in my closet. Hercules was sitting by the table looking up at my computer.

"Great minds think alike," I said to him. I opened the computer and turned it on. Then I lifted Hercules onto my lap. "I think we should start with the high school's website."

He didn't seem to agree with me based on the expression on his furry black-and-white face. Turned out he was right. The records available on the website about the school's various sports teams didn't go back thirty-six years.

I looked at Hercules. "How about the newspaper?" I asked.

He enthusiastically agreed with a loud meow.

"If Ella was a full-term baby, and it seems she was despite what Lily told people, it meant that the tournament was in March."

It took no time to learn that the girls' volleyball team had gone to Green Bay in mid-March. "I thought volleyball was played in the fall," I said.

Hercules didn't seem to know. He hit the touchpad and suddenly we were looking at a photo of the team, a better one than the picture I'd found the last time I looked.

Lily was standing next to Mila. Her blond hair was pulled back in a ponytail and a beautiful smile lit up her face even in the old photograph. Both Ella and Taylor had that same smile.

I kept one hand on Hercules and leaned back in my chair. "I need to talk to Mila Serrano again. I need to figure out what she was keeping to herself."

He seemed to agree.

I also needed to talk to Ann McKinnon, the assistant volleyball coach. I checked the time. If I left now I could stop at the school and possibly find her there. There was an activity program for younger kids at the school on Saturday morning, run by the members of the various sports teams and supervised by the athletic staff. It was another project Everett Henderson had financed. It was possible Ann McKinnon would be there.

I drove down the hill to the high school and parked in the half-empty lot. There was a sign-in desk at the door. Larry

Taylor was sitting behind it. Larry was Harry Taylor's younger brother.

"What are you doing here?" I said. Larry had no children but he would be gaining a stepdaughter, Emmy, when he got married in a couple of months.

"Hey, Kathleen," he said with a smile. "I volunteer here one Saturday a month so we can keep track of who's going in and out and make sure none of the equipment grows legs, if you know what I mean."

"How are the wedding plans coming along?"

He rolled his eyes. "Between my father and Emmy the ceremony gets bigger every day. Georgia is trying to convince me to elope. What about you and Marcus?"

"I'm embarrassed to admit we don't really have any plans made yet," I said.

"Don't let the old man or Emmy find out or the next thing you know you'll be looking at a ceremony with a full orchestra, doves and a chocolate fountain."

"A chocolate fountain isn't the worst idea I've ever heard," I said with a grin.

"Maybe we could get a two-for-one elopement deal." Larry cocked an eyebrow at me.

I laughed. "That's not the worst idea I've ever heard, either."

"Are you picking someone up?" he asked.

"I'm here to see Ann McKinnon," I said.

Larry didn't ask why. He put my name in the logbook and

showed me where to sign. "Since I know you I don't need to see your driver's license. Ann should be in the west gym. Do you know where it is?"

I had been in the building several times. "Up the concourse, turn left, go down the hall to the end and turn right."

"You got it," Larry said.

I walked up the concourse and down the hallway wondering just what I was going to say to Ann McKinnon.

I got to the gym and looked inside. A woman who I guessed had to be the volleyball coach was putting soccer balls in a large mesh bag. I took a deep breath and pushed the door open.

The woman turned and looked over at me. "Can I help you?" she asked.

"Are you Ann McKinnon?" I said. This was where Larry had said I would find her, but I wanted to be sure.

"Who wants to know?" There was a challenge in her voice.

"My name is Kathleen Paulson," I said.

"What do you want?"

"Are you Ann McKinnon?" I stuffed my hands in my pockets and tried to keep the aggravation out of my voice. I only partially succeeded.

I wasn't sure whether or not she would answer. She continued to stuff soccer balls in the bag. Finally, just at the point where the silence was becoming uncomfortable, she said, "Yes."

Ann McKinnon was no more than an inch or so shorter

than me. She wore a black T-shirt and black athletic pants. I knew she had to be close to sixty, although she could easily have passed for several years younger. She had bright blue eyes and her hair was completely white, cut in a shaggy bob with bangs.

"I'd like to talk to you about Lily Abbott," I said.

Ann barely glanced in my direction. "No," she said.

"Why?" I countered, not even trying now to keep the challenge out of my voice.

She shrugged. "I don't want to."

I took a deep breath and let it out slowly. Getting confrontational wasn't going to get me anywhere. "Lily had a daughter," I said. "Her name is Ella King. She has a husband named Keith and a daughter of her own whose name is Taylor. Taylor graduated last year. Ella is my friend. She wants to know who killed her mother. I promised to help her."

Ann finally looked at me. "I don't care what you promised. I answered questions from the police thirty-six years ago and a couple of days ago all over again. Same answers both times. I'm not getting sucked into gossip."

"I'm not looking for gossip. I'm looking for information about the tri-state volleyball tournament the girls went to thirty-six years ago. Why did they go in March? Wasn't volleyball season for the girls in the fall?"

The sound of her clapping echoed around the gym. "Very good," she said. "I see you did your homework. Yes, traditionally the girls' season does take place in the fall, at least around here, but the tri-state was a tournament to scout players to join a program to develop Olympic-level athletes. It was held in March because that's the start of the boys' season."

She pulled the drawstring closed on the top of the ball bag and dragged it toward the open door of the storage room. I glanced inside. I wasn't sure, but it looked like there might have been a washer and dryer against the end wall. "I'm not answering any more questions, Ms. Paulson," she said. "Go away."

Ann stowed the bag of balls. Then she picked up a lone basketball and tossed it over her shoulder. It arced its way through the net without touching the rim. How much practice had it taken to perfect that shot?

"Nice," I said.

She scooped up the ball and tossed it into the storage room without acknowledging I'd spoken. How was I going to get her to talk to me? How could I find some common ground?

There was a bin filled with hockey sticks to my right by the door. Suddenly I had an idea. I checked several sticks and pulled out one I liked the look of.

"How about a little one-on-one?" I said. "First one to three points wins. If you win, I'll leave. If I win, you answer my questions."

That got her attention. She gave me a long, appraising look. "You must think you're pretty good."

I picked up a neon orange ball from the floor and tossed it in her direction. "There's only one way to find out." I watched her face.

She continued to size me up. Then suddenly she grabbed a towel off a stack of mats and tossed it to me. "Wipe your shoes," she said.

I did as I'd been instructed. Then I took off my jacket and left it on the table by the gym door. I walked across the floor toward her and hoped I looked more confident than I felt. I was a good floor hockey player. I'd beaten Marcus multiple times. I'd beaten a lot of people. I'd played dozens of games over the years and I won more often than I lost. But Ann McKinnon was an athlete and, I suspected, deeply competitive.

I was right. The fact that Ann was older didn't slow her down. She was in excellent shape, with lightning-fast reflexes. She faked right, darted left and scored the first goal.

"One down, two to go," she crowed, moving backward away from me with a little dance of victory.

I saw my chance. I got my stick on the ball, nailed it with a blistering slapshot and watched it sail past her into the net.

I held up one finger.

We both scrambled for the ball but Ann got to it first. She fired in the direction of the net but I made a dramatic lunge to keep her from scoring. It left a welt of floor burn on my left forearm.

"Why don't you just let the police do their job?"

I had the ball but I couldn't get around her. It was as though she could somehow read which way I was going to move before I actually did.

"I'm not interfering with what the police do," I said. "I'm trying to help my friend." She blocked me again. I had to be doing something to give myself away. What was it?

"I've already spoken to the police. Why should I talk to you?"

She was trying to distract me.

"Why shouldn't you?" I countered. She was right in my face and I lost my focus for a second. Ann had the ball and didn't waste any time taking a shot. She just missed the net.

This time as we both went after the ball, I watched Ann watching me. Her eyes were focused on my upper body. It was my shoulders, I realized. They were moving before my feet were. They were telegraphing where I was going.

"Everyone says that Lily was a kind person," I said. I let my shoulders turn a fraction to the left and then I darted right, flipping my wrist and stealing the ball away from her.

"Ella is a kind person, a good person. Maybe she got some of that from Lily and certainly she got it from the parents who raised her. She wants to know what happened to her birth mother and I'm going to help her any way I can."

"Good for you," she said. "That doesn't mean the rest of us have to help you." I wasn't sure if I heard sarcasm in her voice or not.

My shirt was damp with sweat and my legs were burning. I promised myself I'd start walking to work a lot more, no matter how cold it was.

Ann was keeping me moving, I realized. She was trying to tire me out so she could win.

"You were more than just a coach to Lily," I said. "You were her friend." I didn't actually know if I was right, but since Ann hadn't been much older than the girls she was working with, I hoped I was right. "Don't you want to know who killed her?"

"After all this time, what difference will that make?" she said.

"It will make a difference to Ella." I whipped the ball into the net in one smooth motion. I was out of breath and every muscle in my body would ache tomorrow, but right now all I needed was to score one more goal.

Ann was determined not to lose to me. She seemed to find an extra reserve of energy. She faked moving around me, then cut in front and, before I realized she was going to take a shot, sent the ball into the net, dead center. She pumped one fist into the air. "One more point, winner takes all," she said.

I realized that right before she took that shot her chin came up. So Ann did have a tell after all.

"You might just be someone looking for information to exploit Lily's daughter," Ann said, bumping me with her hip.

My left foot slid on the hardwood but I managed to stay upright and keep my stick on the ball.

"I'm not," I said, hating how wheezy I sounded. Ann didn't sound like she was exerting any effort at all. "Ask anyone who knows me. If you want a list of references I'll give them to you." I jerked my head toward the door. "Or go out to the desk and talk to Larry Taylor."

Ann cut in front of me again and almost knocked me to the floor. Even so I managed to get a shot off. It went wide of the net. Ann cheered and chased the ball. I positioned myself between her and the goal. She banged into me and almost knocked me to the floor. Even so I managed to take a swipe at the ball, knocking it off track.

"The police will find out what happened to Lily," she said. She was beginning to sweat, literally if not figuratively. "That's their job and surprisingly they're pretty good at it. What do you think you can do without their resources?"

"I can ask questions and talk to people," I said.

Ann laughed as she stretched her arm out and snagged the ball, keeping her stick moving as she turned and darted backward just as easily as she moved forward. "So you honestly think you can learn things the police can't?"

"Sometimes, yes."

Ann suddenly changed direction. I saw her chin come up. I lunged in front of her and managed to get the tip of my stick blade on the ball. It was enough.

I faked right, pivoted left and, instead of rushing the net the way I was guessing she was expecting me to, took a long shot. The ball arced toward the net. Ann charged after it but the ball went into the net in the upper corner.

I thumped my stick on the floor, planted my hands on my thighs and leaned over to catch my breath. I was red-faced and sweating profusely. After a minute I straightened up and pushed my hair off my face.

Ann stretched one arm over her head. She looked at me and I waited to see what she would do. Finally she let out a slow breath, dropped her arm and offered her hand. "You're a lot better than I thought you were."

"And you're just as good as I thought you were," I said, shaking the hand she'd held out.

Ann used the edge of her shirt to wipe her face. She leaned her stick against the net. "What do you want to know?"

"That tournament the team went to in Green Bay—when you were there, did you see Lily with any of the guys from the boys' team?"

Ann immediately shook her head. "We knew the dangers of boys and girls at the same tournament. The girls' team played first, so we only overlapped one day at the hotel. And we watched them like hawks." She pulled one hand back through her hair. "I can promise you that Lily didn't hook up with anyone on the boys' team. Anyway, wasn't she only about seven months pregnant when she disappeared? She couldn't have gotten pregnant back in March if that was the case."

"She might have been further along," I said.

Ann shrugged. "I wouldn't have noticed. Anything medical, forget it. Not my area of expertise. Sorry."

"How can you be so sure Lily didn't connect with any of the boys at that tournament?" I asked. Both my palms were bright red from gripping my stick so tightly.

Ann laughed. "Two ways. First, Lily thought they were all a bunch of jerks, her words. That's because several of the guys had been spouting garbage about girls' sports teams being inferior to boys'. And second, the boys smuggled beer into one of the rooms to celebrate and most of them were drunk. None of them were romancing any girls. The only thing they had their arms around was a garbage can."

The fact that the boys had managed to sneak beer into one of their rooms meant they could just as easily have snuck in a girl. I didn't think the guys' being drunk made Ann's point. I did think, however, that if Lily had hooked up with someone on the boys' volleyball team, it wouldn't have stayed secret very long.

I scooped the ball out of the net and handed to her. "Is it possible Lily could have met some other guy there?"

Her mouth twisted to one side. "Maybe. Yes, we were watching them, but keep in mind teenagers have an amazing capacity to get around rules set by adults. Lily was responsible and trustworthy. It wouldn't have been like her to sneak out, but since she was so responsible we all probably watched her a little less closely than we did some of the others."

She reached for her stick. "I find it hard to think that Lily connected with a guy from another school. I don't see when they would have met. The boys checked in, got room assignments and went right to practice. Meanwhile, the girls had supper followed by a team meeting and then back to the hotel."

"Did you think Lily ran away?" I asked.

Ann nodded. "I really did. I was shocked when her body was found. You know she was fighting with her parents?"

I rubbed my right shoulder with my free hand. "I know," I said.

"I heard Lily say more than once that she just wanted to take off. I thought she did. I always hoped she was somewhere having a good life." She shifted the stick from one hand to the other. "I know it sounds like a bad movie of the week, but are you sure Lily's death wasn't just some random thing? That she wasn't killed by a stranger? Maybe, I don't know, maybe she trusted the wrong person."

"How do you explain the body being found at the co-op store?"

She shrugged. "I can't, but it doesn't mean there isn't an explanation." She walked over to the storage room and tossed the ball inside. I put my stick in the bin by the door.

By unspoken agreement I helped put the rest of the equipment away. "I saw Lily the day she disappeared," Ann said.

She was on the other side of the gym from me and I turned to stare at her. "Where?"

"Here. I was packing equipment for a basketball tournament that was happening right after Christmas. I was the youngest, and a woman to boot, so I got stuck with the job and I wanted to get it done before I left for the holiday." She shrugged one shoulder in a "hey, what can you do?" motion. "Lily saw my car and came and banged on the office window. I let her in. She'd just had another fight with her mother." She stared down at the floor for a moment. "I don't think I helped."

"Why do you say that?" I asked. I picked up three more neon orange balls and dropped them into the bin Ann was using to keep the storage room door open.

"I said maybe her parents were right. The baby would go to a loving family, not some kind of Dickensian orphanage." She held up one hand. "I know I overstepped. She was angry. I always wondered whether what I said helped push Lily to run away. She must have thought no one was on her side. If I'd been more supportive, maybe Lily would have stayed and talked to me or even gone home. All I was thinking about was myself and how I wanted to get out of here, meet my cousin Seb and get to my aunt and uncle's house in Red Wing."

"That's understandable," I said.

"Have you talked to Lily's ex-boyfriend?" Ann asked as we each grabbed an end of the net and carried it to the storage room.

I shook my head. "Not yet."

"I know he wasn't the baby's father, but I never liked him or his asshole friends."

I wasn't sure a teacher should be calling former students assholes.

"He complained a lot about how much time she spent at practice. They'd break up and then he'd sweet-talk his way into her life again. I told her she needed to kick him to the curb. Finally they broke up for good early that spring."

I remembered Marcus saying Bryan James had a *possible* alibi for the time they believed Lily had been killed. Was he any more or less certain by now? I needed to find out.

"Do you remember Lily ever wearing a necklace with a broken-heart pendant?" I asked.

"I don't remember Lily wearing any kind of jewelry," Ann said. "She didn't even have her ears pierced." She frowned. "Is it important?"

I shook my head. "No. It was something I hoped was a lead but it doesn't seem to be." I sighed.

Ann shrugged. "I know I sound like a cynic, but I think it's too late for any kind of justice for Lily. Sometimes the clock runs out and you lose. That's just life."

chapter 14

I thanked Ann for talking to me and picked up my jacket and scarf.

"Maybe you'll give me a rematch at some point," she said with a smile.

I shrugged. "Maybe I will."

I walked back to the main doors, stopping to sign out and say good-bye to Larry. Then I went out to the parking lot, climbed into the truck and slumped back against the seat. My legs were like rubber. I needed a long soak in the bathtub with one of the herbal poultices Rebecca had taught Maggie how to make, but right now I needed to get to Bell's and pick up the photos.

There were only two pictures that turned out, Jon Bell explained. He handed me a paper envelope and I slid them out.

One was of Lily and a young man who had to be her brother, Tim, based on how alike they looked. The other was of Lily alone. She looked so full of life, smiling at the camera and leaning against her big brother, who had slung his arm around her shoulders. Lily was wearing the items of clothing the woman at the bus station and Reverend Hansen had described—the hoodie, the acid-wash jeans, the knit beanie with a pin on the brim. It was the first really good photo of Lily I'd seen. I had to swallow a couple of times before I put the photos back in the envelope.

I didn't see anything about these images that made me think Marcus would want either one, but I still thought I should let him see them first. After that I'd call Emily. She might at least want the one of Tim and Lily. I was hoping I'd be able to give the photo of Lily by herself to Ella.

I put the photos in my bag, paid Jon, and walked up the street to meet Maggie at the co-op store. If Maggie wondered why I was a little flushed, she didn't ask.

We walked around for a while looking in store windows for inspiration. "I'd like to get something cooking related if I could," Maggie said. "At first I thought about a new set of bread pans, but Rebecca really seems to like the ones she has."

Finally, we found the perfect gift in the window of Gunnerson's Antiques. It was a new store opened by Amy Gunnerson, who had decided against going into the family business, a funeral home, the way her siblings had. Amy had a good eye for vintage items, and in the six months the shop had been open, it had already attracted a following among tourists.

The 1950s-era glass rolling pin was part of a window display. "What do you think?" Maggie asked.

"I think you should get it," I said. "Rebecca told me once that she was nervous about using her mother's glass rolling pin when she was a girl because she was always afraid she'd break it. She said her mother noticed and told her that things were meant to be used and enjoyed, and if something did happen, then you'd had the pleasure of using them. I think this rolling pin will bring back some happy memories."

We walked around a little longer and eventually ended up at Eric's for hot chocolate. "How are things going at the store?" I asked.

"Busy," Maggie said, using her spoon to move around the marshmallows floating on the top of her drink. "We've had a lot of Christmas shoppers—tourists as well as people who live here—and I'm happy to say everyone has been very respectful. A lot of them have noticed the plaque but no one has asked any intrusive questions."

"I'm glad," I said, taking a sip of my hot chocolate.

"It couldn't have been planned, could it?" she asked.

I frowned at her across the table. "What couldn't have been planned?" I said.

"Lily's body ending up where it did. There have to be better ways to hide a body."

"I'm not so sure there are," I said, giving voice to a thought I'd had more than once since I'd first uncovered Lily's remains. "Think about it. No one knew what was behind that wall for close to forty years. It was almost a perfect crime."

Maggie leaned back in her chair, both hands wrapped around her mug. "True, but to me it still seems like a spur-of-the-moment thing, which makes me think the murder was spur-of-the-moment as well."

"But the killer had to know that the wall had been taken down and the new drywall was going up. Whoever it was may have taken advantage of the perfect opportunity to hide Lily's body, but they had to know the opportunity was there." I took another sip of my hot chocolate. "What bothers me is, how did Lily get to Red Wing and back again?"

"Maybe with the person who killed her?"

I hunched my shoulders. They were already starting to ache. "That means it was probably someone she knew. A stranger wasn't going to take her to the church and then the bus station. A stranger would ask questions about the baby."

Maggie took a sip of her drink and nodded.

"The problem is I can't figure out who that mysterious person is. What if they're dead?"

"Then at least you can tell Ella that," Maggie said. "It's still an answer."

Hercules was waiting for me in the porch, looking out the window, when I got home.

"How was your afternoon?" I asked as I leaned down to give him a scratch on the top of his head.

"Mrr," he said with what seemed like a shrug. He followed me into the kitchen and looked expectantly at the cupboard where I kept the sardine crackers before looking at me.

"You know Roma says you and your brother have too many treats," I said.

He meowed his agreement and looked at the cupboard again. I hesitated for a moment and then I got him two crackers. I knew that the next time Roma questioned me about how many snacks Hercules and Owen were indulging in, my guilty conscience would give me away.

It was a long shot, but ever since my conversation with Maggie I'd been wondering if Lily's killer could somehow have been connected to the work that was being done on the building. I called Harry.

"You told Marcus that it was probably Idris Blackthorne who took care of the drywall work and the painting back when Lily's body would have been put behind the wall," I said. Idris Blackthorne had been Ruby's grandfather.

"I know it was," Harry said. "The old man remembers there was a bit of an uproar over him getting the job instead of a couple of other people. Say what you will, though, his guys did good work."

"Do you have any idea who would have been working for him?"

"Not a clue. I'm sorry." I pictured him shaking his head. "I doubt the old man knows, either. Ruby might be able to help you, though. I know she got all of her grandfather's papers and things when he died. And it's not like her to throw anything out."

"I'll ask her," I said. "Thanks."

I called Ruby and explained what I was looking for, crossing my fingers—literally—that Harry was right and she still had Idris's papers.

"I have all of my grandfather's things in storage," she said. "He kept meticulous records on everything. I'll check his ledgers for you in the morning."

I thanked her and we said good-bye. I hoped that I was finally getting somewhere and that this wouldn't be another dead end.

Marcus arrived about ten minutes after I'd talked to Ruby, just as Hercules was concluding his very elaborate face-washing ritual. Owen had wandered in to have a drink and meow "hello" and then disappeared, literally, of course. When I showed Marcus the two photos from the disposable camera, he told me I could keep them. "I don't see anything in either one of them that can tell us who killed her," he said. "But thanks for letting me see them. I'd rather have that image of her in my mind."

I decided I would call Emily Abbott in the morning and see if she wanted either of the photos.

"Have you confirmed Bryan James's alibi?" I asked as I cleared the table after supper.

"I guess it depends on how you define 'confirmed,'" he said.

"So you haven't."

"Not to my satisfaction." He was filling the sink with hot, soapy water since my little house didn't have a dishwasher. "He was hanging out with some of his friends—guys from the boys' volleyball team. They're all alibiing each other. The problem I have is they were drinking. Realistically, after all this time, how credible are they?"

I could see his point. "Have you talked to Jake Andersen?" I asked, shaking the place mats over the garbage can before I put them away.

His blue eyes narrowed. "I'm guessing you have," he said.

I nodded.

"Did you learn anything?"

"Not really. It looks as though Jake's alibi and Bryan James's alibi are the same group of guys." I rattled off the names Jake had given me.

Marcus nodded but didn't say anything.

I linked my fingers and tented my hands on the top of my head. "So Jake is Bryan's alibi. Bryan is Jake's alibi and there's not really any way to know if they're covering for one another or telling the truth."

"There might be a way," Marcus said slowly.

I turned to look at him. "What do you mean?"

"One of the guys had his dad's new video camera that night. Nick Gonzalez. He was just shooting video of his buddies goofing off. It wasn't the first time he borrowed the camera, but it was the last time."

"I take it he got caught."

He nodded again. "The next day. But Gonzalez swears he has the videotape. Somewhere."

"Do you believe him?"

"It doesn't much matter. Either the videotape doesn't exist—maybe never did—or he really can't find it. The result is the same. The only alibi any of those men have is very shaky."

Marcus and I went to the Stratton to watch *Miracle on 34th Street* being performed live as a radio play. I was a big fan of the movie from 1947. All the actors were dressed in costumes from the forties and I enjoyed every minute of the production.

The entire left side of my body stiffened up during the time we were in the theater and I struggled to stand up at the end of the night. Marcus reached for my arm to help me to my feet and I winced when his hand closed around my left forearm.

"Are you all right?" he asked, blue eyes narrowed in concern.

"I'm just a bit . . . sore," I said, trying not to groan as we started up the aisle.

"From what?"

"I might have played a little ball hockey."

My left sleeve slid back a little and he noticed the floor burn on my arm.

"Who in heaven's name were you playing with?" he said. "The Incredible Hulk?"

I made a face. "In a way, yes."

As we drove up the hill I checked my phone. There was a message from a number I didn't recognize. It was very difficult to make out—there seemed to be some kind of machinery in the background—and I had to listen twice to figure out it was from Mila Serrano. She wanted to talk to me. Was she going to tell me what I believed she'd kept from me when we talked on Friday?

Once we were back at the house I listened to the message a third time. "Please call me as soon as you get this message," Mila had said, followed by something else that neither Marcus nor I could make out.

I hesitated for a moment because it was late, but she had asked me to call her right away. Whatever she wanted to talk to me about had to be important.

The phone rang five times and I was second-guessing myself about calling when a man answered. "I'm looking for Mila Serrano," I said. "She left me a message to call her."

"Who are you?" the man asked.

I looked uncertainly at Marcus. "My name is Kathleen Paulson," I said. "Is Mila there?"

"Why are you calling?"

Something was wrong. "I already told you. She left me a message asking me to call. To whom am I speaking?"

"This is Officer Keller, Ms. Paulson," he said. I felt a knot of fear settle in my stomach.

"Officer Keller?" I said. "I don't understand. Where's Mila?"

Marcus's head snapped up at the sound of the officer's name.

"Why did Mrs. Serrano want to talk to you?" the officer asked. "It's a bit late for a social call."

I closed my eyes for a second, took a slow breath and let it out again. "I don't know," I said. "That's why I was calling her."

Marcus held out his hand for my phone. I handed it over without saying a word. I knew he had a much better chance of finding out what was going on than I did. He identified himself and asked what was going on. I stood there with my arms folded over my chest and tried not to think the worst.

It turned out that Mila had been taken to the hospital. She'd tried to kill herself.

I stood in the middle of the kitchen floor, arms wrapped around myself, shaking my head. "No," I said. "I don't believe it. I just talked to her yesterday. And she didn't seem suicidal. I would have noticed. Mila was getting ready for an exhibit of her art. Why would she try to kill herself?"

He made a helpless gesture with his hands. "I don't know. I'm going to go see what I can find out."

I put a hand on his arm to stop him. "Do you honestly think Mila tried to kill herself? Honestly? Did you see anything, anything at all that now you're second-guessing? Anything that you dismissed then that now makes you think maybe she would have tried to take her own life?"

For a moment he didn't speak, then he raked a hand back through his hair. "I didn't talk to her," he finally said. "She was on my list but I hadn't gotten to her yet."

"Mila Serrano didn't try to kill herself. I know she didn't," I said. "Somebody did this. The same somebody who killed Lily and hid her body in the wall."

"Kathleen, c'mon. That's a big leap."

I was shaking my head before he finished speaking. "No, it's not. It's the next logical step. Mila was keeping something back when I talked to her. There was something she didn't want to share. Maybe she was protecting someone. Maybe she wasn't sure about what she knew and wanted to . . ." I threw up my hands. "I don't know, maybe make sure she was right before she said anything. Find the person who did this and you'll find the person who killed Lily."

"Kathleen, I need to go see what's going on," he said. I didn't know if he agreed with my logic or not. It didn't matter. I knew I was right. He put on his jacket and boots, kissed me and was gone.

Maggie called early the next morning. I was sitting at the

table with a cup of coffee, trying to decide what I wanted for breakfast. "Is Marcus with you?" she asked.

"No, he isn't," I said.

She hesitated.

"Mags, is this about Mila?" I asked.

"You heard." Her voice was flat.

"I did, and Marcus is looking into what happened."

"She didn't try to kill herself," Maggie said. "You saw Mila on Friday. Did she seem suicidal to you?"

"No, she didn't." Owen had come to sit at my feet and was looking curiously at me. "Marcus will figure this out. I promise."

She sighed softly. "If you hear anything, will you let me know? Please?"

"Of course I will," I said. "And please call me if you hear anything." She promised she would and we said good-bye.

I got up to get more coffee and my phone chimed with a text. It was from Ruby, just three names: Glen Lasko, Peter Moller and Bash LaSalle. I had no idea how I was going to find the men and if they were even in the area—or even alive—but at least my idea hadn't turned out to be a dead end. Yet.

Marcus called about five minutes later. Mila was still unconscious.

"What happened?" I asked. Hercules had joined his brother and they were both eyeing me.

I heard him blow out a breath. "She supposedly tried to hang herself."

"Supposedly. You don't think she tried to kill herself, do you?"

"I'm not sure," he hedged.

I asked him the question that had kept me awake for a large chunk of the night. "Did I say or do something when I talked to Mila that made this happen?"

"No," he said firmly. He paused. "Okay, this is not something you can share with anyone. Understand?"

"I do," I said.

"Mila did not try to kill herself. It looks as though someone choked her from behind with the scarf she was wearing and then, when she passed out, faked the suicide attempt. Two things saved her. One was that the person who tried to kill her didn't do a good job of tying the knot, and the second was that she was found very quickly. The doctors are very cautiously optimistic."

I felt as though an elephant had been sitting on my chest and had now gotten up to stretch his legs.

"Tell me what happened when you talked to Mila," Marcus said. I gave him the basics.

"And why did you get the feeling she wasn't being straight with you?"

I explained how evasive Mila's body language had been and how she hadn't actually answered my question. "Mostly it was just a feeling," I said.

"I trust your instincts," he said.

"I keep thinking maybe Mila did know who Ella's biological father is. Maybe that person is here in town and Mila went to talk to him. Maybe he killed Lily and almost killed Mila. It seems like a big coincidence that Lily's body was found and now someone has tried to kill Mila."

"Yeah, it does." I pictured him nodding as he spoke. "I'm not sure when I'll see you."

"That's okay," I said. "Just find whoever did this."

"I'll do my best. I love you. Stay safe."

I set my phone on the table and stood up. Hercules rubbed against my leg and I leaned down and picked him up. He nuzzled my chin as though he was trying to comfort me.

"I can't help thinking I set something in motion when I talked to Mila," I said. "But I can't stop now. As my mother would say, *Alea iacta est.* The die is cast."

chapter 15

I made scrambled eggs and toast for breakfast and threw in some bits of vegetables I needed to use up, including some wilted spinach, half a soft tomato and three mushrooms that had gotten pushed to the back of the vegetable drawer.

"I should have talked to Bryan James before now," I said to Hercules, who had been lurking around while I cooked, hoping something would find its way onto the floor. "I should have done more than just leave messages." I realized I hadn't taken Lily's ex-boyfriend seriously as a suspect because he wasn't Ella's biological father and I knew he had a possible alibi. Now that I knew how shaky that alibi was, I realized how shortsighted I'd been. Had Bryan talked to Jake? Was that why he hadn't returned my calls?

I brought my computer over to the table, moving my coffee out of the way so no stray paws or tails could knock it over onto the laptop.

Bryan James was easy to find on social media, and as far as I could tell, he was in town, not away at another tournament. I didn't want to just show up on his doorstep, but I wasn't a complete stranger. Face-to-face I'd be a lot harder to ignore.

I put the computer away again and called Emily Abbott to tell her about the photos. "I'd be happy to bring them to you," I said. "Or scan them and text them."

"I suspected that's what was on that old camera," she said. "I took those two photos the day Lily disappeared. Tim could never bear to have them developed."

"I'm sorry," I said. I could hear the pain in her voice.

"You don't need to apologize," Emily said. "It's not your fault." She hesitated for a moment. "They both look happy, don't they, because that's how I remember them looking."

I had to swallow down the lump in my throat before I could answer. "Yes, they do," I said.

"Please give the photographs to Ella King," she said. "I appreciate your offer to scan them but it's not necessary. Lily and Tim were Ella's family, *are* her family, and she deserves to have them."

"I will," I said. I thanked her and we said good-bye. I set the phone on the table and it immediately rang again. I didn't recognize the number but I answered anyway. It was Bryan James.

I was so surprised I had to sit down.

"I got your messages," he said.

"But Jake Andersen told you not to talk to me."

"Something like that." There was silence for a moment. "I'm friends with Mila Serrano. I talked to her on Friday and she said that you're trying to find out what happened to Lily."

"Yes, I am," I said.

"Mila said we should talk."

"Mr. James, have you spoken to Mila since Friday?" I asked.

"No," he said. "And please, call me Bryan. I'm a middle school teacher and basketball coach and I was at a daylong workshop in Minneapolis yesterday. Why?"

So he didn't know. "I'm sorry to have to tell you this," I said, "but Mila is in the hospital."

"What . . . what happened?" He could barely get the words out. If he was acting surprised, he was pretty good at it.

"It appears . . . that she tried to hurt herself."

"Absolutely not." His voice was firm and certain. "Not Mila. She wasn't depressed or suicidal. I just talked to her."

I couldn't tell him what Marcus had told me, but I could say I agreed with him and I did. "The police are still investigating," I added.

"I think we should talk in person," he said. "Would you be willing to meet somewhere in public? My little guy is in Reading Buddies so I'm not a total stranger."

"Yes," I said. If I talked to Bryan James in person I could read his body language and see how he reacted to my questions.

"How about Eric's Place?" Bryan said. "Eric is a friend and he can vouch for me."

"Same here," I said.

We agreed to meet in an hour. "I know what you look like," he said. "And I should say I'm also friends with John Stone. I know you've been involved with situations like Lily Abbott's death before."

I got to Eric's about five minutes early. I asked for a table by the end wall, not over by the window where I usually sat. I explained to Claire that I was waiting for someone.

"Would you like a menu?" she asked.

I shook my head. "Just coffee, please."

Claire had just brought the coffee when a man approached the table. He was heavyset, with salt-and-pepper hair and a matching beard. He introduced himself as Bryan James. I recognized him from his social media and from the library.

I indicated the empty chair opposite and he sat down. Claire came over with a mug and the coffeepot. She clearly knew him. "Would you like anything else?" she asked.

He shook his head. "Thanks, coffee is just fine."

"Let me know when you want a refill," she said and then moved on to another table.

"Thank you for meeting me, Ms. Paulson," Bryan said.

"Please call me Kathleen, "I said. He didn't look like a man who had killed his former girlfriend thirty-six years ago and then tried to do the same to her best friend. On the other hand, I knew looks could be deceiving.

"Please, what can you tell me about Mila? I called the hospital but they wouldn't tell me anything."

I added cream and sugar to my cup. "I don't know a lot. Mila left me a message last evening, and when I called back I found out she was in the hospital."

He scrubbed one hand over his face. "It's just not possible that she tried to hurt herself."

"It doesn't fit with the person I talked to," I said. "Could we start at the beginning? How did you and Lily meet?"

"Chemistry class. I had a whole cheesy pickup line about how the two of us had chemistry. She called me out on that, but we got to be friends and then more."

"The two of you were . . . on and off."

"Oh yeah," he said. "And that was all on me. Lily and I fought about how much time she spent at volleyball practice and about a lot of other things. We finally broke up spring of our senior year."

He stared past me for a moment and gave his head a shake. "I was a jerky teenage boy and all I was thinking about was having fun back then, but I didn't kill Lily."

"Do you have any idea who did?"

He shook his head. "I've been asking myself that question since I heard Lily's body had been found, and I can't come up with a single name. Everyone liked her."

"Her brother thought you'd done something to her," I said.

"Tim Abbott hounded me until the day he died. He was convinced I had hurt Lily in some way. I would never have done that."

I traced the rim of my coffee cup with one finger. "So what were you doing the day Lily disappeared?"

"My mother made me go to church for the longest-night service. To my surprise the building wasn't struck by lightning. After that I hung out with my buddies at a party for a while."

"One of those buddies was Jake Andersen."

"Yes."

"You were drinking?"

He nodded.

That all fit with what I already knew. "Why did Mila call you?" I asked.

"We sort of keep in touch," he said, "but mostly by social media. I was surprised to hear from her. She told me about Ella King being Lily's daughter. Then she said she had talked to you and I should, too."

He looked down at the table, picked up a spoon and flipped it over the back of his fingers before his gaze met mine again. "I had already talked to Jake. He said you were asking questions about what we were doing the night Lily disappeared. I told him Nick—Nick Gonzalez—had a videotape that proved where we were. I'd told the police that. But Jake said Nick couldn't find the tape. He said it was a bad idea to talk to you. I'm sorry. I shouldn't have avoided you."

"Do you know why Mila thought you should talk to me?" I asked.

Bryan shook his head. "She seemed really interested in the snowstorm the night Lily disappeared. She asked if I remembered how bad it was."

"Did you?" I asked.

He played with the spoon then seemed to notice what he was doing and placed both of his hands on the table. "Yeah, I did because I was supposed to get a ride home with one of the guys and his car wouldn't start. We had to walk home. There was an accident near the school that brought down two power poles. Not only did that knock out the electricity for part of town, it also meant the road was blocked and it took us even longer because we had to go a different way. Mila wanted to know if I remembered exactly where the road was blocked and where the detour was."

I waited. His body language told me there was something more coming.

Bryan sighed. "Mila was with us. She couldn't remember where the road was closed or where the detour was set up because she'd been drinking. She didn't drink very often."

"I thought Mila was at some sort of family party," I said.

"She was. After she got home she snuck out to meet us."

I had another mouthful of coffee. It was getting cold. I looked around for Claire. She raised her eyebrows and I nodded. Once Bryan and I both had refills, I looked across the table at him again. "Did Mila say why she wanted to know about the roadblock and the detour?"

"No. But I think it had to do with Lily. I think she remembered something after the two of you talked."

Or maybe while we were talking, I thought.

"What about your friends?" I asked. "Would any of them have hurt Lily?"

He seemed genuinely surprised at the question. "No. No way."

"How about Jake Andersen? I heard he and Lily argued a few days before she disappeared."

Bryan laughed, shaking his head. "Jake was a big blowhard. He liked to stir up trouble. He liked arguing. Yeah, he and Lily got into it about funding for boys' sports versus girls', but no one really took him seriously. Lily didn't stay mad. And anyway, Jake was with the rest of us the night Lily vanished. If you could see that video, you'd see that we were all drunk and stupid."

Video that couldn't be found at the moment.

His expression changed then. "If I thought any of my friends had hurt Lily, I would be the first one to turn them in. Lily was my first love. I know how foolish it sounds now that we know she's been dead all these years, but I always hoped she had just run off and was out there, somewhere, having a great life. I want to know who killed her just as much as anyone else does."

He seemed like a nice guy. There was nothing evasive in his answers to my questions. But I knew appearances could be deceiving. I wasn't ready to write Bryan off as a suspect just because he'd said all the right things.

"Do you have any idea who the father of Lily's baby was?" I asked.

His expression darkened. "No. I tried to get her to tell me, but she wouldn't say, no matter how hard I pushed."

"Could it have been anyone you knew?" I said. "One of your friends, like Jake, maybe?"

He was shaking his head even before I finished speaking. "That's just stupid," he said. "None of the guys would have been sneaking around with Lily. And she thought Jake was juvenile. Never would have happened."

My question had put a damper on the conversation. Luckily, Eric was coming over to us.

"Hi, Kathleen," he said. "How are you?"

"I'm good," I said. "Thank you for the cheese-and-spinach hand pies. I'm sure Susan told you we couldn't pick a favorite between the two recipes."

Eric smiled. "She did."

"Wait a minute," Bryan said. "Spinach-and-cheese hand pies? You've been holding out on me." He was back to the easygoing, friendly man I'd first been talking to.

"I thought you were all about salads these days," Eric said. "You said you were trying to get in shape."

Bryan shook his head. "I said Jamie—my wife," he said in an aside to me—"is trying to get me in shape." He patted his belly. "I keep telling her that round is a shape."

Eric laughed. "I have to get back to the kitchen," he said. "It was good to see you both."

I didn't see anywhere else for the conversation with Bryan to go. I thanked him for answering my questions and asked him to please call me if he thought of anything else.

"I will," he said.

I wasn't certain he would. I waved good-bye to Claire and went out to the truck. Instead of starting it right away, I sat in the driver's seat and thought about what Bryan had told me. Was he right? Did one of the questions I asked stir a memory for Mila? The way Bryan's demeanor had changed when I'd asked about the father of Lily's baby was unsettling. Had Mila remembered something about Bryan? Could he be Lily's killer?

chapter 16

I got home and found Fifi sitting in the driveway staring at the back door. There was no sign of Hercules. "What are you doing here?" I said. Fifi leaned against my leg and I scratched behind his ears. He sighed. After a moment I took him by the collar and walked him next door.

"Thank you, Ms. Paulson," Ronan said, wrapping his arms around the dog's neck.

Marcus was just pulling in as I made my way back to my own yard. He looked tired.

"It's good to see you," he said, leaning down to kiss me. We walked around the house together.

"How's Mila?" I asked as soon as we were inside.

"She's still unconscious, but the doctors are a little more optimistic than they were last night."

"I'm going to hold on to that," I said.

He yawned. "Were you out?" he asked.

"I was just taking Fifi back next door," I said, "but before that I was down at Eric's talking to Bryan James." I explained about the phone call from Lily's former boyfriend. We headed inside and got out of our winter clothing.

"When Mila wakes up we may finally be able to get some answers," Marcus said. He pulled out a chair and sat down. I was heartened that he'd said "when," not "if."

"Have you come up with anyone connected to Lily Abbott who might have hurt Mila?" I asked. I moved behind the chair and began to work on his shoulders. They seemed perpetually tied in knots these days.

"No," he said. "Have you?"

"I don't know." I leaned over to kiss the side of his face. "Did you know Mila talked to Bryan James on Friday? She told him he should talk to me."

"Did she say why?"

I shook my head. "He says she didn't."

"Do you believe him?" He made a face as I worked at a particularly tight spot.

"I don't know. I find it convenient that both his and Jake Andersen's alibis depend on this mysterious videotape no one can find."

Marcus groaned as I concentrated my efforts on one area of

his shoulder. "Has anyone ever told you that you have hands like the Incredible Hulk?"

I kissed the opposite cheek from the one I'd kissed before. "I'm going to take that as a compliment," I said. "I assume you haven't had any luck finding that tape."

"None. Nick Gonzalez says he can't find it, doesn't know what happened to it. He offered to let us look through the boxes in his basement."

"I keep meaning to ask you, did you ever find anything useful from that necklace that Harry found on the floor?" I asked as I worked on a tight area just to the left of his shoulder blade.

He took so long to answer I thought he wasn't going to. "Forensics didn't find anything. No fingerprints. No DNA. And there's nothing that suggests it belonged to Lily. Emily Abbott didn't recognize it and neither did anyone else who knew Lily."

I sighed. "When Harry showed it to me I was so sure it was hers, but Mila didn't remember seeing Lily wearing it and you're right, neither did Emily or Lily's former volleyball coach."

"Not everything is a clue," Marcus said. He shifted in the chair, reached up and pulled me down onto his lap, and for a few minutes I forgot all about necklaces and clues.

Monday morning the quilters had their holiday celebration. They'd made me a table runner and a set of holiday place mats. Their work was beautiful and I was touched by their kindness.

Harry came in just before lunch to check the book drop. It had developed a squeak somewhere inside and the outside handle was loose.

"Easy fix," Harry said.

I felt the tension in my neck ease. The book drop was my nemesis and I had no money in the budget to replace it right now. "Do you have a minute, before you get started?" I asked.

"Sure," Harry said. "What do you need?"

"Information." I pulled my phone out of my pocket and showed him the three workers' names Ruby had texted to me: Glen Lasko, Peter Moller and Bash LaSalle. "Can you tell me anything about these three men?"

"I can tell you that Glen Lasko is dead. Has been for the last ten years. He would have been the supervisor on the project. He'd worked for Idris for years. And I don't see how he could have hurt Lily Abbott."

I frowned. "What do you mean?"

"Glen had arthritis in his hands. Fingers were really twisted. That's why he was working as more of a foreman. Say what you will about Idris Blackthorne, he was loyal to the people who were loyal to him."

"What about the other two?" I asked.

"Both of them left town years ago, as far as I know."

Even though I realized this was a long shot, my heart sank.

Harry swiped a hand over his chin. "But now that I think about it, it seems to me Bash might be back in Red Wing. How about I ask around, quietly, and see what I can find out about either one of them?"

"Please," I said. "I feel like I'm trying to grab a handful of rain. I want to help Ella but I don't seem to be getting anywhere."

"You'll figure it out," he said, giving me a smile. "You always do."

At lunchtime I spent some time online looking for photos from that volleyball tournament the boys' and girls' teams had gone to in Green Bay right after Lily and Bryan broke up. No matter what Bryan had said to me, I still felt there was a possibility that Jake Andersen was Ella's biological father.

All I could find were the official team pictures. There were no informal photographs. From the look of the schedule and what Ann McKinnon had told me, the players hadn't had a lot of downtime. I found a photo of Ann with the other coaches. She was wearing track pants, a T-shirt and a knit beanie. She looked so young—no older, really, than her students. I learned that she had graduated from high school at seventeen. She had done one year in the nursing program at college before switching her major. And she had put together the first aid team for the tournament because she was also a certified first aid instructor.

I frowned at the screen. That didn't make sense. When I

had told Ann that Lily might have been further along in her pregnancy than she was letting on, Ann had claimed ignorance. *Anything medical, forget it. Not my area of expertise.*

She'd lied to me. But why? I needed to talk to Ann again. Maybe I'd stop by the school on the way home and see if she was there. Was it possible that Ann had known a lot more about Lily's pregnancy than she had let on?

After school Riley Hollister came by to see me. The teenager was a math whiz but her tumultuous home life and the unexpected death of her mother had led to her getting into some trouble recently. We had connected over our shared love for books and numbers. I was happy that she seemed to be doing well living with relatives of her late mother along with her little brother, Duncan, while their father, Lonnie, dealt with his drinking issues.

Riley was growing her hair out again—she had shaved her head several months ago—and she seemed calmer, probably because she had no more adult responsibilities, although I knew she still watched over Duncan.

"Lonnie is still in rehab," she said. She refused to call her father by anything other than his first name. Given that he'd been a lousy parent, I couldn't fault her for that. "We went to see him. I don't care, but it's important for Duncan."

"How was it?" I asked.

"He's not as big a dick sober as he is when he's drinking. He said I don't have to forgive him for being a sucky dad because he hasn't given me any reason yet to believe he can do better but he's going to." Riley rolled her eyes. "We'll see."

I noticed the long black-and-gray scarf Riley was wearing. "I like your scarf," I said. "Did Rebecca make it?"

She nodded. "Yeah."

I smiled. "It's Gru's scarf from *Despicable Me*, right?"

"Wait a minute. You know that movie?" Riley said.

"Sure," I said. "I've probably watched it four or five times." I didn't say that it was one of Hercules's favorite movies. "My favorite minion is Kevin."

"Mine is Stuart." Somehow it didn't surprise me that Riley's favorite would be the one-eyed little yellow guy.

"I have something for you," I said. I opened the bottom drawer of my desk and handed a wrapped package to the teen. The red-and-green paper was covered with disco-dancing reindeer. Riley smiled when she saw it.

"It's books, right?" she said.

I smiled. "Maybe."

"I know it is."

"What makes you so sure?"

She held out both hands. "Hello. Librarian. What else are you going to get people for Christmas?"

"Okay, yes, it's books, but you'll have to wait until Christmas to find out which ones." Riley was a voracious reader and I hoped she'd like what I'd chosen.

"I . . . uh, have something for you," she said, ducking her

head. She handed me an envelope tied with a length of silver ribbon. "You can open it now if you want."

I undid the ribbon and lifted the flap of the envelope to find a folded piece of paper inside. It was a certificate that said Riley Hollister was the most improved student for the month of November.

For a moment I couldn't speak.

"Hey, this is a good thing for a change, not a bad thing," Riley said.

"I'm so proud of you," I said. Without thinking about it I threw my arms around her in a hug.

"It's not a big deal," she mumbled.

"It's a huge deal." I looked at the certificate again. Riley was smart, but she'd never done well in school. She dismissed a lot of the assignments as busywork and she challenged her teachers on everything.

Riley stuffed her hands in her pockets. "Dr. Davidson says I could be a vet someday if I want to." Riley volunteered at Roma's clinic and I knew from Roma that Riley was good with the animals, patient and kind.

"You could do anything you set your mind to," I said. I wasn't spouting platitudes. I believed that. I'd learned that Riley could be incredibly focused and determined when she set her mind to something.

"I might be a vet. Or maybe a math teacher."

I must have looked as surprised as I felt at the latter idea.

She just shrugged. "If I was a math teacher I would make the class interesting so more kids would learn."

"I like that idea, too," I said. "I can't wait to see what you eventually choose." I gave her a sly smile. "You like books, so maybe . . . librarian?"

She looked around the room. "Well, by then you'll be too old to get up the stairs, so maybe, yeah." For a moment she was straight-faced, then she laughed.

"Good to know you have my back," I said.

She hesitated and then gave me a quick, hard hug. "I better get going," she said, pulling away. "I have to get to the clinic."

She zippered her jacket and looped her scarf twice more around her neck. I noticed all she had on her feet were a pair of red Converse high-tops.

"Riley, where are your boots?" I asked.

She gave a dismissive wave of her hand—at least she had mittens. "Boots are for dorks. I'm fine. I have two pair of socks inside." She promised to bring Duncan in over the holidays for more books, and then she was gone.

A short time later Susan poked her head in to say that the Cookie Monster tree was missing an eyeball and did we have any more felt to make a new one.

"We do," I said, "but did you check the nearby shelves first?"

Susan frowned at me. "No."

I stood up and stretched. "I'll come look because I need a

break. It's probably around somewhere. We have a couple of patrons who think it's funny to have a one-eyed Cookie Monster."

I followed Susan downstairs and after a quick search found the missing eyeball tucked on the top shelf. I put it back in place, moving both eyes a little higher so they'd be harder to reach. I had just finished when Susan came to tell me I had a visitor. Ann McKinnon was standing at the circulation desk. For a moment it felt as though thinking about her earlier had somehow made her appear in the building.

"Do you have a minute to talk?" she asked with no preamble.

There were only a few people in the library, and the paperwork upstairs on my desk could wait for a few minutes. "I do," I said. "There's something I wanted to ask you." I looked at Susan. "I'm going to take my break now."

"No problem," she said.

I directed Ann over to the meeting room where the quilters had been set up earlier. She wore a heavy black wool coat, some sort of black athletic pants and a pair of black lace-up boots that I recognized as being Black Dog footwear, made in Red Wing. I wondered if there was any chance I could get Riley to wear a pair of boots like that.

She turned to face me, both hands in the pockets of her coat. "You first," she said.

"You lied to me," I said.

Her eyes narrowed. "I don't know what you're talking about."

I held up a finger. "You did one year of nursing school." I held up a second finger. "You're a first aid instructor—or at least you were—and yet you told me medical things weren't your area of expertise."

Color flooded her cheeks. She looked down at her feet for a moment before looking me in the eye again. "You're right. I did lie to you. That's why I'm here. I wanted to come clean before you figured that out." Her mouth twisted to one side. "I guess I'm too late for that."

"So why did you lie?" I asked.

She cleared her throat. "The night Lily disappeared she went off the road because of the bad weather."

"I know," I said.

"She decided to walk to get help, she was close to the school and she saw my car in the parking lot."

"You already told me all of this," I said.

Ann looked away. "Lily was in labor."

I stared at her, openmouthed.

"I delivered the baby."

I couldn't find words for a moment. I didn't know what to do with my hands. "You delivered Lily's baby," I finally managed to say, as though repeating the words would somehow make them make sense. "A full-term baby?"

"You have to understand," she said. "The accident had

knocked out power and phone service to that part of town. I couldn't leave her alone to go get help. I was it. And I did have that year of nursing school and all that first aid training." She pulled a hand back over her hair. "Lily knew that and I've always wondered if that's why she came to me."

None of this made any sense. I had to have missed something. "So you delivered the baby—Ella—and didn't say anything to anyone? Why? You hadn't done anything wrong."

"After the baby was born I sat down for just five minutes. I swear. It was late and I was so damn tired. Lily and the baby were fine, as far as I could tell. The road wasn't cleared, so my plan was to wade through the snow to get help at the fire station. It wasn't that far away."

"You obviously didn't do that."

She stared up at the ceiling. "I fell asleep. When I woke up an hour later Lily and the baby were gone. She left a note, just saying thank you and she was okay. I thought she was with a friend or even with the baby's father. The roads were plowed by then and I drove around looking for them, just to be sure, but I couldn't find them anywhere. I thought . . . I just thought she'd taken the baby and run away."

"Her car was in the ditch. She couldn't have gotten very far. She was carrying *a baby*." I wanted to grab Ann by the shoulders and shake her.

"But I thought somebody came and picked her up. Picked *them* up. When I went outside I could see tire tracks where someone had driven in and stopped in front of the school. And even so, I looked everywhere I could think of. Finally, I just . . . went to my aunt and uncle's."

"Why didn't you call the police? Or Lily's family? Somebody. Anybody." I struggled to control my anger and frustration.

"I didn't know I had a reason to."

"But what about when you did have a reason to? What about when you found out that no one knew where Lily was? You still didn't go to the police."

"I was afraid," Ann blurted. "And yes, stupid. I was only three years older than Lily and a lot of those other girls. You're right. I should have called the police and Lily's family when I woke up and she was gone, but I really did think she was okay."

"But you kept this secret for thirty-six years."

Ann took a deep breath and let it out. "Lily's brother, Tim, came to see me once it became clear that Lily was missing. I was going to tell him everything, and then he said that he was trying to find out where Lily went after she left Mila Serrano's house. He didn't think she'd run away. He was convinced she was dead and whoever she'd been with was the person who killed her. *That was me.* That was me and I had no way to prove I hadn't hurt her!"

"You had no reason to kill Lily," I said. I pulled a hand back through my hair.

"Neither did Bryan James, as far as I'm concerned," Ann said. "He and Lily had been broken up for months, but once Tim Abbott got fixated on Bryan, he wouldn't stop harassing him."

"You could have showed Tim the note Lily left you."

Ann stuffed her hands in her pockets and shook her head. "No, I couldn't. I lost it. When I was out looking for Lily it must have fallen out of my pocket somewhere. I delivered the baby and then both of them disappeared. I knew how that looked. So I did the wrong thing. I kept my mouth shut, and the longer I did, the harder it got to tell the truth. But in my defense I really thought Lily was somewhere safe, and if she didn't want to come back, so be it."

"I understand why you panicked in the moment," I said, "but you've had the last thirty-six years to tell the truth."

"I was stupid and afraid of getting in trouble. I was sending money home to my mother and grandmother. I didn't want to lose my job." She sounded defensive, but not sorry.

"You have to go to the police," I said flatly.

"I'm going to."

"Right now. You have half an hour and then I'll call them myself."

The muscles in her jaw tightened and for a moment I expected her to refuse. "I'll go right now," she finally said. She shifted her gaze back to me. "I truly am sorry. I never meant for any of this to happen."

After she was gone I leaned my head against the wall and

closed my eyes. My head ached and my stomach hurt. I understood that Ann had panicked in the moment, but to keep that kind of secret for thirty-six years? I couldn't help but think that if she had told the truth from the beginning, the police might not have been so quick to label Lily a runaway.

chapter 17

I found it hard to shake the feelings Ann's visit stirred up. I didn't blame her for Lily's death. The blame, the responsibility for that, was all on the person who murdered Lily. But if Ann had told the truth all those years ago, maybe the killer wouldn't have gotten away with murder for so long.

I was the last person out of the building at the end of the day. I stopped to make sure the book drop was working properly. It wasn't sticking or squeaking and the handle was secure. Maybe Harry had solved at least some of my problems with the contraption.

I turned to head down the stairs and caught sight of a figure standing in the parking lot. After a moment I realized that it was Jake Andersen. What was he doing here? Why hadn't he come inside?

Jake was standing by the tailgate of his black truck, hands in his pockets. I walked across the pavement, stopping about ten feet away from him. He made no move to get any closer.

"What are you doing here?" I asked.

"I wanted to talk to you."

"Why didn't you come inside?"

He looked around the empty space. "It's a little more private out here."

"All right," I said. "I'm listening."

His mouth moved as though he was tasting the words before he actually spoke them. "I liked Lily," he finally said.

"You mean romantically."

He nodded. "Yes. I asked her out a couple of times." He paused. "Okay, three times. She turned me down. Every time."

Jake had been just like a six-year-old on the playground, slugging the arm of the little girl he had a crush on, I realized. He'd provoked arguments with Lily because he liked her. I should have figured that out.

He had a small padded envelope tucked under his arm, and he held it out to me.

"What is this?" I asked.

"It's the videotape."

I knew he meant the one Nick Gonzalez had made with his

father's video camera. I stepped close enough to take it from him. "How did you get this?"

"I took it," he said, "but not for the reason you think."

"How do you know what I'm thinking?"

I saw him smile in the gleam from the parking lot lights. "That tape will show that Bryan and I were telling the truth about where we were."

I tucked the padded envelope in the top of my bag. "How long have you had this?" I asked. "And why did you take it?"

His smile faded. "I've had it for a while. I took the tape because there's video of Lily on it. Nick had had the camera at school a couple of days before Christmas break."

"So why are you handing it over now?"

"I heard what happened to Lily's friend Mila. It's not right. Someone has to find the person who killed Lily. And no one should waste time looking at me or Bryan when we really do have alibis."

I thought about first loves and roads not taken. "Thank you," I finally said.

He nodded. "You're welcome."

"You made a copy, didn't you?" I said.

Jake laughed. "Have a good evening, Ms. Paulson," he said. He got in his truck, backed out of the parking spot and drove away.

The moment I got to Marcus's house I handed over the videotape and explained how I came to have it.

"He could have just brought it to the police station," Marcus said.

I shook my head. "I don't think Jake Andersen is the kind of person who does things the easy way very often."

"That tape might eliminate my two best suspects."

"I know," I said as I handed him my coat. It was a long shot, but I was hoping Harry would come up with something.

I pulled out a chair and sat down at the table. "So what's going to happen to Ann McKinnon?" I asked. Ann had kept her word and gone straight to the police department after she'd left the library.

"I'm not sure," he said. "She could be charged with hindering an investigation both for lying when Lily disappeared and for lying again when the body was found."

I sighed. "I understand that Ann was barely an adult when Lily disappeared. I wouldn't want to have to justify and explain some of the choices I made when I was twenty-one, but lying was such a massive thing to do. And then to keep that secret for all these years since."

"I admit it was stupid. She'll likely lose her job over this, at the very least. I think in the moment Ann just panicked, and then the more time went by, the harder it got to tell the truth."

"Is there any news about Mila?" I said.

"She's still unconscious, but the doctors think she could start waking up anytime now."

"Isn't that what they said yesterday?"

He turned the light on in the oven and peered through the

window. The delicious scent that filled the kitchen told me we were having shepherd's pie. "I hate to throw a cliché at you, but I'm going to," he said. "It's a marathon, Kathleen, not a sprint."

Micah padded over and jumped onto my lap. She butted my hand with her head and I began to stroke her soft fur. "I know," I said. "I just keep thinking about how horrible this is for Mila's family."

Marcus straightened up and turned off the oven light. "She's strong and she has a good support system. And *when* she wakes up, maybe we'll get some answers." He leaned against the counter. "I do have some sort-of-bad news. Or maybe I should say it's more like not-exactly-good news."

Micah and I exchanged a look. Neither one of us knew what he was talking about. "What does sort-of-bad news, not-exactly-good news mean? Is it bad news as in Eric is going to stop making pudding cake? Or bad news as in an asteroid is going to strike the Earth tomorrow and all life will be annihilated?"

Marcus shook his head. "Number one, you and Hercules have to stop watching cheesy disaster movies, and number two, it's probably closer to the cake thing."

"You're stalling," I said. "What's the problem?"

"There's an . . . issue with our train tickets."

"What kind of issue?"

He stared up at the ceiling. "We kind of have tickets to Boca Raton, not Boston."

Micah cocked her head to one side. It didn't make any sense

to her, either. "I don't understand how that could happen," I said. "Boca Raton doesn't sound remotely like Boston. It's two words. Only one of them starts with a B. The two places aren't even in the same state. They aren't in the same area of the country."

Marcus nodded. "I know."

"So they just have to give us the correct tickets. Are we leaving at a different time?"

He shook his head.

"No," I said, holding up one hand. "You bought the tickets in good faith. *They* made the mistake, so it's their job to fix it."

"Kathleen, there are no seats to be had on any of the trains to Boston before Christmas because of the airline issues." He blew out a breath. "And I'm the one who made the mistake. I'm sorry. I wasn't paying attention when I bought the tickets."

I closed my eyes for a moment. Micah put a paw on my arm in sympathy, or at least it felt that way. This wasn't a disaster in the vein of an asteroid hurtling toward Earth, I reminded myself. It wasn't even a disaster like Eric not making pudding cake anymore would be. This wasn't a disaster at all. So why did it feel like one?

I looked at Marcus. I had the sudden urge to grab the loaf of French bread on the counter and whack him over the head with it.

"I'm sorry," he repeated. I could see from the expression on his face that he was. "Please say something."

"I was thinking about hitting you with that baguette," I

said. "But then I thought about Ella, who will never get to know her birth family, and Mila, who may not wake up for Christmas, and not going to Boston didn't seem so bad."

I stood up and set Micah on the chair. Then I put both hands on Marcus's shoulders and kissed him. "I know you didn't do it on purpose. We'll do a Mayville Heights Christmas instead."

"We could drive," he said.

I frowned at him. "You hate driving long distances. You can't move around when you get restless and you loathe gas station bathrooms."

"All true. But I love you." He pulled out his phone. I had no idea what he was doing. After a few taps and swipes he looked up at me. "It's a twenty-plus-hour trip, depending on which one of us is driving."

I smiled because I knew he was taking a shot at my lead foot.

"We can drive to Cleveland, which is about the halfway point, spend the night and head out early the next morning. I found us a motel room." He showed me the phone. "I'm going to book it," he said. "So either you're going to Boston for Christmas with me or Micah is."

The cat, with her perfect sense of timing, gave an enthusiastic meow.

I hesitated. Marcus didn't. He tapped the screen. Then he smiled and began to sing a very off-key but enthusiastic rendition of Willie Nelson's "On the Road Again."

The shepherd's pie was ready by the time Marcus's impromptu concert was over—mercifully. Once we'd eaten and cleaned up he suggested a rod hockey rematch. I looked him over, hands on my hips. "I admire your optimism," I said. "We both know you're not going to win but you somehow think there's a tiny possibility that you might."

He waggled his eyebrows at me. "Exactly. I've been practicing."

"With who? Micah?"

"No," he said. "With Brady and Eddie."

"Amateurs," I scoffed.

"Hey, Brady played college hockey and Eddie played in the NHL."

"And both of them have beaten me exactly how many times at this game?"

Marcus didn't say anything.

I smirked at him. Then I put a hand to my ear. "I'm sorry," I said. "I couldn't hear you."

"None," Marcus said. "And has anyone ever told you that you are an obnoxious winner?"

I nodded. "Yes. You. The last time we played."

He glared and pointed a finger at me. "You are going down!"

Micah was sitting by his feet. She looked up at him, then she walked over and sat down next to me.

I beat Marcus two games in a row. I would have beaten him three times, but Eddie called while we were in the middle of the third match—which, for the record, I was leading. Eddie's truck had two flat tires. He was waiting for a tow truck but he needed Marcus to pick up Roma, who was without her own car. It had refused to start that morning.

I gave Micah a scratch under her chin and a kiss on the top of her head and promised I'd make sardine crackers for her soon.

When I got home, Hercules was in the porch seemingly stargazing out the window. I found Owen upstairs rearranging the shoes in my closet. I finished packing for our trip to Boston, with Owen making little muttering comments about what clothes I was choosing to take with me. Did anyone else have a cat who seemed to think he was a fashion maven?

I went back downstairs to see if my favorite flats were in the porch or at the library. I'd turned on the tree lights when I'd gotten home and I found Hercules sitting in front of the tree. Burtis had brought me the tree, cut from his own property. It made the whole house smell wonderful. Maggie had promised to keep the tree watered while we were gone. At first I had decided not to have one at all because we'd be gone for a week. But once Burtis had shown up with the library's tree, I had changed my mind. Looking at my tree now, I was happy I had.

It felt strange in the morning to be home and not at the library. Both cats kept looking quizzically at me as though they were thinking, *What the heck are you doing here on a Tuesday?* Marcus was picking me up just before lunch for the first part of our trip. It would be close to midnight before we got to Cleveland—unless I could convince him to let me drive. After so much hassle, it looked like we were going to make it for Christmas with my family with no more problems.

I called my mom to tell her about our slight change in plans. I got her voice mail and left a message. Then Maggie stopped in to get her instructions about taking care of Owen and Hercules. Roma had read the riot act to her and Marcus about sneaking treats to them.

She put one hand on her chest. "I swear I won't feed them anything but cat food," she said.

Then I caught her winking at Owen and him smiling back at her. "You two could at least pretend you're going to behave," I said.

They gave me their best guileless looks, while Hercules, who had been carefully washing his tail, lifted his head, somewhat confused.

Maggie had just left when Harry called. "I'm sorry," he said. "I do have some information but didn't find anything that helps."

"It's okay," I said. "At best it was a long shot. What did you find out?"

"Peter Moller moved to Florida maybe a dozen years ago and then just seemed to fall off the map. My best guess is he's dead. He doesn't have any family around here and I don't know how you'd ever be able to track him down."

"What about the other man?"

"Bash is dead. Almost five years now. The old man went to his funeral. You can find the obituary on Gunnerson's website. Sebastian LaSalle. Capital L and capital S in LaSalle."

"Thanks for all of this, Harry," I said.

"I wish I could have found something that helped."

"Me too."

"You'll figure it out," he said.

I wished I had as much faith in myself as Harry seemed to have. I thanked him and we said good-bye.

I was at a dead end. I had no way to help Ella. I had no way to find Lily Abbott's killer. I had no suspects. I felt certain Marcus would say that the videotape Jake had given me cleared both Jake and Bryan. Jake had no reason to hand it over if it didn't. I had no idea who Ella's biological father was. I'd thought it was possible that it was Jake, but given that he obviously still had a soft spot for Lily, I found it hard to believe that he wouldn't have admitted they slept together and wouldn't want to know his daughter. And now the names of the three men who had been working on the building all those years ago had led nowhere. Two were dead and the third likely was. And dead men tell no tales.

I leaned against the back of the chair and stared up at the ceiling. Was it worth looking up Sebastian LaSalle's obituary on Gunnerson's website? There was something about the man's name that kept poking my brain. Both Harry and Ruby had referred to him as Bash, which suggested he went by the nickname most of the time. I wouldn't have guessed it was short for Sebastian. And then suddenly I knew what was bothering me. I looked at Hercules as I finally made the connection. "I would have thought Seb," I said out loud.

The cat wrinkled his whiskers at me as though he was confused, which he probably was.

Ann McKinnon had mentioned that she had been going to Red Wing all those years ago *with her cousin Seb.* That was way too much of a coincidence to ignore. I could tie Sebastian—Bash or Seb, whichever nickname you chose—albeit tenuously, to Lily.

So what did I do with this new piece of information? I decided another cup of coffee was in order. Hercules jumped up onto my chair and reached a paw toward my phone.

"Freeze, furball!" I said. He looked at me, then he looked at the phone and meowed.

"There's nothing on my phone that you need."

He reached for the phone again. "Leave that alone," I said firmly. I leaned over and grabbed the phone from the table. He glared at me and jumped down to the floor.

Once I'd poured my coffee I sat at the table again. Hercules immediately launched himself onto my lap. When I'd sat down I'd set my cell on the table once more. He eyed the phone.

"What is it with you and that phone?" I asked.

"Merow," he said. He touched the screen with one paw.

Was he trying to tell me something or was he just being a cat? I decided to give him the benefit of the doubt. "What is it?" I asked. I scrolled through the phone and he stared intently at the screen. Suddenly he let out a loud meow.

Mila's phone message. Was Hercules actually telling me he wanted me to listen to Mila's phone message again? Now? This was the same cat that had led Marcus's father through the rainy woods behind Roma's house to find me after I'd been dropped down an abandoned well. Was it really that far-fetched?

I played the message again. This time something about the noise in the background grabbed my attention. "I think that's a washing machine," I said.

Hercules was busy cleaning his chest, so all I got for acknowledgment was a soft "mrr." I listened again. This time I was certain. The noise I could hear in the background of the message was the sound of a washing machine.

"I think I know where she was," I said. I'd thought I had spotted a washer and dryer in the storage area the day I was at the gym talking to Ann.

"I think Mila was at the school when she called," I said. Had she gone to speak to the coach? Did Ann tell her about delivering the baby? Was that why Mila was calling?

I replayed the message one more time and thought I heard Mila say the words "wrong way."

Wrong way. What did that mean?

My phone wasn't the only thing on the table. The envelope with the photos of Lily was lying there as well. All of a sudden Hercules straightened up and knocked the pictures to the floor. He jumped off my lap, sat down next to the envelope and looked expectantly at me.

Now what was he trying to say?

"We've already look at those photos several times," I said.

He cocked his head to one side as if to say, *Do you really want to do this?*

I leaned over and picked up the envelope. Then I picked up Hercules. Once he was settled again on my lap I set the two photographs on the table in front of us.

"I don't know what I'm supposed to be looking for," I said. Lily smiled at the camera in her hooded sweatshirt and knit beanie with the no-ghosts pin on the brim of her hat. She was wearing black high-tops that made me think of Riley in her red ones instead of a warm pair of boots.

Black high-tops.

Not boots.

I looked at Hercules. "Is this what you wanted me to see?" I asked.

I didn't wait for his answer. I picked him up and went into the living room. I set the cat on the top of one of the two boxes I'd gotten from Emily Abbott. Then I took the lid off the other one.

I sorted through the top couple of layers of clippings while Hercules supervised from his perch on the other box. It only took a couple of minutes to find the article about the woman in the bus station who was certain she'd seen Lily. She'd gotten the hat and the hoodie and even the pin right, but she'd said

Lily had been wearing Black Dog boots. According to Ruth Hansen, her husband had noticed Lily wearing the same boots.

All roads led back to Ann McKinnon. I slumped against the sofa. "It wasn't Lily," I said to Hercules. I rubbed the back of my neck with one hand.

"It couldn't have been Mila because she has dark hair. It couldn't have been Bryan or his friend Jake because neither one of them could pass for a woman."

Black Dog boots and blond hair.

I looked at Hercules. "Ann McKinnon has a pair of Black Dog boots." She'd been wearing them when she came to talk to me at the library. I knew that the footwear, which was still made in Red Wing, had a very loyal following. Was Ann one of those people? And had she had blond hair before she turned white?

I got to my feet. I knew how to find out.

It took about fifteen minutes to find an old photo of Ann McKinnon with the high school volleyball team in which she wasn't wearing a hat like she had been in the photo from the tournament. It didn't really surprise me to see that she'd had blond hair. Ann McKinnon impersonated Lily at the bus station? Ann gave baby Ella to Reverend Hansen?

I slumped down in my seat, resting my head on the back of my chair. I replayed both of my conversations with Ann, remembering what she'd said, picturing her body language. Her chin came up when she wasn't being truthful, I realized, just the way it had when we were playing floor hockey. I could see her in my mind's eye telling me that Lily had left after they argued, which was a lie, I now knew. Just the way it had been when Ann told me she fell asleep after delivering Lily's baby.

It was a lie.

All at once it hit me like a rogue wave rolling over my head. Ann didn't just impersonate Lily—she was also the person who murdered Lily. It was the only explanation that made sense. Bash LaSalle hadn't had anything to do with Lily's death, other than inadvertently providing Ann with a place to hide the body.

I grabbed my phone and called Marcus, but he didn't answer. Then I remembered that he'd said he had a meeting with the prosecuting attorney about a case that was coming to trial early in January. I left a message.

There was a knock at the door then. Mike Justason was standing on my back step. He looked a bit frazzled. His hair was standing on end and part of his jacket collar was caught under his scarf.

"Hey, Kathleen," he said. "Any chance you've seen Fifi?"

I shook my head. "No. Has something happened to him?"

"He ran off. Short version of a long story: I stopped at the Larssons' to drop off a snow shovel. I had Gavin and the dog with me. I told both of them to stay in the truck. Neither of them did. As far as I can tell, something spooked Fifi." He swiped a hand over his mouth. "It could have been anything. You know how he is."

"I'm sorry," I said. "What can I do?"

"Nothing," Mike said. "I was kind of hoping he headed for home and ended up over here for some reason." He shook his head. "Last thing I need to happen right before Christmas."

"Fifi is a smart dog," I said. "I bet he can find his way home."

"Kathleen, that dog is afraid of his own shadow. He could be hiding anywhere."

"Where have you looked so far?" I asked. "I'll help." I'd rather be out helping Mike than sitting in the house wondering when I was going to hear from Marcus.

"Aren't you leaving for Boston today?" he asked.

"Not until lunchtime. I'm all packed. I have time, and an extra set of eyes can't hurt."

"Truth be told, I'm happy to have the help," Mike said. "Thanks."

He asked me to head west. He and the boys were working east, starting on Rebecca and Everett's street because the last time the dog had taken off, that was the direction he'd gone in. I promised I'd call his cell if I saw Fifi.

I put on my coat and boots and grabbed my bag and my keys. Hercules followed me out to the truck. I started to tell him he couldn't come with me and stopped because we both knew that was an exercise in futility.

We drove up and down the hill, watching the sidewalk and people's yards for any sign of Fifi. Hercules stood on his back legs with his front paws on the passenger-side window. Several times I stopped the truck, got out and called for the dog, but there was no sign of him.

Finally I looked over at Hercules. "Another fifteen minutes and we need to head back." He meowed loudly and continued to look out the window.

We were driving down a street that could have been the backdrop for a Christmas card when I thought I saw a flash of dark fur up ahead on the right. Was it possible the dog could have come this far? I slowed down, and as we came around a slight curve in the road, there was Fifi, sitting in the middle of a driveway almost as though he'd been waiting for a ride.

I pulled over, hoping the dog wouldn't run when I got close to him. "Stay here," I said to Hercules.

I got out and walked around the front of the truck. "Fifi," I called. He came right to me and I bent down and wrapped my arms around his neck. "I'm so glad to see you," I said.

He licked my face. I took it that meant he was glad to see me, too.

I took hold of his collar and pulled out my phone to call Mike with the good news, but the call didn't go through. My first thought was that the boys had done something to Mike's phone. It could be sitting in a snowbank somewhere for all I knew.

I decided to put Fifi in the truck. It was just as easy to take him home. Except I couldn't put the dog in the cab with me because Hercules was already there, watching us out of the back window. There was no way I could get us home safely with both of them beside me. And given how Fifi felt about cats, who knew what the stress of being in an enclosed space with Hercules would do to him.

A second call to Mike also failed. I decided the best solution was to tie the dog in the truck bed and drive home slowly. Fifi jumped up onto the back of the truck. I settled him on an old blanket I had used to cover a basket of apples I'd brought home from Harrison Taylor a couple of months ago and then forgotten to put away. Hercules watched through the back window, which made the dog less nervous than I would have expected.

I tied one end of my scarf to Fifi's collar and the other end to the closest tie-down anchor. "Stay there," I said. "We're going home."

He seemed to understand that he was safe and was content to lie on the blanket and sneak glances at Hercules.

I got back in the truck. Hercules glanced out the back window, almost as though he were worried about the dog.

"Fifi is fine," I said. "I'll drive slowly and I'll stick to the quieter streets."

I kept checking the rearview mirror, and Fifi did seem fine. Hercules, on the other hand, seemed tense, if that could be said about a cat. He kept looking from the back window to the windshield, almost as though he expected the police to come along and issue us a ticket.

I spotted the high school up ahead. The parking lot was deserted, not a single car in the space. No one was at the school. I could stop for just a minute and take a look for a dryer vent, just to confirm that I had spotted a washer and a dryer in that storage area before I told Marcus my suspicions in detail.

I pulled into the school driveway, drove to the far end of the lot and parked. "I'll just be two minutes," I said to Hercules, holding up the same number of fingers. Fifi turned his head toward me when I got out of the truck. "I'll be right back," I told him.

I walked around the corner of the building. There was a school bus parked next to a dumpster and in the small gap between the two I could see the dryer vent cover. I wriggled into the space for a closer look. It was definitely a dryer vent. I slipped back out and was on my way back to the truck when I realized I had dropped my glove.

I walked around the building and bent down to pick up the missing glove. My hand was already red and cold. When I straightened up, Ann McKinnon was standing there. I gasped, took a step back without thinking about it and held up one hand. "You startled me," I said.

"What are you doing here?" she asked. She had one hand behind her back.

"I was looking for my neighbor's dog." I tipped my head in the direction of the truck. "I just found him down the street. I pulled in here to get him settled in my truck." Looking at her, all I could think was *this is the person who killed Lily Abbott and stuffed her body behind a wall.*

"I need to explain about yesterday," Ann said.

My mouth was suddenly dry. "I'm sorry," I said. "I'm leaving for Boston for Christmas in a couple of hours. Maybe we can talk when I get back." All I wanted to do was get away from her.

"I need to talk to you now." Ann's hand snaked out and grabbed my arm. Before I could scream she pulled the other hand from behind her back. She was holding a box cutter. "Not a sound," she warned. She twisted my arm up hard behind my back and half walked, half dragged me into the building.

I was in trouble.

chapter 18

Once we were inside the gym Ann let go of me. The only thing I could think of to do in the moment was bluff a confidence I didn't feel. "I understand that you're under a lot of stress right now," I said, "but this isn't the time or the place for us to talk. I have somewhere I have to be."

I turned and walked away from her, hoping she didn't notice how badly my legs were shaking. I took three or four steps back toward the door we'd just come in and I was on the floor. Ann had snagged my ankle with a hockey stick.

"What are you doing?" I said, getting to my feet. I had banged my head and an elbow and they were both throbbing.

"Stop pretending," she said. "I know you figured it out."

I glanced over at the windows, high up in the wall above the bleachers. They hinged out and two of them were open. If I called for help, would anyone hear me? Was anyone other than Hercules and Fifi around to hear me?

"I don't know what you're talking about," I said. Maybe I could bluff my way out of this.

Ann smiled. There wasn't the tiniest bit of warmth in her face. "Yes, you do," she said. "You know I killed Lily."

I was trapped. So much for bluffing. "Yes. I know you killed Lily. And so do the police." At least they did if Marcus had checked his messages by now.

She shook her head. "No. I don't think they do, because if they did, they'd be here instead of you."

"Are you sure you want to take that chance?" I asked. "Just go. I mean it. Go. If you walk out of here right now, you can get away." I held out my phone. "Here. Take my phone. Throw it in a snowbank. Tie me to the bleachers and get out of here."

She tipped her head to one side, a pensive expression on her face, and folded her arms across her chest, still holding the box cutter. "Well, it seems to me that my only problem is you. So if you're gone"—she held out one hand, palm up—"so are all my problems."

"My truck is out in the parking lot with a dog and a cat inside. Anyone who knows me will know that I wouldn't have left them out there for more than a few minutes."

"I can move the truck," she said. "Or even better, I can call the authorities myself once you've gone bye-bye"—she waved with one hand the way a two-year-old might—"and explain how worried I am about you because I discovered your truck and the cat and dog here in the parking lot but there's no sign of you anywhere." She smiled that cold smile again. "Trust me. I can sell it. I've had some practice at that kind of thing."

"Your luck is going to run out. I figured out that you killed Lily. So will other people. You're not going to get away with it."

"I got away with it for thirty-six years. The fact that I'm standing here and not in a jail cell somewhere says that I'm still getting away with it."

Out of the corner of my eye I could see the hockey stick she'd used to pull my foot out from under me lying on the wood floor where she'd dropped it. Could I grab it and use it to keep her at bay long enough to get to the main gym doors? My left arm where I'd hit my elbow was numb all the way to the ends of my fingers. Would that hand still work?

I kept my gaze fixed on her face so I wouldn't give away what I was thinking of doing. "You got away with it because nobody had a reason to suspect you," I said. "It was the one thing I couldn't figure out. The why."

Ann laughed. "It seems you're not as smart as you think you are."

I lunged for the hockey stick, hoping the element of surprise would give me an edge. I managed to grab the blade before she reacted. Aiming the stick like it was a lance and I was a knight on horseback ready to lead a charge against the enemy, I jabbed her hard in the breastbone. She took a couple of off-balance steps backward. It had to have hurt, but ever the jock, she barely grimaced. However, the box cutter dropped out of her hand. I flipped the stick, used my hardest slap shot and set the tool sailing across the gym and through the gap under the storage room doors.

"Next time I'll put your eye out," I said.

She gave her head a little shake. "No, I don't think you will. You don't have it in you. You're too nice." Her eyes flicked right for a moment, taking in a soccer ball a couple of steps away from her. All of a sudden she leaped sideways and kicked it right at me.

Some instinctual part of my brain reacted before the rational part had a chance to. I jumped to the side and the ball whipped by my leg. Without really thinking about it I brandished the hockey stick again and caught her on the left side of her head, narrowly missing her eye.

Her head snapped to one side and she blinked several times.

"You've still got a chance to get out of here," I said. "Or just stay and face what happened. I don't believe Lily's death was premeditated in any way, which works in your favor at least. I think maybe . . . *maybe* it was just an argument that somehow got out of hand."

Ann didn't say anything, but the lines around her mouth tightened. Her hand came up as though she was going to touch the side of her head and then she dropped it again.

"Is what you told me before true?" I asked. "Did Lily come here to talk to you?"

I didn't think she was going to answer and then she nodded. "Her car went into the ditch just up the road, maybe five minutes from here. She'd seen my car in the parking lot, so she walked back here. She didn't realize she was in labor."

"What did you fight about?" I asked. I really was curious. It was the one thing about the murder that didn't make sense. What was Ann's motive?

"We didn't fight about anything," she said, biting off each word. "What happened to Lily was an accident. If anything, it was her fault. Lily wasn't nearly as perfect as everyone seemed to think she was, you know. She was a selfish person." Her chin came up. She was lying.

"Lily was eighteen. We're all a little selfish at that age."

Ann started shaking her head before I finished speaking. "No," she said emphatically. "No. We're *not* all selfish at that age." She took a step closer to me.

I took one backward. I wasn't going to be able to hold her at bay with the hockey stick much longer. I needed to keep her talking and buy myself a little more time.

"She was good, wasn't she, I mean as a volleyball player?" I asked. "Olympic-quality good."

Ann gave an almost infinitesimal nod. I thought she wasn't going to say anything, then she spoke.

"There were several colleges trying to recruit Lily for almost a year. One in particular would have been a perfect fit for her, with the opportunity to get a good education and the chance to play. Lily was going to sign the letter of intent and she'd decided to place the baby for adoption. Then she changed her mind. It was such a stupid choice."

She folded an arm up over her head, lacing her fingers so tightly into her hair I thought she might pull a clump off her head. "We wouldn't have argued if it wasn't for that stupid necklace."

"The one I asked you about?" I said. From the beginning I'd thought it was important.

She nodded.

"So it was Lily's."

"She kept it hidden from everyone. She showed it to me after giving birth. Ella's father had given it to her the night they slept together. They'd been talking to each other all week. She thought it was romantic. She was going to take the baby, get on a bus and go to him." Her voice was getting more agitated. I tried to keep mine steady.

"You tried to talk her out of that."

"I knew what would happen. I tried to make her understand that no guy halfway through college wanted to be saddled with her and a baby, but Lily wouldn't listen."

Ann looked away for a moment. Then her eyes met mine again. "He was one of the officials. I wanted to make her see it wouldn't look good for him if she told the whole world about their love story."

"'The heart wants what it wants, or else it does not care,'" I said softly.

"Emily Dickinson," Ann said. "Ironically, a woman who didn't have a lot of romance in her life."

"You said it wouldn't have been good for the baby's father if the truth of how and when he and Lily met had come out, but it wouldn't have been good for you, either."

Her shoulders went rigid. "What do you mean by that?" she said.

"I mean that Lily got pregnant at the tournament. On your watch. You were supposed to make sure something like that didn't happen."

"And if the boys' coaches had done a better job of supervising *them*, I wouldn't have had to go help when they were all heaving up their guts." There was a flush of color high on both her cheeks. It seemed I might have struck a nerve.

"That can't have taken all night," I said. I just needed to keep her talking. "What did you do after that?"

"Why does that matter?" Ann snapped.

Oh, I had definitely struck a nerve.

"If you have nothing to hide, why not answer the question?" I said.

"Fine," she said through clenched teeth. "I had a drink with one of the other coaches."

I didn't say anything, but I did raise an eyebrow.

"And yes, I spent the night. I spent the night because I'd spent every other minute of that tournament acting like a freaking babysitter cleaning up vomit, putting on Band-Aids and nagging people to eat their damn vegetables!" Anger flashed in her eyes, and her face became even more flushed. "How was I supposed to know Lily was going to stuff a couple of pillows under her blanket and sneak out? She gave me her word. They all did."

"You would have lost your job if Lily had told everyone how and when she ended up pregnant."

"All I asked her to do was keep that part to herself. That's all. Why should I pay the price for what she did? She kept looking at that necklace like it was made of diamonds. So I tried to take it from her. I just wanted her to see it was nothing more than a dime-store trinket. We . . . we struggled and somehow Lily fell and hit her head. I didn't mean to kill her."

I knew that wasn't the entire story because Lily hadn't died from a head injury. She had been suffocated.

"You panicked," I said. "I understand that. Anybody would." Why wasn't Marcus here yet?

Ann raked a hand back through her hair. "I couldn't think straight. By that time the roads really were plowed, although the section where the poles had gone down was still blocked. I decided I would take the baby to the church in Red Wing. We'd gone there when I was a little girl and I lived for a while with my aunt and uncle. I knew the minister and his wife were good people. I was trying to do the right thing."

"So was it before or after that that you realized Lily wasn't actually dead?" I asked.

chapter 19

"I don't know what you're talking about," Ann said, but I knew by the way her gaze slipped away from mine for a moment and by how, once again, her chin came up, that she was lying.

"I believe that she fell and hit her head, and I believe that you thought she was dead. It isn't always easy to find another person's pulse when you're panicked. But she was just unconscious and I'm guessing she began to come to in the car."

Ann's mouth was pulled into a tight, thin line, and one hand squeezed into a white-knuckled fist.

"You could have taken Lily and the baby to the hospital or

the fire station, anywhere there were people, but you didn't." It was impossible to keep the judgment out of my voice.

I tightened my grip on the hockey stick. "You put something over her mouth and nose until she stopped breathing, then you put on Lily's hat and hoodie and wrapped a scarf around your face. Lucky for you the two of you both had blond hair. And most people are not nearly as observant as they like to think they are. We see what we want to see."

"I didn't have any other choice. It was too late then." She wouldn't look at me. "I had to make people believe I was Lily, and despite what you might think of me, I wanted to be sure the baby was safe and taken care of. I thought she would end up with Lily's family." Ann took a step toward me and I moved back again, aware that she was trying to move me back against the bleachers, one small step at a time.

"But she didn't," I said. "She had wonderful parents who loved her, but she didn't get to know her biological grandparents or her uncle and they didn't get to know her."

"That's not my fault," Ann said, dark eyes flashing. "It didn't make any sense when the police said Lily couldn't be the baby's mother, because I knew she was. It was months before I stumbled on the information about the cis-AB allele."

I realized she had gone to the bus station dressed as Lily in case Lily had told one of her friends about her plan to leave town and find the baby's father.

My head ached and my left arm still felt numb. I wiggled my

fingers. At least they were still working. "Why did you leave Lily at the co-op store?" I asked.

"Other than stick Lily's body in a snowbank, I didn't have a lot of choice," Ann said. "And I really thought Lily would be found in a week or so. I didn't intend for it to take so long. Not thirty-six years."

"You knew it would be a good place to hide a body because your cousin was working there."

"You ask too many questions," Ann said. "It's going to get you in trouble one of these days."

"You'd been in the building." I was guessing, but it was a pretty good guess from my perspective. "You wrapped Lily's body in the blankets and the plastic so you wouldn't have to look at her, so you wouldn't have to look at what you'd done."

"Shut up!" Ann shouted. "Shut up! Shut up!" She rubbed the middle of her forehead with the back of her hand. "I'm sick of the sound of your voice. Yeah, I knew about that building because my cousin Seb was working there. And I found out that they were hiding a key outside so if any of the guys got there early they didn't have to stand around in the cold. It's not my fault they made it so easy."

"And you thought you were in the clear until the power went off. And the pipes froze in the old building."

Again she took a step toward me. Again I stepped back. The only thing between us was that hockey stick. "Somehow

Mila figured out it was you, so you made it look as though she had tried to kill herself."

She jabbed a finger at me. "That one is on you. You're the one who talked to her, and then she started asking questions about things that were none of her business."

"She saw you," I said. It was the only thing that made sense. I remembered the words I thought I'd heard on Mila's garbled message: "wrong way."

"She was walking home from some stupid party."

The one she'd snuck out to.

"She realized I'd been driving in the opposite direction from where I said I'd gone. She wanted to know why."

"You shut her up."

"I protected my own life. I've had to dig and scratch for everything I ever got *and* be twice as good to be half as well-thought-of."

She dove for my hockey stick, catching the shaft with one hand and pulling hard. Without really thinking about it, I let go. Ann struggled to keep her balance, teetering backward, one ankle rolling over. She grunted at the pain.

I ran. Despite the twisted ankle and the hit to the head I'd landed with the stick, she was right behind me. *Where was Marcus?*

There was a bin of soccer balls at the end of the stand of bleachers. I grabbed two off the top and hurled one and then the other back at her. She dodged them both, but they did slow her down just a little. I knew I couldn't outrun her to the door.

I might be twenty years younger, but she was strong and fast. And determined in the extreme.

I decided my best chance was to run across and up the bleachers. I was hoping Ann had lost some of her ability to turn quickly when she twisted her ankle. She could push her way through the pain to run, but I was counting on her not being able to pivot the way she had before. I would run up and along the bleachers, zigzagging the way Ronan Justason had done at the library when he and Gavin had been caught playing library Jenga. I could get far enough ahead of Ann to bolt for the main doors and get out.

I didn't think about what I'd do if my plan didn't work.

There was a basketball at the end of the second row of risers. I flung it at Ann and it glanced off her shoulder. Then I ran along the bottom row of the bleachers and headed up the risers, dodging right and left in a random pattern. Ann was falling behind, but she had the last ball I'd thrown at her.

She whipped it at me, getting me on the left side of my back. My arms windmilled as I struggled to stay upright, as I struggled to breathe. I couldn't keep my balance.

I slipped over the edge of the riser. There were no sideguards in place.

Nothing to stop my fall.

Nothing to grab on to.

Somehow, I managed to catch hold of the end of the riser with my right hand and then my left. I hung there, trying to pull some air into my lungs, my legs swinging wildly from side to side. I tried to get one foot on a riser below me, but my boot slipped and the momentum almost made me lose my grip. I was a good ten feet above the gym floor. I struggled to pull myself up, both arms trembling. I didn't think the fall down to the gym floor would kill me, but it would incapacitate me and Ann would do the rest.

And then she was bent over me. She raised her foot to stomp on my fingers.

"Don't do it," I begged. "Please don't." I screamed for help.

A blur of dark fur came flying through the window above us and landed on the top row of the bleachers.

Fifi.

Fifi?

For a moment I thought I was imagining the whole thing, but the dog was real, barking and running toward us. And somehow I got a foot on the end of one of the risers below me and then got the other foot up next to it. Ann's head was still bent over me. I pulled myself up and banged *my* head hard against Ann's forehead. It was enough to knock her off her feet.

Ann crumpled onto the riser below me and Fifi threw his body over her, pinning her down. There was no way Ann could get up with the dog's weight on top of her. I was safe.

Pushing with my feet and gripping the sides of the riser, I managed to climb up onto it, where I lay on my side wheezing a little from the exertion.

Hercules was suddenly next to me. He nuzzled my cheek and meowed.

I reached out to put a hand on his head. "I'm all right."

Below me Ann shook her head and tried to sit up. Fifi growled and bared his teeth. Then he looked at me and wagged his tail.

I leaned over and wrapped my arms around his neck. "You're a good dog," I said.

I sat up and Hercules climbed onto my lap. I stroked his fur, wondering how the two of them had gotten into the building. How had Fifi managed to jump through a window that had to be more than twenty feet above the ground?

All of a sudden I could hear people outside. I yelled for help and a few moments later Marcus and another police officer came through the back gym door. He ran across the gym and bolted up the bleachers.

"Hey," I said, suddenly having to swallow down a rush of tears.

He put a hand on my cheek. "Are you all right?"

I nodded.

"What the hell happened?" he asked. "I got your message but I couldn't find you. Finally Mike Justason called because he said you were looking for his dog and you weren't answering your phone."

Two paramedics were standing at the bottom of the bleachers looking at Fifi. I patted my leg. "C'mon up here," I said to the dog.

He looked at Ann and then looked at me, his expression doubtful.

I patted my leg again. "It's okay now. C'mon."

He climbed up on the bleacher and lay down next to me. I slung my free arm around his neck.

The paramedics started up toward us. "I think there's a big chunk of the story I'm missing," Marcus said. "But it can wait." He gestured to the paramedics. "Ric, would you take a look at Kathleen, please?"

Ric Holm knelt in front of me. "Hey, Kathleen," he said. "Hey, Hercules."

The cat meowed a hello. The two were old friends.

Ric gestured at Fifi. "New member of the family?"

"Next-door neighbor. This is Fifi."

He frowned. "Fifi?"

I nodded, which made me wince.

"Okay," he said. He looked at Marcus. "I'm just going to check her head first."

For once I didn't argue. I was pretty sure Ric was going to say I had a concussion, because when Fifi came flying through that window I would have sworn that Hercules was riding on his back.

chapter 20

Ric checked me over carefully. "You don't have a concussion, as far as I can tell," he said.

I had no nausea, no dizziness, no double vision. I wasn't confused or disoriented. The top of my head was tender, but I didn't even have a headache.

"I feel all right," I said. I could see the concern in Marcus's eyes. "I promise I would say so if I didn't. My elbow hurts a lot worse than my head does."

"You know what symptoms to look out for," Ric said.

Marcus nodded.

"If you have any doubts, throw her over your shoulder and take her to the emergency room." He looked at me. "Kathleen, if you feel sick. If you get any kind of a headache or any problems with your vision, go to the hospital. Please."

"I will," I said. I was grateful to be okay. I was grateful to be alive.

Ric went on to explain that my elbow was sprained, not broken or even dislocated. He wrapped it, put my arm in a sling and gave me instructions about icing it over the next few days. Then he reached into his kit and pulled out a small brown paper bag I immediately recognized as being from the pet food company a colleague of Roma's had started.

Hercules recognized the package, too. His whiskers twitched and he licked his lips. Ric took out two crackers and set them on the riser next to Hercules. The cat meowed a thank-you.

"You're welcome," Ric said.

He turned to Fifi and set four crackers down for the dog. "He's bigger," Ric said to me by way of explanation. The dog's tail began to wag in appreciation.

Ric smiled, closed the top of the bag and tucked it back in with his supplies. "Thanks to my many, *many* encounters with you and Hercules and Owen, I carry a bag of these treats all the time. Turns out it's a good way to make friends."

Ann was taken out of the gym on a stretcher. She did have a concussion and possibly a broken ankle. Marcus helped me climb down off the bleachers. I held Hercules against my side with my bandaged arm and Fifi stayed close by my other side.

"How did they get in here?" Marcus asked.

"I assume the usual way for Hercules," I said, "and I know it doesn't make any sense, but Fifi jumped in through the window."

He looked around the gym and then up at the open windows high above us over the bleachers. "It's not possible," he said. "That window has to be over twenty feet high. No dog can jump that high. Fifi isn't a kangaroo."

I reached down and patted the dog's flank. "Kangaroos actually can't jump much higher than about six feet," I said. "A snow leopard, on the other hand, can make a vertical jump of about twenty feet."

Marcus smiled. "Well, I don't think Fifi is part snow leopard, so there has to be another explanation."

Once we were outside, Marcus looked around and very quickly pieced together what had happened.

Fifi had chewed through my scarf. Based on the bit of fluff stuck to Hercules's ear, he'd probably had some help.

Marcus pointed to a trail of pawprints on the ground. "See? He jumped to the top of the dumpster right there. I'd say it's four, maybe four and a half feet high. Then he leaped onto the top of the school bus. That's a jump of about six feet. Doable for a dog of his strength and size."

Fifi woofed his agreement.

Marcus took several steps backward to get a better look at the roof of the bus. "Based on the paw prints, he got a running start, ran the length of the bus and launched himself through the window."

That last jump had to be close to nine feet. I didn't want to think about what it would have meant for both of us if Fifi hadn't made it. I smiled down at him and patted his side again. "You are a very resourceful dog," I told him.

Hercules nuzzled my chin, a little jealous, I guessed, over all the attention the dog was getting.

"Yes, and you were very resourceful as well," I said. I couldn't see any paw prints anywhere that belonged to Hercules, and I wondered if maybe I hadn't imagined him on the dog's back after all.

"I just have one thing I need to do and then I'm taking you home," Marcus said. "Don't move."

"I'm not going anywhere," I said. I was happy to stand there, wrapped in my warm coat and Marcus's big scarf with Fifi and Hercules to keep me company.

Mike Justason came around the end of the building, escorted by a police officer, just as Marcus returned.

"Detective Gordon," the officer called.

Marcus turned and the young woman pointed at Mike. Marcus nodded and waved Mike over.

Fifi looked up at me. "It's okay. Go," I said.

He gave a sharp bark and raced across the snow-dusted parking lot, tail wagging. Mike leaned over to throw one arm around Fifi and run his other hand over the dog's fur to make sure he was okay.

Marcus and I walked over to join them.

"Kathleen, are you all right?" Mike asked. His hair was

standing up as though he'd run a hand through it multiple times.

"I'm fine," I said.

He gestured at my left arm. "No offense, but you don't exactly look fine."

"It's nothing serious. Just a sprained elbow." I smiled at Fifi and reached over to give the top of his head a scratch. "Things could have been a lot worse, if it wasn't for him."

Mike looked confused, his eyes darting from me to the dog and back again.

Marcus gave him a brief explanation of how Ann McKinnon dragged me inside the gym and how Fifi had jumped through the window and distracted her.

"Ann McKinnon killed someone and lied about it for thirty-six years?" Mike said. He swiped a hand over his mouth. "I had no idea."

"No one did," I said.

He looked down at the dog. "I don't think I'm going to be the one eating that steak I had planned for dinner."

"He earned it," I said. "And a whole lot more."

"I'm just glad you're all right." He looked down at the dog and jerked his head in the direction of the front of the building. "Let's go."

Fifi looked at Hercules. "Woof!" he said.

"Merow," the cat replied.

Mike frowned. "Hang on a minute." He pointed between them. "What's this?"

"I'm not sure," I said. "They seem to have worked together and now I'm not sure that world domination might not be next."

Mike and Fifi left after I hugged the dog one last time. Then Marcus walked me across the parking lot toward a large white SUV.

"Where's your car?" I said.

"I'm using this one," he said. He kept walking. I didn't.

"*Why* are you using this one?" I asked.

He stopped and turned around. "Okay. First of all, I'm fine."

Hercules and I exchanged a look. "I can see that you're fine. You haven't answered my question. Why are you driving this car? Where's yours?"

He raked a hand back through his hair. "It kind of went in the ditch this morning."

I frowned. "Kind of? What happened?"

"I went off the road this morning. The car slid into the ditch and ended up on its roof."

I closed the distance between us and put my free hand against his cheek. "You're really all right?"

He nodded. "I am. I promise. But my car isn't drivable. It has some front-end damage." He gestured at the white SUV. "You'll like this. It has great seats."

He got me—and Hercules—settled in the big Ford. The seats were comfortable.

"You orchestrated my rescue, didn't you?" I said to the cat. He ducked his head modestly and then glanced up to see if I'd noticed. I wrapped my good arm around him and kissed the top of his furry head. "I love you," I said. "I don't think there's a steak in your future, but I'm pretty sure there's going to be some salmon."

Marcus got in the driver's side and immediately turned to me. "Are you sure you're okay?"

I nodded. "I promise I'm fine. Ric would have pushed hard for a hospital visit if he'd thought I wasn't."

He looked out the windshield. "I'm so sorry I didn't answer when you called. I'm sorry I spent so long in that meeting."

I reached across Hercules and put my hand on his arm.

"Hey, don't do that," I said. "Ann McKinnon killed Lily. That's why all this"—I tried to gesture with my left hand but didn't really succeed—"happened. And now, at last, Lily will finally get some justice and Ella will know more of her story."

Marcus smiled. "I love you," he said.

I smiled back at him. "I love you, too."

"We need to set a date. The sooner the better, as far as I'm concerned."

"I'd marry you right now in this parking lot if there was someone here to perform the ceremony," I said.

Hercules meowed loudly.

"Yeah, I'm pretty sure you're not licensed to officiate, at least in this state," Marcus said.

I leaned back against the seat. "Your car isn't drivable."

"I'm sorry," he said. "I can't find a rental anywhere. I don't suppose you want to take your truck to Boston?" He gave my hand a squeeze and fastened his seat belt.

My head was starting to ache now and my elbow was throbbing. I wasn't sure I could spend twenty minutes driving in my truck let alone twenty hours. "I think it's time to admit defeat," I said. "I really had my heart set on having Christmas in Boston with you and my family, but after today it doesn't seem quite so important."

"We'll have a good one, I promise."

I looked over at the gold signet ring he wore, the ring that had belonged to his father and his grandfather and that I had given to him when *I* proposed. "As long as you're there," I said. "That's the only present I need."

After Marcus made me lunch and Maggie and Roma arrived to fuss over me, I called my mom, curled up in the big wing chair in the living room with Owen stretched out over my legs and Hercules sprawled across my lap.

Roma had offered her SUV for the drive to Boston, but my right hip was bruised from above the hip bone down to the top of my thigh. Sitting on it for more than a few minutes was really uncomfortable.

"Hi, Katydid," Mom said. "Are you and Marcus on the way?"

I swallowed back the sudden prickle of tears. "Not exactly," I said. I explained what happened, how Marcus had gone in the ditch, how I'd gone out to help Mike look for Fifi, how I'd found the dog at the school, how Ann had ambushed me and even how Fifi and Hercules had come to my rescue. "I'm sorry," I said.

"But you're both okay?" Mom asked.

I nodded even though she couldn't see me. "Except for a sore elbow and a bruised hip, I'm fine."

"That's what matters. We'll miss you and Marcus like crazy, but I promise we'll see you soon."

Just the sound of her voice made me feel better. It wasn't like being wrapped in one of her hugs, but it was close.

Right before supper, Ella showed up at my door. Marcus had his head in my refrigerator trying to decide what he was going to make, with two furry sidekicks adding their suggestions.

"I'll get that," I said, getting to my feet when I heard the knock.

Marcus straightened up and closed the refrigerator door. "No, you won't," he said. He made a shooing motion with one hand. "Sit."

I made a face at him but I did sit back down.

Ella looked a little nervous when she stepped into the kitchen. "Hi," she said. "Am I interrupting anything?"

I stood up again. “No,” I said. “I’m glad you’re here.”

She gestured at my arm still in the sling and the large pillow on my chair. “You’re hurt.”

I shook my head. “It’s just a sprained elbow with a big bandage that makes it look worse than it is.” I indicated the table. “Please. Sit down.”

She shook her head. “No. I’m not staying. I just wanted to thank you. I can’t believe Ann McKinnon killed my mother. She was Taylor’s gym teacher.”

I nodded. “I know. Based on everyone’s reaction, she was a good teacher.”

“So Ann was the one who took me to the Hansens?” Her hands were stuffed in the pockets of her quilted jacket and she was restless, shifting her weight from one foot to the other. Ella needed time to work through all the emotions that learning someone she knew had killed Lily had stirred up.

“She wanted to make sure you were safe and she knew they were trustworthy.” Hercules came and leaned against my leg.

She exhaled softly. “I suppose I should be grateful for that, but right now I can’t be.”

“No one expects you to be,” I said.

“We have something that belongs to Lily,” Marcus said.

Ella stared at him, her expression a mix of surprise and uncertainty. “Really?”

“It’s a necklace that we think your biological father gave her,” I said.

Tears filled her eyes and she pressed a hand against her mouth for a moment. "I can't . . . I can't believe it."

"I promise I'll get it to you as soon as I can," Marcus said.

She nodded. "Thank you."

"It's a long shot," I said, "but it might help you find him."

One tear slid down her cheek and she swiped it away. Then she threw her arms around me and hugged me. It made everything else that had happened that day worthwhile.

Marcus and I were "discussing" whether or not the sling and the compression bandage should come off before I went in the bathtub when his phone rang. I thought I had made a good argument for soaking my elbow in the hot water, and he was mostly acting like a large, stubborn rock.

"Don't go anywhere," he said as he reached for his phone. "I need to get this."

I slid my arm out of the sling. It was still stiff and sore, but it moved a lot better than I'd expected it to.

The phone call was brief. Marcus set his phone on the table and turned back around. He was smiling.

"What?" I said.

"Mila Serrano has regained consciousness."

My breath caught in my chest. "She's all right?" If this wasn't Christmas magic, it was close.

He nodded. "She's talking and she asked to speak to me."

"Go," I said. "I'm fine."

He reached for his phone again. "I'll see if Rebecca will come over while I'm gone."

I put my good hand on my hip and winced just a little. "Marcus, I don't need a babysitter. I won't get in the bathtub. I won't do anything. I'll make hot chocolate and watch *Miracle on 34th Street* with Hercules until you come back."

The cat poked his head around the living room doorway at the sound of his name.

"I know you don't need a babysitter," he said. "Humor me because *I* need it. It's possible that the only reason we're standing here like this is because of that cat"—he pointed at Hercules, who immediately adopted his innocent "who, me?" expression—"and Mike Justason's dog. So I'm calling Rebecca because it will make me feel better."

This time it was me who wrapped my arms around him. And it was actually me who called Rebecca.

Rebecca said she was happy to come keep me company for a while. She came with half a loaf of cinnamon bread and a poultice for my elbow. We ate toasted cinnamon bread and watched *Miracle on 34th Street*. I'm not sure if it was the toast, the company or the poultice, but by the time Marcus got back, my arm felt a lot better.

Once Rebecca was gone, we sat at the kitchen table and he told me about his conversation with Mila. She had told him that she didn't know anything about Ella's father. "She'd suspected that Lily met him when they were playing at the tournament in Green Bay." He glanced over at the toaster. The kitchen had smelled so good when he got back he'd decided he needed to try a piece of Rebecca's bread.

"But why didn't Mila tell you that when Lily's body was found?"

"We hadn't had a chance to talk to her before she was hurt, remember? You had, but she wasn't sure whether or not to tell you her suspicion."

I'd been certain Mila had been hiding something. I wish I'd guessed what it was.

"And she confirmed what Ann told you," Marcus said. "After Mila talked to you, she started thinking about the night Lily disappeared and how she'd seen Ann's car go by when she was walking home from that party. She realized Ann had been headed in the opposite direction from where she'd told everyone she'd been going. It didn't make sense."

"So she went to talk to her old coach," I said.

He nodded as he got to his feet. "It didn't occur to her that Ann had killed Lily. It was just a detail that didn't make sense to her."

He got a plate from the cupboard and a knife from the drawer below it.

"So we don't know anything about Ella's father," I said.

He smiled. "Actually, we do. I learned a lot from Ann McKinnon. She said that Lily had told her that he had grown up in pretty rough circumstances, but he had been accepted into medical school at Stanford. She didn't even know his last name, but the closer she got to having the baby, the more she romanticized everything. She decided she'd go to California, show up at the school and find him."

I stared at him. "With a baby?"

Marcus nodded. "Like I said, it seemed she romanticized the whole thing."

"Why didn't he come forward when Lily went missing?" I asked.

"I don't know for sure, but I'm guessing he didn't know, assuming he really was at Stanford."

The toaster popped and the scent of cinnamon and raisins filled the kitchen. Marcus buttered his toast, cut it into four pieces and came back to the table. "Do you think if Lily had somehow made it to California she would have gotten her happy ending?"

"Probably not," I said, even as a tiny voice inside me whispered, *I hope so.*

chapter 21

Even though I wasn't working, there was no way I was missing the Christmas story time with Harrison Taylor on Wednesday afternoon. The old man looked like a greeting card version of Santa Claus with his snowy white beard and warm smile. He was wearing a red sweater and a faux-fur-trimmed Santa hat, and some of the little ones seemed convinced that he really was Kris Kringle.

Harrison's granddaughter, Mariah, had come to help hand out holiday cookies along with Riley Hollister and Ella's daughter, Taylor. Ella was there as well. Marcus had gotten the necklace to her and she was wearing it, reaching up, every once in a while, to touch the tiny half heart as if to reassure herself that it was there.

Once story time started, I asked Ella to come upstairs to my office. "Okay," she said, a small frown creasing her forehead.

Susan was waiting for us, looking a little nervous. A state I'd never seen her in before.

"What's going on?" Ella asked.

Susan slipped a finger under the gold chain around *her* neck and pulled the necklace she was wearing out from under her sweater. "This is what's going on," she said.

When I'd arrived at the library at lunchtime, Susan had been waiting for me. She'd asked if we could talk. She was uncharacteristically serious, which made me wonder if something was wrong. Once we were in my office, she asked if it was true that there had been a necklace found at the same time as Lily's body, a gold necklace with a broken-heart pendant.

"It's true," I'd said. "Why are you asking?"

Susan had pulled her own necklace out from under her sweater. "This is why," she'd said. It looked like the mirror image of the pendant Harry had found.

Susan undid the clasp of her necklace now and handed it to Ella.

"I don't understand," Ella said, shaking her head.

"I think the two pieces fit together," she said.

With shaking fingers Ella pushed the two heart halves together. They fit perfectly. "How . . . how can this be happening?" she asked.

Susan swallowed a couple of times before she spoke. "My necklace was given to me by my father. His name was Christopher and he died when I was thirteen. He was born in Mayville Heights and moved to Green Bay when he was two. He went to school in California. That's where I grew up. I knew this was where my dad was born, and when I met Eric, and by some weird quirk of fate he was from Mayville Heights, I felt as though the universe was telling me this was where I was supposed to be. I'll do a DNA test, but I'm certain that we're half sisters."

Ella pulled one hand into a fist and pressed it against her mouth.

"The first time I got my heart broken—just a few months before he died—my father told me about this girl he'd met back before medical school. He said he didn't have much time with her but he never forgot her." Susan put a hand on her chest.

"I think he was talking about Lily." She smiled. "Dad . . . *our* dad was funny and loving, and yeah, he could be mercurial and complicated sometimes. He was also a good doctor and a talented musician. When he gave me the necklace he told me he was giving me a piece of his heart, and I'd like to think Lily always had a little piece of it as well."

Tears slipped down Ella's cheeks. I blinked away some of my own.

"If Dad had known you existed, he would have been happy," Susan continued. "I'm so sorry he didn't get to know you and you didn't get to know him. But you and I do have time to get to know each other better. If you want to."

Ella nodded. "Yes, I want to," she said. "Growing up I wanted a sister."

Susan laughed. "When I was growing up I wanted a cat, but I have a feeling a sister will be even better."

I slipped out of my office to give the two of them some privacy. Harrison was just finishing the story. I stood there watching him, charmed by what an engaging storyteller he was and grateful that I'd convinced the old man to let his son Larry videotape the whole thing.

Finally Harrison closed the book. "Merry Christmas, everyone," he said. The kids cheered, which might have had a little bit to do with the fact that they knew that cookies were next. Behind me I heard a voice say, "Merry Christmas, Katydid."

I turned around to find Mom and Dad *and* Ethan and Sarah smiling at me. Then I was wrapped in hugs and laughter and all four of them talking at once. Ethan was grinning, unable—as usual—to stand still for more than a few seconds. Sarah had cut her hair and I caught a glimpse of a henna tattoo snaking up her left arm. My dad was as handsome as ever, his hair a little grayer but otherwise reassuringly the same. My mother kept her arms around my shoulders and I leaned my head against hers.

"How did you do this?" I asked. "I don't understand."

"This was all your mother," Dad said, reaching over to lay a hand on my injured arm. "We flew down on the private jet owned by the production company for *The Wild and the Wonderful*."

I lifted my head to look at Mom. "What did you do?" I said.

She shrugged one shoulder. "I made a business deal. I'm going back to the show for three months for a proverbial king's ransom."

My mother had done a short stint on the popular soap opera *The Wild and the Wonderful* several years ago. Fans loved her and clamored for her long-term return. The amount of money they offered to get her back kept increasing, but she wasn't willing to commit to that kind of contract. She had, however, been back for several short-term visits, and every time, the ratings went up. Once again the producers had been trying to lure her back, promising everything from more money to a personal chef.

"To show their appreciation, they let us tag along on a flight the company jet was already making from New York to Minneapolis," she said. "It was only a short drive from Boston to New York."

"Yeah, and from now on, I'm traveling this way," Ethan said.

"Dream on," Sarah said, nudging him with her hip.

I looked at Mom. "You did this for me? You're going back to the show for me?"

"Making that much money and flying on a private plane isn't exactly a hardship." She smiled. "And I would do anything for you." She kissed my forehead. "Merry Christmas, Katydid."

We were surrounded then by everyone who wanted to say hello, and all four of them were quickly pulled into hugs and conversations. I was content to lean against Marcus with his arm around me and watch.

I had wanted to be in Boston for Christmas so very much. I'd wanted to be home. Now I saw Maggie and Mom deep in conversation, probably about the soap—Maggie was a big fan. Ethan and Sarah were talking with Harry, likely about music, based on the way my brother's hands were moving. My dad was charming Mary as only he could.

I looked past them to see Emmy dragging Harrison off to see the Cookie Monster tree. She was already calling him Gramps, the title he'd officially have in less than two months. Riley had her arms around Duncan's neck, laughing about something as she talked to Levi. And Susan and Ella were with Taylor, who looked a little confused and a lot happy. There was enough Christmas magic in the room to light up every Christmas tree in town.

"Are you all right?" Marcus asked.

I nodded. "I wanted to be home for Christmas," I said. "And I am."

acknowledgments

Thank you to my editor, Jessica Wade, and her assistant, Gabbie Pachon, whose hard work makes me look good. Thanks as well to my agent, Kim Lionetti, who has been an advocate for Kathleen, Owen and Hercules from the beginning. A huge thank-you to all the readers who have spread the word about the Magical Cats.

And last, but never least, thank you to Patrick and Lauren, who always have my back and my heart.

If you love Sofie Kelly's Magical Cats Mysteries,
read on for an excerpt of the first book in Sofie Ryan's
New York Times bestselling Second Chance Cat Mysteries . . .

the whole cat and caboodle

Available wherever books are sold.

Elvis was sitting in the middle of my desk when I opened the door to my office. The cat, not the King of Rock and Roll, although the cat had an air of entitlement about him sometimes, as though he thought he was royalty. He had one jet-black paw on top of a small cardboard box—my new business cards, I was hoping.

"How did you get in here?" I asked.

His ears twitched but he didn't look at me. His green eyes were fixed on the vintage Wonder Woman lunch box in my hand. I was having an early lunch, and Elvis seemed to want one as well.

"No," I said firmly. I dropped onto the retro red womb chair I'd brought up from the shop downstairs, kicked off my sneakers, and propped my feet on the matching footstool. The chair was so comfortable. To me, the round shape was like being cupped in a soft, warm giant hand. I knew the chair had to go back down to the shop, but I was still trying to figure out a way to keep it for myself.

Before I could get my sandwich out of the yellow vinyl lunch box, the big black cat landed on my lap. He wiggled his back end, curled his tail around his feet and looked from the bag to me.

"No," I said again. Like that was going to stop him.

He tipped his head to one side and gave me a pitiful look made all the sadder because he had a fairly awesome scar cutting across the bridge of his nose.

I took my sandwich out of the lunch can. It was roast beef on a hard roll with mustard, tomatoes and dill pickles. The cat's whiskers quivered. "One bite," I said sternly. "Cats eat cat food. People eat people food. Do you want to end up looking like the real Elvis in his chunky days?"

He shook his head, as if to say, "Don't be ridiculous."

I pulled a tiny bit of meat out of the roll and held it out. Elvis ate it from my hand, licked two of my fingers and then made a rumbly noise in his throat that sounded a lot like a sigh of satisfaction. He jumped over to the footstool, settled himself next to my feet and began to wash his face. After a couple of passes over his fur with one paw he paused and looked at me, eyes narrowed—his way of saying, "Are you going to eat that or what?"

I ate.

By the time I'd finished my sandwich Elvis had finished his meticulous grooming of his face, paws and chest. I patted my legs. "C'mon over," I said.

He swiped a paw at my jeans. There was no way he was going to hop onto my lap if he thought he might get a crumb on his inky black fur. I made an elaborate show of brushing off both legs. "Better?" I asked.

Elvis meowed his approval and walked his way up my legs, poking my thighs with his front paws—no claws, thankfully—and wiggling his back end until he was comfortable.

I reached for the box on my desk, keeping one hand on the cat. I'd guessed correctly. My new business cards were inside. I pulled one out and Elvis leaned sideways for a look. The cards were thick brown recycled card stock, with SECOND CHANCE, THE REPURPOSE SHOP, angled across the top in heavy red letters, and SARAH GRAYSON and my contact information, all in black, in the bottom right corner.

Second Chance was a cross between an antiques store and a thrift shop. We sold furniture and housewares—many things repurposed from their original use, like the tub chair that in its previous life had actually been a tub. As for the name, the business was sort of a second chance—for the cat and for me. We'd been open only a few months and I was amazed at how busy we already were.

The shop was in a redbrick building from the late 1800s on Mill Street, in downtown North Harbor, Maine, just where the street curved and began to climb uphill. We were about a twenty-minute walk from the harbor front and easily accessed from the highway—the best of both worlds. My grandmother held the mortgage on the property and I wanted to pay her back as quickly as I could.

"What do you think?" I said, scratching behind Elvis's right ear. He made a murping sound, cat-speak for "good," and lifted his chin. I switched to stroking the fur on his chest.

He started to purr, eyes closed. It sounded a lot like there was a gas-powered generator running in the room.

"Mac and I went to look at the Harrington house," I said to him. "I have to put together an offer, but there are some pieces I want to buy, and you're definitely going with me next time." Eighty-year-old Mabel Harrington was on a cruise with her new beau, a ninety-one-year-old retired doctor with a bad toupee and lots of money. They were moving to Florida when the cruise was over.

One green eye winked open and fixed on my face. Elvis's unofficial job at Second Chance was rodent wrangler.

"Given all the squeaks and scrambling sounds I heard when I poked my head through the trapdoor to the attic, I'm pretty sure the place is the hotel for some kind of mouse convention."

Elvis straightened up, opened his other eye, and licked his lips. Chasing mice, birds, bats and the occasional bug was his idea of a very good time.

I'd had Elvis for about four months. As far as I could find out, the cat had spent several weeks on his own, scrounging around downtown North Harbor.

The town sits on the midcoast of Maine. "Where the hills touch the sea" is the way it's been described for the past 250 years. North Harbor stretches from the Swift Hills in the north to the Atlantic Ocean in the south. It was settled by Alexander Swift in the late 1760s. It's full of beautiful historic buildings, award-winning restaurants and quirky little shops. Where else could you buy a blueberry muffin, a rare book and fishing gear all on the same street?

The town's population is about thirteen thousand, but that more than triples in the summer with tourists and summer residents. It grew by one black cat one evening in late May. Elvis just appeared at The Black Bear. Sam, who owns the pub, and his pickup band, The Hairy Bananas—long story on the name—were doing their Elvis Presley medley when Sam noticed a black cat sitting just inside the front door. He swore the cat stayed put through the entire set and left only when they launched into their version of the Stones' "Satisfaction."

The cat was back the next morning, in the narrow alley beside the shop, watching Sam as he took a pile of cardboard boxes to the recycling bin. "Hey, Elvis. Want some breakfast?" Sam had asked after tossing the last flattened box in the bin. To his surprise, the cat walked up to him and meowed a loud yes.

He showed up at the pub about every third day for the next couple of weeks. The cat clearly wasn't wild—he didn't run from people—but no one seemed to know whom Elvis (the name had stuck) belonged to. The scar on his nose wasn't new; neither were a couple of others on his back, hidden by his fur.

Then someone remembered a guy in a van who had stayed two nights at the campgrounds up on Mount Batten. He'd had a cat with him. It was black. Or black and white. Or possibly gray. But it definitely had had a scar on its nose. Or it had been missing an ear. Or maybe part of its tail.

Elvis was still perched on my lap, staring off into space, thinking about stalking rodents out at the old Harrington house, I was guessing.

I glanced over at the carton sitting on the walnut sideboard that I used for storage in the office. The fact that it was still there meant that Arthur Fenety hadn't come in while Mac and I had been gone. I was glad. I was hoping I'd be at the shop when Fenety came back for the silver tea service that was packed in the box.

A couple of days prior he had brought the tea set into my shop. Fenety had a charming story about the ornate pieces that he said had belonged to his mother. A bit too charming for my taste, like the man himself. Arthur Fenety was somewhere in his seventies, tall with a full head of white hair, a matching mustache and an engaging smile to go with his polished demeanor. He could have gotten a lot more for the tea set at an antiques store or an auction. Something about the whole transaction felt off.

Elvis had been sitting on the counter by the cash register and Fenety had reached over to stroke his fur. The cat didn't so much as twitch a whisker, but his ears had flattened and he'd looked at the older man with his green eyes half-lidded, pupils narrowed. He was the picture of skepticism.

The day after he'd brought the pieces in, Fenety had called to ask if he could buy them back. The more I thought about it, the more suspicious the whole thing felt. The tea set hadn't been on the list of stolen items from the most recent police update, but I still had a niggling feeling about it and Arthur Fenety.

"Time to do some work," I said to Elvis. "Let's go downstairs and see what's happening in the store."

The cat jumped down to the floor and shook himself, and then he had to pause and pass a paw over his face. Elvis knew *store* meant "people," especially tourists, and *tourists* meant "new people who would generally take one look at the scar on his face and be overcome with the urge to stroke his fur and tell him what a sweet kitty he was."

I put on some lipstick and gave my head a shake. I'd gotten my thick, dark brown hair from my father and my dark eyes from my mom. I'd just cut my hair in long layers to my shoulders a couple of weeks previous. If we were moving furniture or I was going for a run I could still pull it back in a ponytail. Otherwise I could pretty much shake my head and my hair looked okay.

One of my part-time staff members, Avery, was by the cash register downstairs, nestling three mismatched soup bowls that had gotten a second life as herb planters into a box half-filled with shredded paper. Her hair was the color of cranberry sauce, and she'd shown up that morning with elaborate henna tattoos covering the backs of both hands. They were beautiful. (She claimed the look was all part of her "rebellious teenager" phase.) Avery worked afternoons in the store—her progressive private school had only morning classes—and full days when there was no school, like today.

I'd had a few rebellious moments myself as a teenager, so Avery's style didn't bother me. She was smart and hardworking, and even though one of the main reasons I'd hired her was because she was the granddaughter of one of my gram's closest friends, I kept her because she did a good job. And my customers seemed to like her.

Mac, the store's resident jack-of-all-trades, was showing a customer a tall metal postman's desk that we'd reclaimed from the basement of a house near the harbor. We'd had to cut the desk apart to get it up the narrow, cramped steps and through the door to the kitchen. Mac had banged out all the dents, put everything back together and then painted the piece a deep sky blue, even though I'd voted for basic black. I watched him hand the customer a tape measure, then give me a knowing smile across the room.

I could see the muscles in his arms move under his long-sleeved gray T-shirt. He was tall and fit with close-cropped black hair and light brown skin. Avery had given Mac the nickname Wall Street. He'd been a financial planner but had ditched his high-powered life to come to Maine and sail. In his free time he crewed for pretty much anyone who asked. There were eight windjammer schooners based in North Harbor, along with dozens of other sailing vessels. Mac was looking for space where he could build his own boat. He worked for me because he said he liked fixing things.

Second Chance had been open for a little less than four months. The main floor was one big open area, with some storage behind the staircase to the second floor. My office was under the eaves on the second floor. There was also a minuscule staff room and one other large space that was being used for storage.

Some things we offered in the shop were vintage kitsch, like my yellow vinyl Wonder Woman lunch box—with matching thermos. Some things were like Elvis—working on a new incarnation, like the electric blue shelving unit that used to be a floor-model TV console. Everything in the store was on its second or sometimes third life.

Our stock came from lots of different places: flea markets, yard sales, people looking to downsize. Mac had even trash-picked a metal bed frame that we'd sold for a very nice profit. A couple of Dumpster divers had been stopping by fairly regularly and in the last month I'd bought items from the estates of three different people. So far, rummaging around in boxes and closets I'd found half a dozen wills, a diamond ring, a set of false teeth, a stuffed armadillo and a box of ashes that thankfully were the remains of someone's long-ago love letters and not, well, the remains of someone.

We sold some items in the store on consignment. Others, like the post office desk, we'd buy outright and refurbish. Mac could repair just about anything, and I was pretty good at coming up with new ways to use old things. And if I ran out of ideas, I could just call my mom, who was a master at giving new life to other people's discards.

Elvis had headed for a couple that was browsing near the guitars on the back wall. The young woman crouched down, stroking his fur and making sympathetic noises about his nose. The young man moved a couple of steps sideways to take a closer look at a Washburn mandolin from the '70s, with a spruce top and ebony fingerboard.

Avery had finished with the customer at the counter. She walked over and lifted the mandolin down from its place on the wall and handed it to the young man. "Why don't you give it a try?" she said. I knew as soon as he had it in his hands he'd be sold.

Avery glanced down at Elvis. He tipped his furry head to one side, leaning into the hand of the young woman who was scratching the top of his head, commanding all her attention, and it almost looked as though he winked at Avery.

A musical instrument was the reason I'd ended up with Elvis—that and his slightly devious nature. I'd taken a guitar down to Sam for a second opinion on what it was worth. Sam Newman and my dad had grown up together. I could play, and I knew a little about some of the older models, but Sam knew more about guitars than anyone I'd ever met. I'd found him sitting in one of the back booths with a cup of coffee and a pile of sheet music. The cat was on the opposite banquette, eating what looked suspiciously to me like scrambled eggs and salami.

Sam had moved his mug and the music out of the way, and I'd set the guitar case on the table. Elvis studied me for a moment and then went back to his breakfast.

"Who's your friend?" I asked, tipping my head toward the cat.

"That's Elvis," Sam said, flipping open the latches on the battered Tolex case with his long fingers. He was tall and lean, his shaggy hair a mix of blond and white.

"Really?" I said. "The King of Rock and Roll was reincarnated as a cat?"

Sam looked at me over the top of his dollar-store reading glasses. "Ha, ha. You're so funny."

I made a face at him. Elvis was watching me again. "Move over." I gestured with one hand. To my surprise the cat obligingly scooted around to the other side of the plate. "Thank you," I said, sliding onto the burgundy vinyl. He dipped his head, almost as though he were saying, "You're welcome," and went back to his scrambled eggs. They were definitely Sam's specialty. I could smell the salami.

"Is this the cat I've been hearing about?" I asked.

Sam was engrossed in examining the vintage Fender. "What? Oh yeah, it is."

Elvis's ears twitched, as though he knew we were talking about him.

"Why Elvis?"

Sam shrugged. "He doesn't seem to like the Stones, so naming him Mick was kinda out of the question." He waved a hand in the direction of the bar. "There's coffee."

That was Sam's way of telling me to stop talking so he could focus his full attention on the candy apple red Stratocaster. I got up and went behind the bar for the coffee, careful to keep the mug well out of the way of the old guitar when I brought it back to the table. Elvis had finished eating and was washing his face.

"What do you think?" I asked after a couple of minutes of silence. Sam's head was bent over the neck of the guitar, examining the fret board.

"Gimme a second," he said.

I waited, and after another minute or so he straightened up, pulling a hand over the back of his neck. "So, tell me what you think," he said, setting his glasses on the table.

I put my coffee cup on the floor beside my feet before I answered. "Based on what the homeowner told me it's a 1966. It belonged to her husband. It's not mint, but it's in good shape. There's some buckle wear on the back, but overall it's been taken care of. I think it's the real thing and I think it could bring twelve to fifteen thousand."

Beside me Elvis gave a loud meow.

"The cat agrees," I said.

"That makes three of us, then," Sam said.

I grinned at him across the table. "Thanks."

When I got up to leave, Elvis jumped down and followed me. "I think you made a friend," Sam said. He walked me out to my truck, set the guitar carefully on the passenger's side, and then wrapped me in a bear hug. He smelled like coffee and Old Spice. "Come by Saturday night, if you're free," he said. "I think you'll like the band."

"Old stuff?" I asked, pulling my keys out of the pocket of my jeans.

"Hey, it's gotta be rock-and-roll music if you wanna dance with me," he said, raising his eyebrows and giving me a sly smile. He looked down at Elvis, who had been sitting by the truck, watching us. "C'mon, you. You're gonna get turned into roadkill if you stay here." He reached for the cat, who jumped up onto the front seat.

"Hey, get down from there," I said.

Elvis ignored me, made his way along the black vinyl seat and settled himself on the passenger's side, next to the guitar case.

"No, no, no, you can't come with me." I leaned into the truck to grab him, but he slipped off the seat, onto the floor mat. With the guitar there I couldn't reach him.

Behind me, I could hear Sam laughing.

I blew my hair out of my face, backed out of the truck and glared at Sam. "Your cat's in my truck. Do something!"

He folded his arms over his chest. "He's not my cat. I'm pretty sure he's your cat now."

"I don't want a cat."

"Tell him that," Sam said with a shrug.

I stuck my head back through the open driver's door. "I don't want a cat," I said.

Ensconced out of my reach in the little lean-to made by the guitar case, Elvis looked up from washing his face—again—and meowed once and went back to it.

"I have a dog," I warned. "A big, mean one with big, mean teeth." The cat's whiskers didn't so much as quiver.

Sam leaned over my shoulder. "No, she doesn't," he said.

I elbowed him. "You're not helping."

He laughed. "Look, the cat likes you." He rolled his eyes. "Lord knows why. Take him. Do you want him to just keep living on the street?"

"No," I mumbled. I glanced in the truck again. Elvis, with some kind of uncanny timing, chose that moment to tip his head to one side and look up at me with his big green eyes. With his scarred nose he looked . . . lonely.

"What am I going to do with a cat?" I said, bouncing the keys in my right hand.

Sam shrugged. "Feed him. Talk to him. Scratch under his chin. He likes that."

I glanced at the cat again. He still had that lonely, slightly pathetic look going.

"You two will make a great team," Sam said. "Like Lennon and McCartney or Jagger and Richards."

"SpongeBob and Patrick," I muttered.

"Exactly," Sam said.

I was pretty sure I was being conned, but, like it or not, I had a cat.

I looked over now toward the end wall of the store. My cat had apparently helped sell a mandolin. The young man was headed to the cash register with it. Elvis made his way over to me.

I leaned over to stroke the top of his head. "Nice work," I whispered. I wasn't imagining the cat smile he gave me.

The woman who had been looking at the post office desk was headed for the door, but there was a certain smugness to Mac's expression that told me he'd made the sale. I walked over to him. "Go ahead, say 'I told you so,'" I said.

He folded his arms over his chest. "I can't. I'm fairly certain she's going to buy it. She just wishes it were black."

I laughed. "I guess black really is the new black," I said. "I'm about ready to leave. I have to pick up Charlotte, and Avery is going to get her grandmother. Do you need anything before I go?"

I was doing a workshop on color-washing furniture for a group of seniors over at Legacy Place. North Harbor was full of beautiful old buildings. It was part of the town's charm. The top floors of the old chocolate factory had been converted into seniors' apartments. There were a couple of community rooms on the main level, where the residents had various classes like French and yoga and got together to socialize. We were using one of them for the workshop since many of the class participants lived in the building. Eventually I wanted to renovate part of the old garage next to the Second Chance building for workshops; for now, when I did classes for the general public, I had to settle for renting space at the high school. Luckily the hourly rate was pretty good. This workshop was a freebie my gram had nudged me into doing.

Mac shook his head. "I've got everything covered." He narrowed his brown eyes at me. "Are you sure it's a good idea to make Avery go with you?"

"Actually she volunteered."

"Avery volunteered to help you teach a workshop for a bunch of senior citizens?" One eyebrow shot up. "Seriously?"

"Seriously. She's good with older people. They'll be feeding her cookies and exclaiming over her hair color, and before you know it she'll have wangled an invitation to go prowl around someone's attic." Avery had a thing for vintage jewelry, and thanks to her grandmother Liz's friends, was building a nice collection.

I pressed my hands into the small of my back and stretched. I was still kinked from crawling around that old house all morning. "You know, I used to hang around with some of those same women when I was Avery's age." I'd spent my summers in North Harbor with my grandmother as far back as I could remember. The rest of the time I'd lived first in upstate New York and then in New Hampshire. "Liz taught me how to wax my legs and put on false eyelashes."

"I could have gone the rest of my life not knowing that," Mac said dryly.

"And I know the secret to Charlotte's potpie," I teased.

"You're not going to say it's love, are you?"

I shook my head and grinned. "Nope. Actually it's bacon fat."

My father had been an only child and so was my mother, so I didn't have a gaggle of cousins to hang out with in the summer. My grandmother's friends, Charlotte, Liz and Rose had become a kind of surrogate extended family, a trio of indulgent aunts. When I'd decided to open Second Chance, they'd been almost as pleased as my grandmother, and Charlotte and Rose had come to work for me part-time. Now with Gram out of town on her honeymoon, the three women fed me, gently nagged me about working too much and pointed out every single man between twenty-five and, well, death. When Gram had asked me to offer one of my workshops to her friends, how could I say no?

I glanced at my watch. "I don't expect to be more than a couple of hours," I said. "And I have my cell."

"Elvis and I can hold down the fort," Mac said. "Are you going to take another look at that SUV?"

I'd been thinking about replacing the aging truck we used to move furniture with an SUV, if I could get it for the right price. "I might," I said.

"Well, take your time," Mac said. "It's Monday afternoon. Nothing ever happens in this town on a Monday."

Of course he was wrong.

SOFIE KELLY is a *New York Times* bestselling author and mixed-media artist who lives on the East Coast with her husband and daughter. She writes the *New York Times* bestselling Magical Cats Mysteries (*Paws to Remember*, *Whiskers and Lies*, and *Hooked on a Feline*) and, as Sofie Ryan, writes the *New York Times* bestselling Second Chance Cat Mysteries (*Fur Love or Money*, *Scaredy Cat*, and *Totally Pawstruck*).

VISIT SOFIE KELLY ONLINE

SofieKelly.com

NEW YORK TIMES BESTSELLING AUTHOR

SOFIE KELLY

"Kelly is a brilliant storyteller."
—Socrates' Book Reviews

For a complete list of titles,
please visit prh.com/sofiekelly